MOON STRUCK

Moonstruck
Moonstruck Book 1
USA Today Bestselling Author
Heather Young-Nichols

heatheryoungnichols.com

Also by Heather Young-Nichols

Rules of the Game

Kissing the Player

Wanting the Player

Moonstruck

Moonstruck

Moontouched

The Empowered Series

The Gremlin Prince

The Goblin War

The Gorgon Sacrifice

Shadow Coven

Haunted Magic

Cursed Magic

Stolen Magic

Fated Magic

Forever 18

Forever Grayson

Forever London

Forever Lennox

Heavy Hitter

Pushing Daisies

Daisy

Van

Bonham

Daltrey

Mack

Courting Chaos

Cross

Ransom

Booker

Dixon

Finding Love

Making Her Mine

Making Him Hers

Harbor Point
Love by the Slice
Love by the Mile
Love by the Rules

Gambling on Love
Highest Bidder
Highest Stakes
Highest Reward

Holiday Bites
All I Want
All of Me

The Fallout Series
Last Good Thing
Last First Kiss
Last Chance Love

With J.A. Hardt

Bound by Magic

With Amelia J. Matthews

Dirt on the Diamond

After Office Hours: Seducing the Professor

Chapter One

THE WORLD SPUN around me when really I was the one spinning.

I was only allowed to lose control in small moments like this. Henry Davis' daughter must always be in control.

My best friend Olivia and I only had this careless moment to let go and twirl to the music flowing from the house. We spun so fast—faster than we probably should have—until we each had absolutely no breath left.

At eight, we would throw our hands out against the sky until gravity hit with a vengeance and we smacked to the ground full force. Falling now that we were twenty-one would've been inappropriate but my father was too busy to notice the spinning.

"I can't believe I still love to do that," Olivia said beside me once we stopped, each of us laughing too hard to keep going.

"Me too," I said back.

We shuffled over to the side of my father's crowded ballroom to watch the others dance. Some of the girls pretended to be happy watching and that's where they differed. While they pretended, I was actually perfectly happy to be alone—watching. That way I didn't have to deal with one detestable boy or another trying to sneak a feel. Or more. Something they wouldn't dare do if my father was near. I didn't need that kind of headache added to the one already called my life.

Our grand ballroom was filled to the rafters with friends and business associates of Father's who came in celebration of the official start to the season. We always hosted the first party, at least as long as I remembered. My father wouldn't stand to be second to anyone and there wasn't a soul who would refuse his invitation. Either out of fear of him or of becoming socially ostracized.

The 1923 summer season promised to be spectacular if tonight's party indicated anything.

Even in the dim glow of the heavy chandeliers

over our heads, one man caught my attention. I'd never seen him before so he stood out.

Tall, long, and lean. Well-fitting dark suit. His face was so striking. I'd almost call him beautiful. The entire room disappeared around us leaving me the luxury to watch him without worrying who might notice. It was like we were the only two people in the room.

The music faded from my ears. This stranger became my entire focus.

"Elizabeth Davis, who are you staring at?" Olivia's voice snapped me right back to reality.

"What?" My gaze jumped to her. "No one."

Olivia had her chocolate hair pinned elegantly to her head much like I did. Her hazel eyes sparkled in the moonlight. Brown hair and eyes could've been seen as mousy or dull. Olivia was anything but. She was also taller than me by several inches.

"Who holds your attention, Lizzie?" Olivia stood close behind me and peered over my shoulder to follow my line of sight. I tried to shift so she'd end up seeing one of the McCray boys but it didn't work.

She knew me far too well.

"No one." I began fiddling with the extravagant dress my father insisted I wear. A nervous habit Father tried to *teach* away.

Though I was much more comfortable in trousers, Father didn't allow that. A proper girl always wore dresses. Long ones at that. In a time when women went carousing, chopping off their hair, and raising hemlines, he tightened his control of my every move.

I really missed having a mother.

"You can't lie to me." Her eyes scanned the area again. "Is it that tall drink of water over there?" She nodded toward the man I'd been staring at. "Who is he?"

"I don't know." I did my best to look uninterested because I shouldn't have bothered being interested. My father would decide who I married and it wouldn't matter if I preferred someone else. I had no say.

Ball gowns swished from side to side taking up every iota of space as women unintentionally swayed to the music. Even mine. It was a beautiful satin in light rose made for only me. But I didn't even get to pick it. The ridiculous contraption had been laced so tightly it barely allowed me to breathe and it made my breasts swell creating the illusion I had more than I actually did. Every single time I noticed it, a blush crept up my chest and neck so I tried not to notice.

My father still believed in corsets.

The walls began closing in on me.

I needed to get out of that room.

Too many people along with a firm layer of whalebone crushing my lungs, and it wouldn't be long before I passed out if I didn't get some space.

"I think I'll get some air," I said in the middle of her chatter.

Olivia's father had already made her match and it was all she talked about. Boring.

I couldn't bring myself to care about any road that led to a husband.

If I had my way I'd never marry. I longed for a life where I could be *me,* not the me my father decided I should be.

The summer night had cooled from the heat of the day.

I welcomed the slight breeze that lifted my hair off my bare shoulders. Against my better judgment, as I left, I turned casually for one last glimpse of the beautiful stranger.

He saw me.

I knew he had when he started pushing his way through the crowd. He hopped around some. Skirted around others to make his way across the room.

Instead of continuing to watch him, I turned my

face up toward the moon and it's bright, not quite full shape.

I used the moon as a distraction and not even a successful one. I still stood there trying not to hope that the handsome stranger would follow me out there. Pointless to hope. Even if he followed me outside, I had no idea how to talk to a man. My stomach pitched at the thought.

"Lovely night," a deep voice said from right beside me, tickling across my skin.

It was him. His presence reached out for me.

"Yes, the air has cooled nicely." *Don't look at him. Don't look at him.* His voice sounded like his face looked. Beautiful and manly, deep and seductive.

As if I had any idea what seduction sounded like.

"I noticed you didn't dance." He leaned casually on his forearms against the balcony railing. His movements were fluid, full of purpose.

At best he made me feel like a child beside him.

My movements were stilted, unsure, and instead of confidence, I exuded insecurity. I shook my head and hoped he wouldn't notice.

"I'm sorry for the men if you've denied them all," he said still watching me.

The corners of my mouth turned up slightly.

"No one has asked." Somehow, without even trying, he'd put me at ease. I was never at ease among strangers.

Who was I kidding? I wasn't at ease around most friends.

Olivia being the rare exception.

"I find that hard to believe."

"It's true." With a newfound boldness, I leaned in toward him and, in a mock whisper, said, "I'm the unruly daughter of Henry Davis. More trouble than I'm worth."

"I highly doubt that," he said smirking at me.

His voice warmed my body like the summer sun making my breath catch in my throat.

I didn't know how he did it but within moments I was calm and comfortable, chatting with him as if old friends. He pointed out different dancing couples, laughing with me at some of the more inept young man as they stepped on some poor young woman's feet.

But I'd forgotten to ask his name and he hadn't offered. I wanted to ask, even though it went completely against my upbringing because a proper young lady did not make herself available in any capacity to the opposite sex.

"Elizabeth, I've been looking for you."

I snapped my head around and my entire body became rigid and pencil straight to my full, albeit lacking, height. Father used to call me the runt of the litter but as an only child, there was no litter.

"Father." I took a large step away from the stranger while trying to gauge Father's mood, "I... "

"It's time for bed," he ordered. I'd been hoping to avoid him the entire evening but especially once Orin spoke to me. I hadn't had as much fun at any function in my life.

"I had hoped to... "

"I said it's time for you to retire." His voice barely rose but the master of subtlety added enough edge to remind me of the consequences of disobeying.

The man beside me may not have been able to hear it but I did. As if he had to remind me.

I nodded curtly and started toward the house but I still hadn't gotten the man's name and I knew my father wouldn't fault me for being polite. Not in public at least.

This was worth the risk.

"It was nice to meet you, Mr... "

He reached out slowly taking my hand in his before lightly touching it to his lips quickly. My heart jumped violently in my chest. I couldn't believe he'd kissed my hand with my father standing right there.

In some circles that may have been acceptable but not in mine.

At least not with me.

"Vilkatas. The pleasure was mine, Miss Davis. I think I'll take a walk around the garden. It's such a lovely night." He winked. The movement was so fast, almost as if I didn't see it at all, but I still chose to believe he had. No one had ever winked at me in that way and I liked it.

"It's quite beautiful."

The stern look on my father's face when he cleared his throat got me moving quickly. He didn't usually punish me with an audience but I never wanted to test him. That would bring with it such humiliation that I didn't think I'd survive.

Within minutes I stood alone in my room listening to the music drift up from the party along with the laughter of those without such a strict parent. Olivia would be allowed to stay until the party ended. I didn't want to chance any more trouble so I quickly caught her attention when I got to the stairs and waved my goodbye.

She'd understand.

As I removed one of the few things of my mother's that *he* allowed me to keep, a set of diamond earrings, I replayed every word Mr. Vilkatas said to me and wished more than ever I'd gotten his first name. Then I realized what he'd said.

He'd be in the garden.

Waiting for me? Was that why he winked?

An unfamiliar level of anticipation suddenly took me over.

One so strong that it terrified me.

Chapter Two

As MUCH AS sneaking out of my room to see a man I'd just met scared me, I had to admit, I was also excited.

I was going to do it. Sneak out of my house to meet a strange man in the garden. My father's anger would be of epic proportions if he ever found out but I didn't care. I needed to see him again.

Sure, I'd be chancing my freedom by leaving my room after Father sent me to bed yet, still, I pushed my bedroom door open and slipped out of my room praying no one would hear me. I barely allowed each foot to touch the hardwood floor as I raced down the hall above the party.

If I was seen, I'd pay the price.

I held my breath, my heart pounding until I was safely outside in the cover of darkness where no one would see me. I used the shadows to my advantage and made it to the high hedges that formed the boundaries of the garden.

What was I doing?

Running outside, risking life and limb to meet a man that may or may not be waiting to see me.

Turning back was out of the question because it may have been sad but this was the greatest adventure I'd had in my life.

At the entrance of the garden, I stopped and listened for any sound of someone inside—or someone following me.

When I heard nothing, I pushed forward.

I scanned from side to side, searching the shadows but saw no one. Another two steps forward and there was still no one.

I must've misunderstood what Mr. Vilkatas meant when he said he was going to take in the garden. I'd been sure he gave me a thinly veiled suggestion that I meet him but obviously, he hadn't. I was wrong. As I turned to go back inside, I saw him leaning against a marble statue. His legs crossed at the ankles. His arms over his chest. Long and lean but the epitome of strength.

"You're here." The sound of my voice surprised me. The words came out throaty, breathless. Running wasn't exactly ideal when you were being crushed to death by your clothing.

"You sound surprised," he said back. "I told you I would be. Though I didn't know *you'd* come."

"I mean I shouldn't have." That was an understatement. The mere idea of Father's anger if he should find out made me shiver. I pushed it aside to the back of my mind. This is where I wanted to be.

"That's right." He pushed off the statue he'd been leaning against and began slowly toward me, like a predator stalking his prey yet he didn't just scare me. He terrified me. "You were sent to bed."

"Yes."

"But you didn't listen." He watched me in a way no one ever had. As if trying to see my soul or whatever deep-seated secret my heart contained.

There was little of either my soul or secrets to see.

I was nothing more than my father's daughter waiting to become someone's wife. The new liberties afforded women, such as the right to vote, didn't extend to me.

I smiled anyway. "No."

"Is that a habit of yours?" He stopped once his

body hovered so near mine that I had to tilt my head up to look him in the eyes. My knees needed a little extra encouragement to keep me standing. This was what they meant when they said week-kneed. "It won't bother me if it is. I just want to be prepared for how much trouble you'll be."

"It's not a habit. Actually, I don't think I've ever done anything to defy my father. He doesn't... I don't try to make him unhappy." My answer surprised him. He tried to keep his calm cool façade in place but failed. His eyes sparkled with the angry truth. He knew what I meant—that Father liked to rule with an iron hand.

"You took your hair down," he finally said pointing at the curls hanging down my back because I'd removed all the pins that had been cutting into my scalp.

"I was getting ready for bed." I quickly swept my fingers through the wild locks which didn't help.

I couldn't really do anything more to make it look more appropriate. Honestly, I didn't even care. Something about this man made me want to throw all the rules out the window. "I hadn't gotten to changing yet," I said as a way to explain the formal dress. Then realized what I'd said and burned with embarrassment.

"It's lovely." He pulled my hands away from my hair and looked from my eyes to my hair and back again like he wanted to touch the cascading curls himself.

I held my breath to see if he'd do it. I didn't have a single thing to say and it frustrated me.

He made me want to escape in the night, not caring that I'd escaped the house with wild abandon and I still didn't know why. But this man looked at me with kinder eyes than any man I'd ever met, certainly without any of the hatred and hardness that was a constant presence in my own father's face.

I needed to work up the courage to speak my mind with him.

"My name is Elizabeth," I finally choked out. I didn't like the person I was showing him. I wanted the girl from the balcony back. The one that had snuck out of her bedroom. "I know it's proper for you to call me Miss Davis, but my name is Elizabeth."

"I'm Orin." He smiled at me like he didn't have a care in the world like he wasn't concerned with being caught in the garden with me. Of course why would he be? Men didn't have the same rules as women.

I smiled back and bit my bottom lip.

His name was Orin.

We strolled around the vast greenery. I brushed my fingers across the leaves of a lower hanging tree and anything else to distract me from staring at his face and to keep me from fidgeting. It was hard to not stare at him, as beautiful as it was.

"I don't know your family. Are you from here?" I asked.

"We used to be." He walked beside me with his hands clasped behind his back. Orin stood over a head taller and his broad shoulders made him intimidating. I didn't feel intimidated. "The family moved away years ago."

"Return to your ancestral home?" I teased hoping that was actually the case. I didn't want him to tell me he was only visiting. That he'd be leaving soon. I may not have really known him yet but the idea of him not being there made my stomach ache. Not that it mattered, I told myself. It couldn't matter.

"Something like that."

The moment of relaxation didn't last. Someone fell out of the bush right in front of me. A large imposing body with glassy eyes scanned over me then to Orin.

Noah's pungent breath hit me, smelling so strongly of whiskey that I had to cover my mouth and nose to keep from gagging. He'd surprised me but this didn't shock me.

Noah Underwood spent most of his time drunk most days. Everyone knew this.

"What do we have here?" He slurred and swayed with each unsteady step toward us.

"Noah... I came out for some air. My room was stifling." He took another step closer which didn't clear up whether he believed me or if he'd even heard me. I dropped my hand from my face either way. With him around, I needed to have both hands free.

"And him?" he asked pointing at Orin.

"He... " Because I hadn't caused any trouble in my life, I'd never learned to think on my feet. Not when it counted. I had no lie to tell Noah yet telling him the truth wouldn't be smart either.

"I didn't feel a young lady should be unaccompanied at night." Orin's hands dropped to his sides as mine had.

I'd been around enough boys at school that I recognized the precursors of a fight. Tension rolled off Orin like waves hitting the shore.

"Better alone than with a stranger." Noah grabbed my left wrist squeezing so tightly my veins pushed against the skin. My pulse pounded in my fingertips under the pressure. "I'll take it from here." He yanked me toward him so violently my arm threatened to come out of the socket as my feet stumbled against the ground.

I wasn't ready for that.

"No, you're drunk," I said trying to pull my arm out of his grasp but his hand didn't budge. "And hurting me." My teeth ground together to keep the tears pooling in my eyes from falling. He really was hurting me and the smug look on his face said he was enjoying the power he had over me. No matter what I did, he wouldn't let go.

A knot formed in my chest as I got a glimpse of my future. A future I didn't want.

Orin's hand slapped loudly over Noah's wrist, much the way Noah's was around mine. The pressure of Orin's massive, muscular hand must've been immense because Noah released me involuntarily.

"I suggest you find somewhere to sleep it off." Orin's words came through clenched teeth.

Noah stumbled back after seeing something in Orin's eyes that I hadn't. Sizing the both of them up put Orin on the winning end if a fight actually broke out. Noah had been pampered his entire life, not strong. He was soft, entitled, and drunk.

Orin was none of those things.

His whole life, Noah only fought someone smaller, weaker. Someone he'd easily beat.

"Sure," Noah said. "You'll be mine soon enough." It sounded much more like a warning than anything else. "Then I'll take my time with you. But you better come to me untouched." He stumbled awkwardly back out the way he came.

I wanted to throw up.

I swallowed hard and stood there rubbing my already bruising forearm. I was like a ripe peach that way.

Bruised easily.

"Who was that?" Orin stared down at me with obvious anger at a moment I wished I could hide.

Unfortunately, the moon was bright enough I didn't even have the cover of darkness on my side. He watched the moisture form in my eyes, the pain in my face as I rubbed the area that had been squeezed so brutally. Nor would I be able to hide the humiliation running through me at the fact that Noah had put something so private out in the world for Orin to hear.

"Noah Underwood. The son of one of my father's friends."

"What did he mean?" he asked softly.

This man I didn't know treated me with a kindness that made keeping my tears from falling impossible.

Exactly what every man wanted to see.

After plopping down on the stone bench sitting nearby, Orin followed but still kept the appropriate distance.

For a moment, I really wished someone wanted to be inappropriate with me for more than their own gratification like Noah. To experience some sort of pleasure for once in my life. If anyone heard those thoughts... I didn't want to think about what would've happened.

"About what?" I asked hoping that I was wrong about what he wanted to know.

"I think you know."

Sighing, I saw no reason not to answer him. It was inevitable. My entire life was inevitable. "My father and his have been negotiating. I'm pretty sure I'll soon be told that I'm marrying Noah in the near future."

"I see." He straightened his back so he was sitting at his absolute tallest.

"I don't want it. I don't want to marry Noah Underwood." I sobbed once before reigning it back in. "He is not... a nice man or a suitable husband but I can't say that to my father."

"What do you mean *not a nice man?*"

"He's horrible to women but knows no one will say anything because of who his father is. And... there is at least one woman he sees already. I don't think that will change once he's actually married." I didn't care about what Noah did or didn't do except for the fact that I'd soon be part of what he did. It made me sick to my stomach. I wasn't an object to be used. However, I happened to be the only one who thought that way.

"Sees?"

I caught his eye while drawing out the word. "*Sees.*"

"Oh, I see."

My brows shot up playfully.

"I don't mean see... I... understand," he said sounding a little flustered.

Giggling under my breath, I wiped the moisture from my cheeks.

Those few moments in the garden with Orin before Noah's interruption were some of the most carefree I'd ever had. They didn't mean anything and I'd likely never speak to him alone again, but it was something to me.

A memory that, for me and him, no one could take away.

"I can make sure he doesn't hurt you." He glanced at me then to the entrance where I'd originally come from like he wanted to ensure no one would overhear. "If that's what you want."

Chapter Three

Orin could make sure Noah never hurt me. That was what he said though I didn't know how.

I smiled up at Orin and his offer. If only I really could escape Noah, my father, and almost everything else in my world. I'd jump at the chance but the reality was, there was no escaping.

"If you made him disappear completely, that would be great," I finally quipped.

Noah was my reality. He was my future and there was no way to change that.

He wouldn't be able to actually get Noah out of my life but the offer meant everything to me. It was crazy. Orin didn't know me, yet had already treated me better than anyone in my life and I hated to know this was about to end.

It had to but that didn't make it easy.

"I better get back to my room before my father checks in on me," I told him quietly. "Will I see you again?"

"If you want to."

I smiled over at him. Those were the words I wanted to hear.

Of course, I wanted to see him again.

I raced back inside, taking the quickest way that also put me at the most risk of being caught. I had no idea how much time passed out in the garden or how much trouble I was already in. Once safely back in my room, I yanked my dress off quickly, hoping Father hadn't noticed I ever left my room. Then I hopped into bed as if I'd been there the entire night.

My heart thumped erratically against my chest as I tossed and turned, unable to fall asleep. Sneaking out to meet a stranger may not be an adventure for most people, Olivia included, but for me... it was everything. The most excitement I'd ever had and the only thing I'd ever done just for myself.

After what seemed like forever, I tossed my blanket off and quietly walked to the window for another look at the garden.

As I stood there, the shadows moved. Or rather someone in the shadows moved.

With the party still in full swing, it could've been anyone but somehow I knew it was Orin. Without looking up at me, he couldn't know I saw him and wanted to keep watching but he stopped and turned my way.

I pushed the window open and leaned on my elbows on the sill, locking eyes with him, wishing he was still close enough to touch.

The next several days passed without any sign of Orin.

My father continued his negotiation with Noah's father to see how many goats he'd have to exchange for me to marry his son. I'd guess not many but marriage to them was more about the financial burdens than anything else.

Noah would agree without question because he'd do whatever made his life easiest. Going against his father's money wouldn't do that but having me to manage his house and spread my legs whenever he chose would. That last part made my stomach roll.

I didn't want to be Noah Underwood's wife. Didn't want him to touch me in even the most innocent way let alone intimately.

It was my job to make sure my father's house ran

smoothly. I probably should've been grateful that he bothered keeping me in the first place since to him I was nothing more than what killed my mother.

I'd just finished up our plans for dinner with the cook that night when Father came through the front door causing my footsteps to quicken on instinct.

I wanted to get to my room before he saw me.

After pushing my bedroom door open, I found a small, beautiful bouquet of wildflowers with bursts of red, yellow, and purple, lying on my bed.

I checked behind the drapes and anywhere else I could think of. No one was there. But the windows were open.

The possibility existed that someone climbed through. But how? I was on the second floor with nothing to use as a makeshift ladder anywhere close by. Orin was the only person who'd be so nice but without some sort of special ability, he couldn't scale the side of my house.

Mystery or not, they smelled wonderful.

"Elizabeth!" My name echoed through the halls jerking me back to my reality.

He was headed up the stairs toward me. Years of experience gave me the ability to determine his exact location using the echo of his voice.

I spun around my room, looking for a place to

hide the bouquet so that he wouldn't see them and ask questions. Everywhere was too obvious.

As I ran out of time, I tossed them into the bathroom attached to my bedroom then scurried out of the room hoping he'd never make it inside in the first place.

"Yes, Father," I said, out of breath as I skidded to a stop at the bottom of the stairs willing my heart to slow down.

"We're leaving in one hour," he said without looking my way.

His instructions were absolute, giving me no choice but to obey. I hated asking follow-up questions yet he hadn't said where we were going.

"Where are we going?" I asked quickly. He scowled. "So I know how to dress," I added quickly.

"The Franklin house."

I nodded then moved quickly all while maintaining what he called my 'ladylike manners' back up the stairs. All the while I barked instructions at two of our housekeepers.

The Franklin's perfectly manicured lawn was being trampled by a wave of guests with croquet mallets that smacked against balls while laughter filled the afternoon air. I loved these events because, at the very least, I'd get to spend time with

Olivia, a luxury we were afforded less and less often.

I stood in a group of girls sipping lemonade in the summer heat as we watched over a group of younger children, jealous as the young men were allowed to loosen their collars while we women had to sit and suffer under the stifling heat.

It wasn't fair.

As I scanned the crowd, I found all the same familiar faces until coming to an abrupt stop on his long, lean frame casually leaning against a tree in the shade.

Orin stared right back as if he didn't care who saw, his eyes so intense that my face flushed from more than the heat. I had to look away.

The feeling of butterflies in my stomach was new and exciting.

I liked it.

"What is it about him?" Olivia asked beside me.

"Nothing."

She tried to hold back a smile and said, "He's quite handsome."

"I hadn't noticed," I lied then pried my eyes from him just to have them snap right back.

"That's why the two of you are staring at each other like you're the only two people left in the world." The trio of girls around us giggled. We weren't alone and gossip would cause problems.

"Liv, she's practically promised to Noah Underwood," our friend, Ellie, reminded her.

I groaned not because she was wrong but because she was right. I needed to remember that and act like it before I caused myself even more trouble.

To end the conversation, I walked away from the group.

The crowd of people acted like I was invisible as I made my way through the crowd. Still, extra planning went into making it look like I was wandering aimlessly and didn't have a destination in mind.

It was a terrible idea but I needed to be closer. Wanted to look into his dark eyes and listen to his deep voice.

Orin moved as I did, pausing when I paused until I hit the edge of the pond where I slipped off my shoes. I only intended to cool off a little. No one should fault me that. Southern summers came early and with a vengeance of heat that unparalleled everything else. The cool water brought with it the relief I'd been searching for.

The water gave me such wonderful relief that I wet my hands then pressed them against my neck and slid my feet into the water. Then I unbuttoned the top two buttons on my blouse.

"It's warm today." His voice jolted me even though I'd known it was coming.

I expected to be blinded by the sun when I looked up to him. Instead, he blocked it out completely and made it so I couldn't clearly see his face.

"Yes, it is."

Orin dropped down beside me as close as he possible without looking suspicious should anyone see us together. "Are you having a good time?"

"Not really," I answered honestly. "You?"

"Better now," he said with equal honesty.

I smiled but his words made me blush.

"Where are you from? No one seems to know anything about you." I wanted the focus off me and that was the first question that came to mind.

"Have you been asking?" His lips curved into a smile when I didn't answer. "Here, my family originally but if you mean me specifically, I was born in Boston."

"I've never been there. My father doesn't take me with him when he goes away."

Orin looked out over the water watching the long

grass across from us sway back and forth as if playing pat-a-cake.

"Where's your mother?" he asked.

The question surprised me. He hadn't yet asked about my family situation and I wasn't sure I wanted him to.

"She died." He waited patiently for an explanation. "Childbirth. With me." I sighed. "I don't know why I'm telling you this. It really isn't proper."

Orin's laughter filled the air. It was the first time such a deep vibration erupted from him. He'd smiled a lot but there hadn't been a real laugh until right then. "Are you worried about what is proper?"

"No, but I should be." I took a breath to calm my nerves. "How old are you?"

"Twenty-five. Practically an old man."

I snickered. Twenty-five wasn't old.

We continued to talk, mostly about nothing important at all until my father called my name.

Damn.

I hadn't meant to stay away long enough for anyone to notice.

Hopping up, I pulled my stockings and shoes on. If Father came to the top of the small hill that gave Orin and me a small amount of privacy and saw us together... I couldn't chance that.

"I have to go," I said quickly. He stood up beside me. "We're having a dinner tonight, nothing formal. You should come."

He didn't have the chance to answer before I ran off in the direction of my father. He couldn't catch me. Not if I still wanted to spend any more time with Orin.

I didn't enjoy playing hostess even when it was only a dozen people. It made Father happy so I did it without complaining but I hated everyone watching me like they were waiting for me to mess up or drop something. It would've been better if Olivia's family was here.

But Orin showed up to dinner and that fact alone made it a better night.

We glanced at each other with shy smiles every chance we got over dinner, something Olivia called flirting. I'd never done it before and even if I wasn't very good at it, I enjoyed these tiny moments with Orin so much.

Orin approached me after dinner as if he didn't care that so many pairs of eyes would be on us.

"Miss Davis, that was lovely." He said sounding very formal as if he were any other guest.

"I didn't do any of it."

"I was speaking more of the view than the meal."

I couldn't not grin like an utter fool at that. His words caressed me as much as a hand would. However, my smile fell when I saw my father over Orin's shoulder.

"My father's coming with Mr. Underwood."

I sighed and took two large steps away from the security of Orin's bubble. Orin turned toward them then backed away so he'd still be able to hear what they said but not look like he was part of the suddenly forming group.

"Elizabeth, it's been decided." Whatever my father was talking about, he showed no sign of whether what had been decided was a good thing or bad.

I knew what he was talking about and my stomach turned, my mouth watered. I was going to vomit. A combination of fear and resignation of what my life would soon become turned my stomach sour.

"What has?" I asked anyway in a desperate attempt to deny reality, praying he meant anything else.

"Mr. Underwood and I have come to an agreement. Noah and you will be married at the end of the season."

Applause erupted from all around us as my eyes filled with tears that I absolutely couldn't let fall.

That would be embarrassing to my father but it wasn't like I could totally control it either.

What a pathetic life I had. The masters of my universe slapped each other on the back with large grins on their faces like they'd just discovered the cure for polio.

I swallowed hard. Knowing it was the wrong decision, I still couldn't let my only opportunity pass me by. My hands shook as I tried to steel myself against his reaction.

"Father." My words came out weak. I needed to sound stronger. After swallowing hard, I steeled my nerves. "I don't want to marry Noah Underwood."

The world stopped.

His smile fell as he turned toward me slowly. Mr. Underwood folded his arms over his chest and chuckled quietly the way one would a child that said something naughty.

It was the slow that was terrifying.

If I could've shoved those words back in my mouth, I would have.

In that moment, I didn't feel brave. I felt very, very small.

Chapter Four

"The decision has been made." There was an unspoken warning in Father's words.

I'd keep my mouth shut and not embarrass him.

Or else.

Working on being brave, I swallowed hard again then took a deep breath, steeling myself to do something I'd never done before.

Stand up for myself.

"I don't love him. I won't ever love him," I said.

He snorted as if to say that love had no place in a marriage. He'd said it before. "Elizabeth, you will marry him at the end of the season."

"But, Father..."

His hand sliced through the air, cutting through

the tension I'd created then slammed into my cheek in an explosion of fire and pain.

Tears fell even though I tried to stop them so he wouldn't get the satisfaction.

I covered the fire burning my skin with my hand trying to douse it. Unsuccessfully. Father knew exactly what he was doing both in the best placement of a slap to the face to ensure maximum pain but also when to use corporal punishment for maximum personal effect.

Orin took two steps toward me but I shook my head slowly to stop him.

Anything he did would make it worse but I could see him wrestle with having to stand by and watch what was happening to me.

"You will be married at the end of the season," Father said again through clenched teeth.

I couldn't move.

I stood there for an agonizing amount of time waiting for him to walk away from me as I'd never be allowed to walk away from him.

He glared at me for an eternity before finally turning away.

I bolted in a full run as best I could with heels on toward Franklin's garden wanting to release all the energy suddenly filling my body. It also allowed me to let the damn holding back my emotions break.

By the time I threw my hands out in front of me to brace myself against a statue, I was fully sobbing. I slid down onto my knees, not caring about the dirt or who saw me or just how un-ladylike my behavior was.

I couldn't be bothered to care about the quick footsteps that followed me.

It took five deep breaths to calm myself down.

Orin touched my shoulder and I flinched. I knew it was him. No one else would've followed me other than Olivia and his steps were much heavier than hers but my legs were too weak from the run to stand so Orin squatted down beside me.

"Are you all right?" he asked. Something about his voice calmed me.

"No, Orin, I'm not. I don't want to marry him."

He stood and lifted me off the ground like I weighed nothing then set me on that stone bench then took the spot right beside me.

"Why is your father making you marry him if you don't want to?"

"He thinks Noah is a good match. It's all about social standing. It's like selling me to the highest bidder and I hate it. My mother would never have let this happen." I know she wouldn't have. I don't think. I didn't know her but she would've protected me.

"You're really going to have to marry him?"

"Yes." Tears filled my eyes once more. I swallowed hard and decided to work on that bravery. "Unless..."

"Unless?"

"Perhaps if someone else wanted me... even then he probably wouldn't go against his word to Mr. Underwood... but he might." I paused watching for any kind of reaction but that stone face remained firm. He was excellent at not showing any emotion and I wished it was something he could've taught me. I didn't know Orin yet but I would've married him if given the choice. "But there isn't anyone anyway."

"What would your father do if your fiancé wasn't around?"

I rolled my eyes. "Noah will always be around." When it came to our fathers, Noah was even more of a coward than I was.

We fell quiet again.

I never had any idea what Orin had on his mind.

Since my experience with men was limited to my father, I couldn't even venture a guess.

"Orin." My voice broke on his name. "Why can't you do it?"

His eyebrows shot up. "Do what?"

"We talk. You treat me like a real person. Orin, are you interested at all?" The forwardness of my question surprised me. With extremely limited time, he was my only hope. He clasped my hand between both of his and looked at me. Really looked at me and if trying to find something specific.

Even this small touch sent my heart racing. His touch traveled to dark corners of my body that I didn't even know I had.

"Yes." His eyes closed like he'd confessed something terrible. As if being interested in me was something horrible he didn't want to admit.

"Then you... "

"I can't explain it to you, Elizabeth but I can't ask for your hand."

I yanked my fingers back from him and stood up, intending to stomp my way back toward the house. He said he was interested in me yet couldn't marry me to keep me from the despicable Noah Underwood. Anger like never before filled me.

Apparently, it wasn't only my father keeping me from happiness.

"Let's leave then," I yelled as I put distance between us but then turned back toward him fully aware of how desperate I sounded and probably looked. "We can leave town and no one would find us."

Orin grabbed my arm, dragging me to him until we were only a breath apart.

"I can't do that. Trust my words when I say I wish I could but it's impossible." I did trust his words. Trust him. That was part of the problem.

If I hadn't met him, I never would have tried to get out of the arrangement or complain about it in any way. I would've lived my sad, pathetic life doing exactly what was expected of me.

"I hate this," I said sadly.

Orin took my face in his hands and slowly, slower than I imagined possible, touched his lips to mine.

Warmth blanketed me, bringing my body alive for the first time.

In my regular life, I'd been dormant before this moment, gliding through life but not living it. Not having kissed anyone before, I had no idea what I was doing yet I pushed up to my toes so that I could reach him better, taste him more.

I feared he'd end this as quickly as he'd started it.

Instead, he wrapped his arms around my waist, lifting me effortlessly up to him.

I clung to his shoulders as his tongue pushed my lips apart.

Olivia had kissed boys this way and told me about it in detail but I had to believe it hadn't been like this. Otherwise, she never would have kissed another.

His mouth was warm and wet against mine and he tasted like sweet lemonade. Before I had my fill, my feet touched the ground and there was far too much space between us. My head buzzed with excitement—and something else.

At least I'd be able to remember this moment on the nights with Noah that I was going to hate.

"I'm sorry. I shouldn't have done that," he said then ran his tongue over his bottom lip. His words broke through the fog that clouded my head.

"I'm not." I smiled softly. "You know." I slipped my arm through his as we slowly walked back toward the entrance of the garden. "If I have to marry him, then I'll also have to... "

"Stop right there." His face was dead serious, his

jaw tightened. "I don't want to think about that right now. Or ever."

"Orin, will you explain it to me one day?" I laid my head on his muscular arm while taking the smallest steps possible. "Why you would kiss me but not keep me from marrying someone else? Someone horrible?"

"The marriage will not take place, I promise you."

I stopped. He sounded so sure that I wouldn't be marrying Noah that it caught me by surprise.

"The only thing that could keep me from marrying him is if someone made my father a better offer but you won't do that will you?"

"I... really wish I could explain but no I can't."

"Fine." I began my walk again. "But just so you know, even if Noah decided to run away with the circus, my father will marry me off to someone."

Orin stiffened and I felt his gaze on me all the way back to the house.

We were out there so long that the other guests had left and we'd been alone without knowing it.

Even my father left as if he didn't even remember I came with him.

I'd been left—forgotten.

. . .

The only thing that got me through the next days was meeting Orin in the garden after my father retired for the night. I shouldn't have done it but if I was going to become someone's wife, I wanted to be Elizabeth for at least a few moments first.

The world constantly changed around me but suffrage hadn't come to the Davis house.

I wasn't living.

I was existing.

The more Orin and I met in the garden for a late-night chat, the closer we became. The more attached I became and I began to question whether it was the best idea to continue.

Yet I couldn't resist seeing him one more time.

"Have you changed your mind, Lizzie?" he asked as we walked arm in arm through the garden under only a sliver of moonlight. I didn't know for sure what he was referring to because the last thing he'd said before that was about missing the brightness of the full moon. I missed his brightness.

"Not that I know of."

"Your betrothal?"

I perked up at the mention of my upcoming marriage. We didn't discuss any of that in our late-night conversations since he assured me that I wasn't going to marry Noah Underwood.

"Why would I change my mind? He's not the man I'd choose to marry."

I dreamed of falling in love with my future husband the way I'd hoped my mother had with my father. I'd been told more than once that her death had changed him and not for the better.

He stopped the both of us to pull me to him, his face searching mine so intently I almost became uncomfortable.

"Elizabeth... " The moon danced on his dark eyes.

"Will you ask for my hand?" I almost wished I could take that question back. Since I already knew the answer, there'd been no point in asking it. Yet I still asked.

His face relaxed and he took a big step away putting a little distance between us.

Distance I didn't want.

"No."

"Then what's the point to all this?" I yelled. I shouldn't have. Anyone could overhear us but the frustration of being so close to exactly what I wanted yet so far from having it pushed me over the edge. There were times I cursed the day I met Orin Vilkatas because without him I would've still been resigned to the life I'd been assigned. "Why not just let him have me and be done with it? Especially if you won't even tell me why you don't want me. I'm not asking you to love me. Just care enough not to let me live this pitiful existence."

"This isn't about not caring for you," he roared back. "I want you but we can't be together." His jaw set firmly in his universal sign that he wouldn't be giving me anything more than that.

"I guess there's no reason to continue to meet then, is there?" I said it but absolutely didn't mean it. Those moments with Orin at night were the only happy ones of my day but I couldn't turn back to him. Those moments were almost gone since we only had a finite number of them left but that hurt even more.

I climbed the stairs back to my bedroom long before I normally would've after seeing Orin. Each and every time my room seemed smaller when I returned. More confining.

As I lay in bed willing myself to fall asleep, something tapped against my window.

At first, I ignored it.

Until a rain of pebbles hit my window sounding exactly like hail yet it hadn't begun storming outside.

Then two loud, angry voices rose up from the

backyard. One distinctly my father's. The other most definitely Orin's.

I scrambled out of bed and ran to the window.

Father didn't even know about Orin.

Oh god...maybe he did.

The dark night with only a half-moon illuminating the yard made it easy for me to step out on the balcony without being seen.

The two of them were toe to toe, angry and loud. My father's hand fisted Orin's shirt as he pushed Orin away.

"Stay away from her," Father said in his angriest voice.

"I need to speak with your daughter," Orin said back, tone and volume equal as if he wasn't worried about the unspoken threat against him.

My father wasn't used to anyone not listening to his every command.

"Get off my property." That ended the conversation as far as Father was concerned because he turned back into the house locking the door and turning off the outside light.

Orin glanced up at me like he knew I was there the entire time then began to walk backward toward the garden. When he made it halfway to the tree line, I decided to go back inside. I wanted to watch until he disappeared but didn't think it was the best idea. Made me seem even more desperate than I was. Finally, I couldn't help myself.

I spun on my toes, hoping I'd still be able to make out his form in the dark—a scream strangled in my throat when I slammed into a large, solid mass.

Chapter Five

SOMETHING COVERED MY MOUTH, silencing the scream about to break free. Strong arms wrapped around me and Orin's scent surrounded me. When he finally lowered his hand, he still held onto my elbow.

"You scared the life out of me," I said breathlessly.

"Sorry." His lips curled, and he didn't look the least bit sorry.

"How did you get up here?" I whispered. It still sounded too loud to my ears. "You were almost to the trees."

"I'm quick." Orin rested his body against the wall. The weight of his gaze forced goosebumps to cover my body. "I forgot to do something today."

"What's that?"

His smile melted my heart. All man. All forbidden. Completely exciting.

He cupped my face with his hands then pushed his lips softly against mine.

This kiss was intriguing.

His taste had to be all his own. I couldn't imagine anyone else smelling and tasting as he did. I wasn't an expert in this area, having only done this once, but this one seemed different, almost desperate as he pushed against me like he didn't want to let me go. One of his hands sneaked up my spine, clasping the back of my neck so I'd stay exactly where he wanted me.

I should've been scared at how tightly he held me.

But I wasn't.

I didn't want to move and instead wrapped my arms around his waist holding him as tightly as he held me. He wouldn't stay long but I'd hold onto him as long as he was there.

Early the next afternoon I met Olivia at the park with two girls we'd known since we were little. I wasn't allowed to do a lot but meeting my friends occasionally was one of the things approved by my father. Plus he had eyes all over town that were connected to mouths that wouldn't hesitate to tell him if I got up to something I wasn't supposed to. I never did because he'd trained me to live in fear. Of him.

Dark gray clouds began rolling in so we parted to try to make it home before the storm began.

When the sky opened up to unleash a torrent of rain and the sound of fury itself rumbled above me, I was on the sidewalk too far from home and didn't have an umbrella or even a jacket with me to try to block it all out.

The sidewalk got slick with water. As I hurried along, already soaked to the bone, my shoe slipped off the edge of the pavement sinking the heel into the muddy area beside it.

It was like a knife cutting soft butter.

"Oh good grief," I said with a groan trying to yank my shoe out of the mud with everything I had.

Four attempts got the damn thing free as the rain picked up causing everything around me to disappear. Visibility was gone beyond my own hand in front of my face.

Still, I kept pushing forward. I needed to get home.

I wrapped my arms around myself as I stumbled. It took four steps to regain balance and keep from falling flat on my face.

I needed to find somewhere to wait out the storm.

It took me a minute to get my bearing to see exactly how far I'd gone and I realized Orin's house was pretty close. I'd never been there but he told me about it in one of our late-night talks.

With each of the steps leading up his porch, my heart thudded harder and harder in my chest.

What if he already had company?

What if he hadn't really meant I'd be welcome anytime?

In all likelihood when he told me where he lived, he never would've considered I'd have the kind of freedom that would lead me to his porch. I never thought I'd be standing her either.

Pushing away all my nerves, I knocked anyway.

When no one answered, I pounded on the wood much harder.

Still nothing. At least he had a covered porch to protect me from the rain, though I shivered from the cold. The roof wrapped around the side of the house to the back as I slowly walked around to knock again only this time on the back door.

Definitely not home.

Without him there, I'd still wait out the rain before making the walk home. I sat on the chair next to the door and began to shiver given the fierceness of the downpour leaving me completely drenched and the cooling temperature.

I pulled my legs up to my chest wrapping my arms around them making myself the tightest ball of a person possible to help keep some body heat in.

As I sat there vibrating, I let my eyes wander over the area where Orin spent his time. His back-yard opened into a heavily wooded area. On the top step, outside the rain, sat a small pile of clothes. It didn't make sense. No one would be drying clothes in the middle of the rain.

"Lizzie!" Orin called snapping my attention to where he emerged from the tree line.

On instinct, I jumped to my feet but barely saw him through the curtain of rain.

Finally, he made his way through the haze.

I'd recognize his voice anywhere but I watched him. My gaze started at his face, the chiseled lines with water dripping from the edges. Down to his bare chest that made my insides tighten. I'd never seen him without a shirt on. Then even lower—

"Oh!" A rush of blood burned up my face as I spun on my heel to turn my back toward him.

I'd never seen a naked man before and honestly, it was one of the things that worried me about getting married. He climbed the steps and stopped behind me.

"You're naked," I said stating the obvious.

"I didn't expect anyone to be on my porch when I returned," he said back with humor in his voice, highlighting how much he enjoyed my embarrassment.

Having absolutely no self-control when it came to him, I turned my head to glance over my shoulder to see if he'd finished dressing.

He hadn't. My heart pounded against my chest and I bit my lips together.

A large grin spread across his face.

He caught me trying to get another peek at him naked. I could've rolled over and died right there. Instead of acknowledging it, I turned away again and closed my eyes.

"You can turn around now," he said.

He was still shirtless when I faced him. Staring at his naked chest didn't seem like the best idea but

I'd never seen a man without his shirt before. Not even my father.

Yet it was.

I shivered again almost violently from the breeze and the all-encompassing nature of his presence.

"You're freezing," he said with eyes wide as he realized how wet my clothes were.

"I-I-I... " My teeth smacked together. "Am."

"Come on." He pulled me by the arm through the back door, the kitchen, and into the front room. He didn't have an overly large house but still more like a home than the one I'd grown up in. Cozy and inviting. "You need to get out of those wet clothes."

My eyes grew wide and my stomach dropped at the suggestion.

The thought scared me to death but it also intrigued me. He watched all the thoughts and scenarios go through my head and chuckled.

"You're soaking wet and going to get sick. I'll get something for you to put on." He climbed the stairs at the back of the room, moved around above me, and tumbled back down with a shirt in his hand. It'd be much too large for me but the idea of having something of his against my skin warmed me in more ways than one.

Orin turned his back to me, stacking wood in the

fireplace, then lit it, filling the room with warmth while I removed my clothes and put his shirt on. I pulled the fabric to my nose inhaling his scent. Clean and all man. Nothing artificial among the soapy scent. All Orin.

"All set," I said so he'd turn back around. Which he did with a thick blanket in hand. He wrapped it around me before setting me gently on the couch. Orin held me tightly to him, my head on his shoulder as if we did this all the time.

I wanted to pretend that we did even when I knew the punishment if we were caught.

"You didn't peek," I said quietly.

If stories were to be believed, men couldn't help themselves around women so showing any amount of skin could have turned one into a lustful beast. Yet it didn't do that to him.

"No."

"Why?" Apparently, in a matter of weeks, I'd turned into a harlot that said whatever came to mind, which included being almost naked under the blanket in a room with a man I wasn't married to. I'd taken everything off. Not just the outer layer.

Who had I become?

"Wouldn't be right." He paused. "But you did."

I dropped my hand to his chest, choosing to

ignore the truth he'd just spoken. "You are so warm." Again he said nothing. "Why were you in the woods without clothing?" Again nothing. "More things you can't tell me about?"

"Yes."

We fell quiet while he stroked my hair and removed the pin that had been holding a nice summer style but now my hair lay in clumps all over after being caught in the rain. I moved away to the edge of the couch, frustrated by him keeping secrets more than anything.

"I don't understand any of this, Orin."

"I know." He sighed. It sounded more like a growl. "It would be easier if we didn't see each other anymore."

I forced myself off the couch and paced the floor in front of the fire. The heat from the flames licked my bare legs both relaxing me and egging on my internal fire.

"Yes, it would." I didn't want that. He remained still, waiting for me because I had more to say. "That's not what I want but Orin you say things to me acting as if you care and then pull away. Is this all in my head?" Tears formed in my eyes as I made my voice bolder and louder. I wanted answers from him even if I already knew he wouldn't give them. "Here

I am half-naked in front of you and nothing. No reaction." I popped the top two buttons open having no idea what I was doing. "Nothing."

Orin leapt from his seat, pulling me against his body firmly as he backed me into the wall at the same time. His lips pressed against mine like he couldn't get close enough. He devoured me and when his tongue licked at my bottom lip, I allowed him in.

I wrapped my left leg around his waist at the same time his hand slid up my thigh. But he stopped short of where I wanted him to be.

If I couldn't have him, I at least wanted him to be my first. Noah Underwood didn't deserve to be.

Something about Orin made me want to throw caution to the wind and be the type of girl my father wouldn't even let me speak to. The kind of girl who might let a boy go further than she should without being married.

Orin pulled back, putting enough space between us to catch our breaths. My heartbeat erratically in my ears drowning out everything else. He groaned as he slammed his balled-up hand against the wall beside us.

Hard.

"Not no reaction," he growled, his breath feathering against my cheek and he sounded like he'd swallowed a handful of gravel. He pressed against me and the evidence of his desire pressed against me too. At least, I thought that was what I was feeling.

"Orin, please. Take me away from here. Somewhere we can be together. Please!"

"I don't think you understand how difficult this entire situation is." He moved away from me back to the couch. "You couldn't possibly."

"Answer one question. Please." I sat back down facing him. "Is it all my imagination? Between us?"

Orin mulled over his answer before giving it. He looked like a man trying to figure out what he *should* say instead of the truth. I wanted the truth.

"No," he finally answered.

"So you... "

"I love you, Elizabeth. I love you enough to want a normal life for you."

Whatever that meant. "I wouldn't get that from you?"

"No."

Spurred on with a newfound boldness due to his admission, I leaned in to initiate a kiss for the very first time in my life. A soft, quick kiss that meant the entire world to me.

"One day, Orin Vilkatas, you will tell me what's going on."

"You are confident of that?" He smiled sadly.

"Yes." I climbed onto his lap. "Because I will marry you but I will not willingly spend the rest of my life with someone who keeps secrets."

Chapter Six

Orin laughed loudly at my declaration and said, "It's late."

"My father is in the city until Thursday. He'll never know when I get home."

He grabbed my hips with his large hands when I moved in to do the one thing I wished I could do for the rest of my life, the one thing I loved doing more than anything else—kissing Orin slow and hard until he lifted me off him into the seat beside him. When I looked over at him with a raised eyebrow, I didn't get the chance to ask why he did it before he answered.

"To keep you marriable and me out of trouble, I think you should stay there."

His words made a smile creep slowly across my lips. The idea that he might have to use some control over his more natural urges around me wasn't something I allowed myself to hope for. Secrets aside, and Orin seemed to have more than his share, I wanted to be with him.

We sat there listening to the burning wood snap and pop as we sat there. Us together was enough.

My Father's house had a more comfortable feel to it when he was away. I almost wished he'd spend more time traveling but in the summer we hosted Sunday lunch with his friends and he wouldn't miss it. Sunday service where I listened to a sermon that I'd forget the moment we left the building was as mandatory as the lunch.

I wasn't sure I believed in God.

A kind, loving God wouldn't have taken my mother from me, leaving me alone in a world dominated by men. That God wouldn't want a person to waste her life because they'd been born a woman.

At least I didn't think He would.

I only stayed long enough for the rain to stop and my clothes to dry enough that it wasn't so uncomfortable to put them back on.

It was still a long walk home.

. . .

Orin came to Sunday lunch again this week like he didn't mind taking the chance that someone might notice the quick looks we gave each other. Father paid such little attention to the guest list that he'd never know Orin wasn't on it. In fact, since everyone in our circle came, he would probably assume Orin was one of them. Or that his family was.

I knew nothing about Orin's family. Nobody seemed to know anything, actually. Even Olivia's grandmother, who usually had all the information on everyone, didn't have any on them.

Finally, lunch ended as had cleanup—which was my job to supervise—so I could join Olivia and the other girls.

Whispers followed my footsteps. Something in the pit of my stomach told me to turn the other way and ignore them. That I wouldn't want to hear what the latest gossip was about.

But I just couldn't ignore it.

"What's everyone talking about?" I asked as soon as I was close enough to the girls standing in the shade of our largest tree. No one answered me. They avoided making eye contact. "Olivia?"

She sighed then looked me in the eye. "Lizzie, no one has seen him in almost a week."

"Who?" I glanced at Orin as if to reassure myself it wasn't him.

"Noah. Hadn't you noticed? The last person to see him said he was leaving a gin joint but now he hasn't been home and his father can't find him." She leaned in closer. "I overheard Mr. Underwood and your father talking."

This was exactly the kind of stress I didn't need. Father's anger never meant anything good. And this anger, which was over something I had nothing to do with, would no doubt fall on me. Nodding, I said, "That sounds like Noah. I'm sure he's somewhere sleeping off one hangover after another."

Alcohol may have been illegal but that made no difference to men like Noah. Or a lot of people actually. I thought people were drinking more since prohibition started, actually.

"He's probably hung up in a whorehouse," Jane said. Her face dropped immediately after the words were out and she saw me. I could only shrug. Both because she was probably right and because I couldn't bring myself to care. "Sorry."

"Come on, Lizzie." Olivia took my arm, leading her away from the group. I needed to make her understand that she didn't have to protect me from the truth. "Now you have to tell me what is going on?"

"What do you mean?" I turned my focus on the grass swaying in the breeze rather than her face. Olivia could read me like no one else I knew and I truly didn't want her to see that I knew exactly what she was talking about.

"You know perfectly well to what I am referring to. Or whom to be more precise."

"Orin?" The corners of my mouth flirted with a smile. It felt good to think I could talk to my best friend about him. Like I was revealing a surprise Christmas present but knew I couldn't reveal too much even to her. She may have been my best friend but she was also pretty weak under the pressure of her parents and would crack like a walnut if they started asking questions.

"Yes." We both glanced his way as if afraid he might overhear though he was all the way across the yard from us. "Well, isn't that a silly grin he has?"

"I know," I whispered. "If I didn't know better, I'd swear he can hear us."

"Stop avoiding my question. What is going on?" Olivia nudged me with her elbow.

"Nothing specific."

Olivia tugged my arm so I'd walk with her. No

one could overhear our entire conversation that way. It was a tactic we'd used many times in the past. "Do you like him?"

"Yes."

"And he you?"

"He seems to."

"But?"

"My father has already decided that I'm marrying Noah. It's not like I can do anything about it."

"You know, there is a whole group of women, who live their lives how they want. They don't marry someone just because their father says."

"Wouldn't that be a dream?"

Four men raced across the yard in between Olivia and me. The previously lazy afternoon was replaced with a hurried frenzy where I couldn't make out what any of them were saying even though they were basically yelling.

Olivia and I looked at each other when those men stopped in front of my father and Mr. Underwood. Their frenzied whispers caused Olivia and me to hurry toward them. Whatever was happening, it wasn't good.

I just wanted to be close enough to eavesdrop.

"Colin, any news?" Mr. Underwood asked one of

the younger men. Colin Stone was three years ahead of me in school and close friends with Noah's older brother.

"Sir, we've tracked him to," Colin glanced around taking note of us women. "Some rather less than pleasant establishments."

"That decides it," my father cut him off and began walking away.

"Henry, I will fix this. My son will be ready to marry your daughter." Mr. Underwood wasn't the type to beg but I'm pretty sure this was the closest he'd ever come.

"Leonard, I will not have my daughter marry a man who wastes his family's fortune. I have backup arraignments. I believe I will now utilize that plan."

The look on Olivia's face probably mirrored mine. Or at least her face showed what I felt. Eyes wide in surprise, mouth slightly open in disbelief. Noah was a lot of things but rebellious against his father wasn't one of them.

"You're breaking our agreement?" Mr. Underwood asked. With these men, the masters of their own little universes, a rift wouldn't be something either would take lightly.

"She will marry Bradley Johnson. His family has made significant advancements in business and he isn't out squandering it. They will be able to live up to their financial obligations."

It was me. I was a financial obligation. While normally the woman's family paid a dowry, or at least in old times they did, my father was deemed too important to have to do that. No. Somehow his business would benefit with my marriage.

"Henry—"

"It's done, Leonard." Father stormed away leaving most of the crowd speechless and unsure of what they should each do.

Me included.

My future had changed before my very eyes without a word, agreement, or anything else from me.

"Bradley? Lizzie, Bradley?" Olivia asked as if I'd have any explanation. Her eyes filled with tears as she turned away and my stomach vaulted.

"I... I... didn't know. Olivia, I would never—"

"Doesn't matter does it?" Her face had changed when she looked at me again.

The sympathetic friend had disappeared even though her situation wasn't much different from mine. Though, her father took her opinion into consideration whereas mine just wanted me gone.

She'd wanted to marry Bradley but her family had other ideas.

"It isn't my choice," I told her though she should've already known that. "I would never choose Bradley if for no other reason than how you feel about him."

Olivia's tear-filled eyes overflowed and the one friend I ever had, the one person I actually trusted before Orin came along, stomped away angry for something I had no power over.

I searched the crowd for Orin, the only other person who'd listen to me, but he, too, had disappeared.

I was alone.

Finally, by mid-afternoon, the last stragglers left. Whether they'd been hanging around because they lacked anything else to do or they hoped for more drama, I couldn't say but incredible relief washed over me when they finally left.

Instead of going inside to face my now changed path in life, I ran off in the other direction.

My shoes smacked the pavement again and again as I pushed myself harder.

I couldn't stop, wouldn't stop even when my chest felt like it would explode.

I'd known where I was going without thinking about it. I needed to talk to Orin.

I gasped for air while pounding on his door.

"What is with this man?" I muttered when he didn't answer after a second round of knocking.

So I did what I did last time and walked around to the back of the house hoping to find him. I tried again on the back door but obviously, he wasn't home.

I could sit there and wait, again, or go back to my house.

Since I had no idea where he'd gone or when he'd be back, I opted for the latter—begrudgingly.

This time I walked much slower as I left. Even stopped long enough to look back at the house I silently promised I'd never return to. If I couldn't be with him, there was no point in torturing myself. Desperation turned into resignation.

I'd always been resigned to my fate and sometimes I wished I'd never met Orin Vilkatas because then I never would have even dreamed that my life could be different.

I'd turned around the side of the house when the back door squeaked open.

Orin strode out, his normal confident self, and

walked into the woods, disappearing into the massive trees.

What? Had he been in the house ignoring me?

Being ignored didn't sit well with me.

I followed him, partly out of curiosity and partly out of anger. And not at all with the hope of catching him naked in the woods again.

At all.

When he stopped, I froze, hoping he wouldn't turn and catch me.

He bent over something. Something I couldn't make out but a tuft of brown fur peeked out from the side.

He ignored me to take care of a dead animal.

I opened my mouth to say... something but his name caught in my throat—a hard lump unable to be swallowed.

Everything came into focus. Acid formed in my stomach and my mouth watered because I was about to throw up.

That dead animal had a human face.

Chapter Seven

My brain didn't fully process what I saw.

But I did know I needed to get out of there, away from Orin and the body lying on the ground. Hopefully, before he realized I'd seen anything. That person I'd thought was on animal was my unwanted fiancé. Noah Underwood.

I took the first step backward tentatively. Careful, purposeful, and slowly so as to not make a sound.

Then another.

And another.

Then a twig snapped under my weight.

Orin's head snapped up. He spun around to face me.

My heart thumped so hard I was sure he could

hear it or even see it pound against my chest as we stood there, a moment of tension passing between us.

I spun around and bolted, running at my fullest speed.

He was faster and stronger but I didn't want to die in the forest behind his house like the person back there lying in the dirt. I hadn't even had a chance to live yet.

The muscles in my legs lengthened and snapped back as I pushed myself harder than I ever had in my life. I cursed the heels I wore as they caught on the underbrush and slowed me down.

I'd gotten across the edge of the woods before Orin grabbed my arm and pulled the both of us to the ground.

I punched and kicked with everything I had and broke away.

But Orin yanked on my ankle to keep me on the ground.

"Lizzie... stop... "

I didn't stop. "Why would you kill him? Why would you do that?"

I kicked and flailed. He grunted when I landed a hit.

Orin wrapped his strong arms around my body

and lifted me off the ground so that my feet swung in the air and all chance of escape disappeared.

"Lizzie, please. Stop."

"Let me go," I begged. "Please let me go."

As the adrenaline in my veins receded, my body began giving out.

My only hope was that the begging worked and Orin would let me go.

His grip loosened so that the very tips of my toes touched the ground. Inch by inch he continued to lower me until I could fully stand on my own. He held my arms to keep me from running.

"What are you doing here?" he demanded, his voice rougher, sharper than he'd ever spoken to me before.

Words refused to form in my mouth when I tried to answer. Instead, I stood there with my lips opening and closing like a fish out of water gulping for air. The fear took over my body and nothing else worked.

Everything about him softened. When he saw the terror in my eyes, his changed from the animal I saw in the woods to the man I thought I knew.

"Lizzie, what are you doing here?" he asked more gently.

I pulled my arms toward my body. This time he

let me go and I started to cry. "I didn't see anything," I said with a sob. "I promise. Just let me go."

"Lizzie." Orin took another step closer. "I'm—I'm not going to hurt you."

"Please," I said again barely able to bring my eyes up to his.

I had no more fight in me. Nothing left to give. I could only hope he'd take pity.

He must've seen that in me, my terror and lack of fight because he nodded his permission.

As quickly as my body allowed, I turned and pushed myself to take one step after another until I knew for sure he was no longer behind me.

And I didn't look back.

Somehow I found my way home with no idea how I actually got there. I walked but saw none of the familiar markers along the way. I walked in a haze and when I arrived, realized I'd been gone for hours. Half expected to see my father waiting with a punishment ready to be laid with an iron fist but he was nowhere to be seen.

And I wasn't going to go looking.

I'd meant what I said to Orin. I wasn't going to tell anyone. It made me feel awful but I'd have to explain what I was doing in the woods not to mention if Orin was a cold-blooded killer, it was a bad idea to tell what I saw. For a fleeting moment, I considered that he'd solved my problem. I wasn't proud of it.

Instead, I shut my bedroom door and locked it, something I wasn't supposed to do but somehow it made me feel safer.

Unfortunately, I couldn't fall asleep. My body begged to be taken into the dark yet still I laid there listening to the breeze outside hit the windows.

The room heated up so I pushed open the window nearest my bed for air.

Still, I could not sleep.

Especially with the wind whistling against the house.

It had to be the wind.

Yet the wind wouldn't whistle a familiar tune. It wouldn't have a rhythm.

When hopped off the bed and peered out the window, trying to remain in the shadow so that if someone was down there, they wouldn't see me.

Orin lingered where the garden met the back-yard, bathed in the white light of the moon. Something was strange about him. He shined brighter under the moonlight than anyone I'd ever seen. Most had their skin tone washed out by the bright hue but for him, it was almost as if it enhanced everything.

When I blinked hard, thinking my eyes played a trick on me, he was gone.

He probably hadn't meant to be seen.

Then he tapped on the balcony door.

My body froze as I fell back against the wall and held in a large breath as if the person on the other side would hear me if I simply breathed.

He tapped again.

I didn't know what to do.

Drawn to opening the door and hearing what Orin had to say, the vision of Noah Underwood dead on the ground ran through my mind. Something I'd never forget and I couldn't do it. I couldn't open the door and let Orin in.

Finally, the tapping ended.

In the morning, as the sun came up, I still laid in bed staring at the ceiling.

I'd fallen asleep eventually but hadn't stayed that way very long. Too many thoughts running rampantly through my head. But not regret over Noah's death.

Did I want him dead? No, of course not. Could I bring myself to cry over the fact that he was? Also no.

"Elizabeth," my father's voice boomed through the door after one loud knock.

Ignoring him wasn't an option, so I got out of

bed, straightened my dressing gown, and opened the door.

"I'll be in the city for a few days. Mrs. Atherton will be here for you."

Meaning the woman who organized the house had money if I needed anything, the same arrangement whenever he left town. No idea why he needed to remind me every single time.

"Yes, Father."

Without a good-bye or a kind word, he trudged down the hall, turned the corner, and disappeared.

I dropped back onto my bed, wrapped the blanket all the way around myself so tightly I could barely breathe.

Then I cried.

Orin had been the one bright light in my otherwise lackluster life. I'd fallen in love with him and it had happened so quickly. I always imagined love to be something that took time to grow like a small ember growing into a forest fire. And that was probably true. My feelings for him would have probably grown even stronger if I'd been allowed to let them.

Another knock on the door broke that momentary solitude. I ignored it.

"Elizabeth, I'm going to the market," Mrs. Atherton called from the other side.

"Thank you," I mumbled because it wasn't her fault I felt the way I did.

There was a long pause. "Elizabeth, are you feeling well?"

"Yes, Mrs. Atherton. I'm just tired." I listened as she clunked down the hall until I could no longer hear her.

Two days passed with me on that bed inside my own little world. No one came to check on me other than the daily knock from Mrs. Atherton asking if I wanted my meals in my room that day and I was thankful. At least until the maid came to clean the room and I realized what day it was. I also received a not so gentle reminder from Father's secretary that my presence would be expected at a dinner. To represent him in his absence and to not embarrass him with my behavior nor by failing to show up.

Bradley would also be at the dinner. His whole family would be which meant his mother would be watching us closely.

He was a decent enough man, much better than Noah and I knew he'd give me a good life. A life I didn't want but still a good one.

I had to fight my way out of the hole I'd masterfully created to put myself together enough that I'd be considered presentable.

The pale blue dress my father had recently given me—not out of love but rather because others had noticed how often my dresses had repeated themselves—was actually the most beautiful dress I'd ever owned.

One last look at myself and I left my room.

Then the house.

I was on a mission to find Orin Vilkatas.

Chapter Eight

When I got to Orin's house, I didn't even bother with the front door, instead going right around the back. If I'd learned anything about Orin it was that he wouldn't answer. He never had before.

The knob on the back door turned on the first try.

I stepped inside and paused, listening for any noise or slight movement that would tell me Orin was home. The air was completely still, silent almost eerie.

Alone in his house for the first time, I walked from room to room taking in his space. Orin spent his time here, though he hadn't done much to personalize the space. It remained a normal house that gave no indication of the murderous beast who apparently lived there.

Could I get over that? Act like it never happened. That Orin hadn't killed a man I'd grown up with. A man I hated but still knew.

I stopped roaming and took a seat on the sofa to wait. I started to feel like an invader of his privacy as time passed.

The summer sun heated the living room but I didn't know if I should open a window so I didn't. I sat there letting a fine sheen of perspiration form on my forehead. One drop ran down the back of my neck.

I'd almost hit my limit of patience when the lock on the front door disengaged and the door opened.

Orin walked through the small entryway and turned left into the kitchen carrying several grocery bags as if they weighed nothing.

I watched without moving as he set the items on the counter. He didn't look my way or acknowledge my presence.

He went about unpacking the groceries not knowing I watched his every move.

"Do you have a habit of breaking into people's houses, Elizabeth?" His voice startled me but melted my insides at the same time.

"The door wasn't locked." Which wasn't really a reason.

No one locked their doors much which didn't mean a person should enter anyone's house without permission.

"I guess it wasn't." Orin continued working, opening one cupboard then the other than the icebox.

"I thought we could talk." I stood and walked toward him.

He didn't turn immediately then his shoulders slumped a little and he let out a small sigh.

"Are you hungry?" he asked.

"Actually, I am. I haven't had a thing to eat in days."

Orin began to work on making me a sandwich with left-over chicken.

If nothing else, it would give me something else to do than awkwardly stare at the man. Seeing him wasn't helping me understand what I was feeling anyway.

The meat stacked bread tasted delicious, however, even with such small bites, the food hit my stomach like a brick. I didn't want to vomit right there in his kitchen.

"So... " I trailed off still unsure of how to start this.

"What do you want to ask?" Orin removed my plate and his, dropping them into the sink as he spoke.

"Orin. You know." I moved to stand in front of him.

"Right," he said quietly.

I tapped my toes against the bottom of a nearby chair as butterflies took over. I wanted answers but I didn't want answers. Whatever he said could change everything but I didn't know if I wanted that change.

"Did you kill him?" I finally asked.

His eyes bore into me but it didn't feel aggressive. More like reluctance over whether to answer or not. Or how to answer.

"Yes," he finally said quietly.

I'd already known the answer yet actually hearing him admit it was so much worse than expected.

"Why?"

"I didn't mean to." He never flinched, never looked away. "What I mean to say is that I didn't intend to. I just wanted to scare him off, make him leave town. Get him to leave you alone. You said you'd like him to disappear."

Dear god, I did say that.

I closed my eyes and took two breaths trying not to react before getting all of the information.

"Then what happened?"

"Damn it, Lizzie." His voice rose and his hands slammed the counter causing me to stumble back slightly. I was standing in front of a man who just told me he committed murder. Seeing my reaction, he relaxed his body and brought his tone back to normal. "I'd rather not give you all the details."

"What were you doing in the woods?"

He turned his back to me because I was asking about Noah's body.

"Orin, I want to know."

"I was burying him."

Did murderers bury their victims?

"Is this... was this the first time you've done that?" I couldn't even bring myself to say the words.

"No." He sighed. "But I only meant to scare him. He'd been drinking and... inappropriate with a *very* young woman when I found him and I lost my temper. I just wanted to protect her."

He lost his temper. That wasn't a reason to kill someone but the stories about how *inappropriate* Noah could be with women had made it even to me. It was one of the reasons I worried about marrying the man. On at least one occasion, he'd hurt someone. Noah's father had to pay for silence but still, the rumors always swirled around him.

"What was he doing exactly?" I asked.

Orin's eyes darkened. "I'd rather not tell you. But she was very young, Elizabeth. Much younger than you."

My stomach tightened so hard that nausea rolled over me. "And when you killed before, was it also to protect someone?"

Orin's gaze met mine. "Yes. Every time."

After moving closer to Orin, I laid a hand gently on his shoulder. He didn't react, didn't flinch at the closeness or my touch. He stood there waiting for me to decide what I wanted to do.

"I love you, Orin. I've spent these last days thinking that you're a bad guy. I believe you when you say that you did it to protect someone. My guess is that Noah brought it on himself if you confronted him and he lost his temper. I'll believe you didn't have a choice. You won't have me as your wife, but I'd like you in my life as long as possible. I need something good at least for a little while." If the situation was as Orin said, I couldn't fault him for protecting someone.

"It isn't a good idea." He turned to look me in the eye.

"Will you hurt me, Orin?"

"Of course not."

"Then I'm sure." I pushed up onto my toes and quickly kissed him on the cheek. Supposed to be quick, once my lips touched his skin they stayed there longer than they should've. "So we're clear. No matter what I say, don't ever do that again. Understand?"

He smiled sadly. "I understand."

"Good. Now I have to find Olivia to see if she hates me." I started walking toward the door with my arm threaded through his. I didn't want to let go. This was as close as I'd ever get to him and I didn't want it to end.

"Why would she hate you?"

"She had hoped to marry Bradley Johnson but got promised to someone else. Bradley turned out to be my father's second choice for me. Now with Noah..." I wet my lips and wanted to kick myself. "Bradley has now been chosen for me."

Orin stopped me at the door. "Is he a good man?"

I sighed. "Yes, he is kind and decent. I could do worse." We faced each other with an awkward silence hanging in the air. "With my father out of town, you could take me out properly."

"On a date?" I didn't know what that meant and I pinched my face together in confusion. "It's the new way of courting."

"Tonight?"

It must've been the hopeful sound to the question that made him smile.

"I'll pick you up," he said still smiling.

"No." I stopped him. "We'll meet. I don't want the staff to see you. A few would definitely tell my father."

He nodded with a smile.

On my way back home, I searched each face I passed for Olivia. I didn't want to have to go to her house but I would if necessary.

Instead, I found her alone in a window seat of a small café sipping a glass of lemonade.

"Olivia." I approached her quietly from behind. "Can we talk?"

"I can't imagine you'd have much to say."

My best friend didn't look up at me but I slid into the booth across from her anyway. She could be mad at me for something I had no control over or we could talk.

"I don't have a choice in this decision, Olivia. If I

did do you think I would choose someone you wanted for yourself. I like Bradley the way I like Mrs. Atherton."

"But not the way you like Orin, right?" She finally glanced up at me.

"Yes, exactly."

Olivia sighed, her eyes changed from those of anger to those of resignation. "I know, Lizzie. It just took me by surprise and my brain got the better of me imagining... never mind."

I swallowed hard because I knew exactly what she was thinking. The same thing I'd imagined a hundred times myself. As a wife, I would be expected to share not only a life but also a bed. I'd imagined the things Noah liked to do to women and every single time I thought of it, my stomach threatened to revolt. Less so with Bradley but I still didn't want to be with him.

"So we're all right then?" I asked.

"Of course," Olivia finally gave me the forgiveness I didn't actually need.

The waitress swooped in filling Olivia's glass and bringing me one without me having to ask. We spent a lot of time here over the years.

"I haven't seen you in town for a while," Olivia said with a raised eyebrow.

"I've been dealing with some things."

"Orin?" She gave me this smile. Like she knew a secret. She did though I never told her anything specific.

"Among other things."

"What is going on with the two of you? Your father will be angry if he finds out you're seeing each other."

I couldn't help but smile. "I know but I'm doing everything he has ever asked of me and I will marry Bradley as he wishes if it comes to that. Right now is the only time in my life that I can do even a little something for myself. I'm going to take the opportunity."

"You're making it harder on yourself. You'll fall more in love with him and still have to give him up."

"I'm willing to take that chance." I slid out of my seat to stand without taking even a sip of the lemonade the waitress brought me. "I have to get home." After hugging her quickly, I left to make the walk back. It was slow, liberating even.

Time was something I usually had far too much of but tonight I was very thankful for it.

I didn't need to rush as I prepared for my evening with Orin. I went through dozens of outfits before deciding on one. Put my hair back into a proper bun and even smeared a bit of cosmetics across my face. Father hated the "face paint" which I so rarely had the opportunity to wear. I could usually get away with the smallest amount for balls or parties because it was expected.

I carried my shoes in one hand as I made my way to the front door. Didn't want the smack of heels against the hardwood flooring to alert the staff that I left and force them to make a report to my father.

Almost to the door, Mrs. Atherton appeared from nowhere, not only scaring the wits out of me but also causing me to second-guess the sneaking out part of my plan.

"Are you out for the evening?" Her gray hair speckled among the black, twisted into braids, and pinned to the back of her head. Her face wrinkled with time yet retained a soft smile that had always lifted my spirits. I hadn't grown up with a mother, Mrs. Atherton was the closest thing.

"Yes," I said back. "With Father away, I thought I'd take in a film."

I shifted my weight from foot to foot and my palms began to sweat. Lying or not saying the complete truth was new to me.

"I think that sounds wonderful." A smile cracked her face even further. "Enjoy yourself, Elizabeth."

I gave her a nod then closed the door behind me.

When I arrived, Orin stood, leaning against a brick wall at the corner near the restaurant. Our predetermined meeting place.

He didn't see me at first. It gave me the opportunity to really look at him.

His short black hair wasn't tamed into submission like a lot of the men my age. He let his flop a little more naturally. Lean muscles rippled from beneath a short-sleeved shirt making him look manly with his arms crossed casually.

Finally, he turned and saw me then smiled. A smile I only ever saw him give me and no one else. A smile that set my insides on fire.

"Hi," I said ignoring the butterflies in my stomach.

When his lips parted, I knew I was in trouble in more ways than one.

Chapter Nine

"You're beautiful," Orin said quietly as he cupped my face, his thumbs running the length of my jaw. In this spot and with the shadow, no one would have seen us.

I smiled shyly at the compliment. I'd never been told that before.

"Thank you." I laced my arm through his like we did this all the time as we make the short walk to the restaurant forgetting to worry if my small taste of independence would get back to my father. I'd be out his hair soon enough.

"Oh, no," I said, tensing and pulling him away from the entrance.

"What's wrong?"

"That man." I pointed inside quickly. "Is Herbert Wilmington. He's a friend of my father's."

"I see. I'm being hidden." His brows furrowed.

"Orin, no. Well, I guess yes you are but only—"

His face broke into a wide smile. "Lizzie, I'm teasing you."

We stood at an impasse.

We couldn't go inside but I didn't want to go home either.

My brain went crazy trying to come up with ideas of how to salvage the night. Spending this time with Orin was what I wanted.

He was forbidden.

Yet I still wanted him.

"I have an idea." Orin took my hand pulling me faster than my feet wanted to move.

"Where are we going?" I asked through a giggle.

I really liked this spontaneous, playful side of him.

"Come with me."

I had a hard time keeping up with Orin's long stride given my much shorter legs. He walked fast while it looked like I was running.

We stopped at the cafe where I'd found Olivia earlier.

"Wait here," he said suddenly then disappeared inside.

When he returned with a brown bag in his hand, Orin pulled me by the hand again until we stopped in front of a shiny dark Packard. He slid behind the steering wheel but I stood beside it. Father had a car and while I'd been in it only on very special occasions and I was never allowed with anyone else.

"Get in," he urged.

"I—I'm not allowed. Or I've never been allowed."

His eyes narrowed. "Get in," he said again watching me with those deep eyes that made it almost impossible to say no.

Once I situated myself on the front seat, the car jerked into motion making me squeal. The car didn't have a top and it was an impossible job to keep my hair from becoming a rat's nest. Though the breeze was refreshing with the summer heat.

Orin drove us out of town right to the edge of the lake. Somewhere quiet and beautiful and we'd be alone. After stopping, he got out without a word and took the bag with him.

I assumed he wanted me to follow so I did right up until he found the spot he was looking for and plopped to the ground. There was something freeing about not having to worry about getting dirty or what Father might say.

Still, I moved carefully to not expose myself. With the rising temperatures, I'd been allowed to wear dresses with slightly shorter hems. Thinner fabrics as well. Made things less constrictive and less stifling.

"Do you mind a picnic?" he asked.

I smiled widely at him and shook my head. "I prefer it actually."

A half a sandwich and four bites of pie later, I watched as he finished everything else. He obviously had a healthy appetite but his body sure didn't show it. Total darkness moved in with only the moon to light the sky. Not full but big enough we could easily see each other.

More than once as we talked, Orin brushed a strand of hair away from my face. I wasn't entirely sure it was necessary but still very glad he did it. Each touch of his skin against mine reminded my body that I was alive. That I was a woman and he was a man.

The later the night got the closer Orin moved toward me until the only way to be closer would be for me to sit in his lap.

Surprisingly that idea didn't bother me.

Excited me actually.

I had no idea what happened to the chaste, well-mannered girl my father had raised.

"You're quite relaxed." I pulled at the waist of my skirt, a nervous habit I'd picked up years before. Idle hands got me into trouble.

"Am I?"

"Yes. You're normally more guarded."

"I hadn't realized but can only assume it's your influence." Orin swallowed, his heavy gaze landing directly on me. "It's getting late." His voice quite deep, husky, and his breath hit my bare neck making me shiver in the heat. "I should probably get you home."

"That would be the proper thing to do." I bit back a smile as looked up at him. "Do you know that you're very bright at night?"

His laugh came out like a bark in the night. "What do you mean?"

"Most people look pale in the moonlight but you're bright." Like a halo surrounding him.

"Always?" he asked brow furrowed like he was trying to figure something out.

"No, sometimes you're brighter than others. Hasn't anyone ever told you that?"

"No." He fell silent, staring out over the water.

Then he stood and pulled me along with him back to his automobile.

This time he drove much slower, which was fine with me because I was in no rush to return home. But we were quieter as well.

I'd steal as many glances as I dared because I didn't want to forget how he looked, acted, or sounded that night. This night would have to get me through years of being a dutiful wife but it seemed like every time I looked his way, he was watching me. He should've been watching the road but the car never strayed.

When he turned into our driveway, I didn't think to stop him from going all the way to the house.

Mrs. Atherton and the staff would likely be asleep so there shouldn't have been anything to worry about anyway.

Orin hopped out of the car and came around to open my door before I even had a chance to.

We walked slowly to the front of the car.

I didn't want the night to end but it had to.

"I had a lot of fun tonight," I said doing my best to keep anything other than happiness from my voice.

"Me too," he murmured.

"Did I say something wrong back there?"

"Of course not. Why would you think that?"

"You've been very quiet since the lake."

Without answering, Orin pulled me into his arms and kissed me fully on the mouth.

Heat crept up my chest and face under the weight of his mouth but no chance would I pull away.

His lips and tongue coaxed my mouth open, the heat from his skin sinking into mine. Or perhaps my heat sinking into him.

When his tongue brushed against mine I savored it, committing this moment to memory so I'd never forget.

When he began to pull away, a small groan escaped right into his mouth causing him to chuckle quietly.

I enjoyed that far too much and he knew it.

"Good night, Lizzie," he whispered, his voice taking on a completely new quality that I had no way of deciphering.

"Good night," I said back, surprised at how foreign I sounded to myself.

He kissed the tip of my nose before getting back in the Packard and driving off into the night.

. . .

We saw each other every day that my father was gone.

I'd meet Orin in town early then we'd spend the day having what was, for me, an adventure. It wasn't hard to make happen because I'd never been allowed to do anything.

I'd return home late where it seemed no one noticed my absence.

Orin ignited in me an overwhelming desire that I'd been told didn't exist. It probably wouldn't in my married life.

Unless something changed, I wasn't marrying Orin.

Unfortunately, I still had to deal with Bradley Johnson. I was expected to spend time with him but I didn't want to be away from Orin.

I had the rest of my life for Bradley and only this small window of opportunity with Orin.

"So," Orin's deep voice broke through the relaxed walk toward my house two nights before my father's return. "Tomorrow is our last night before we go back into hiding."

I shook my head immediately and wrinkled my brows. "No. Remember I have to attend the Parson's function with Bradley tomorrow night."

His face fell. "I don't recall that."

"My father made it clear. I must attend in his place. 'Don't embarrass me' were his words." I cringed both on the inside and the outside.

"Oh." Orin didn't look at me for several minutes. "Can I see you after?"

"It'll be late." I shifted from one foot to another.

A plan hatched from desperation and wasn't about to change my mind now.

No matter how nervous it made me.

"Lizzie... "

"Orin," I snapped cutting him off. "Not tomorrow."

This time he was the one to crease his eyebrows. "I *am* invited to that party."

Hadn't thought of that. Of course, he was. I couldn't have him there.

"Please," I begged. "Don't come."

"What's going on, Lizzie?"

"Nothing."

He came closer to me until his breath feathered across my face.

"Suddenly you don't want me around?"

"What?" My eyes bulged at the suggestion. "I do. I just... it's just... " My toes tapped with nervous energy. I sighed deeply which came out more like a groan. "I have to get used to the life that's been chosen for me. That life includes this type of event with Bradley. I can't be his fiancé if you're there watching me. This is something I have to do."

"So this is it, then?" He moved in closer lightly tracing his fingertips up my arms leaving goose bumps in their wake causing me to shiver even in the summer heat.

"I think you're the brightest I've ever seen you tonight," I said quietly before thinking about it.

The moon was almost full and he'd been walking around with a sheen of brightness surrounding him.

"But you're going to miss tomorrow." He raised an eyebrow as if to challenge me.

I had no idea what he meant but I really wanted to know what was so special about tomorrow.

Chapter Ten

WORDS STOPPED FORMING.

Something deep in my stomach began throbbing, pulsating faster than my heart.

Sick at the thought of not seeing Orin tomorrow but I had no choice. I'd miss tomorrow and the next day and the one after that.

My eyes stung. I hoped he wouldn't see under the cover of darkness. But the moon was so bright.

Too bright. Nothing could be hidden.

"I better go inside," I said softly, my voice cracking.

He didn't agree or disagree and instead brought me even closer. His mouth covered mine with such intensity, I quickly lost my breath.

There were two things behind that kiss. A

goodbye of some kind but also a reminder of what he and I could be.

Tears filled my eyes. I kept them at bay until I securely shut the door to my bedroom and I was alone. Then they fell in sheets, streaking my face and ruining the make-up I'd put on so carefully earlier.

My chest rose and fell rapidly until I was almost unable to breathe,

I wrapped myself back into the safety of a cocoon of blankets.

Our clandestine rendezvous had come to an end as I always knew it would but that didn't make it any easier.

What little sleep I got that night was restless. I tossed and turned like a ship riding out a storm. I woke so many times through the night and at one point imagined Orin had come into my room. A dream or wishful thinking.

Or possibly a hopeful illusion.

Bradley collected me right on time the next day for the Parsons' late afternoon lawn party.

Already in full swing when we arrived, nobody really noticed us. The problem with my situation was that I liked Bradley. He'd been a good friend since childhood when he would choose to play with Olivia and me instead of the other boys.

We chose a table away from where most people lingered. Bradley and I made easy and light conversation about nothing important. Bradley was more laid back around us girls and never tried to show off like some of the other boys.

"Are you all right?" Bradley asked while I pushed food around my plate.

"I'm fine."

"You seem distracted."

Of course, I was. This life of parties and socializing was the life I'd live in the future but I just wanted to be back at the lake with Orin eating a picnic. I wanted something of my own.

"Has your father said when we are to be married?" I asked instead. "My father doesn't always tell me when plans change."

"Three weeks," he answered.

"That's soon." It was very soon. My father probably didn't want to chance having to find yet another man who'd take me. Bradley held steady so I wouldn't know if that was a good thing to him or bad. "Not even waiting until the end of the season are they?" he asked referring to our parents.

"I think he might be afraid that I'll chase you away somehow."

Bradley released a laugh.

"Not possible. We may not be in love, but I can think of worse people to spend my life with."

"Me, too." That was the truth.

We fell silent again and danced two songs to make sure everyone knew we'd been there. I wouldn't miss being required to attend these events once we were able to make our own decisions to not go. I didn't think Bradley would either. He didn't come off as being the most comfortable at this type of thing. Sure, we'd still have to go to some but we wouldn't be obligated to make it our lives.

Scratch that, once Bradley could decide for the two of us to not go. We made our public appearance; my father would be satisfied so we were free to leave.

"Would you like to sit in the garden for a while?" I asked when we reached the house.

"Elizabeth, you don't have to go through the motions with me. I understand what's going on."

My eyes opened widely. He couldn't possibly know what I had planned.

"W-what do you mean?" I stammered.

"Your father is forcing you to marry me as my father is forcing me to marry you. I don't mind of course, since we couldn't work something out with Olivia's family, it doesn't really matter. You don't have to pretend that this is a love match."

"You love her?" His feelings on the matter had never been clear. Of course, why would I have known even if they had been? Though I knew immediately that I'd never tell Olivia. That would just break her heart.

"I thought it would be nice. As you said we will be married and you've been a good friend, Bradley."

He agreed with my reasons and we made our way to the back garden.

Once we were out of the view of anyone toward the house, the large topiaries loomed over us like buildings. I veered us to the left which led to a small crisp pond reflecting the full moon.

"It's really beautiful out here," Bradley said before sitting beside me on a stone bench.

I toed off my heels to rest my feet against the brick path while I worked up the courage to do what I set out to do.

"My mother did all this," I said. "I don't think *he* wanted to let it go. She was very proud of it I'm told."

I glanced from him to my feet several times.

My heart beat rapidly, erratic and hard.

With trembling fingers, I removed the two pins holding my hair in place releasing a cascade of golden waves past my shoulders. Then I shook it out to make sure it was all free.

Bradley continued to prattle on about his job—working for his father at his garment business—but my ears no longer heard him. My focus zoomed in strictly on the plan I'd formed lying in bed late one night.

After taking a few deeps breaths, I interrupted his current story.

"Bradley." I touched his arm lightly to get him to turn my way. "There is another reason I asked you out here."

He raised an eyebrow. "And that is?"

My shaking fingers undid the top button of my dress. Then the next and the next to expose the tops of my breasts which swelled and sunk with each heavy breath giving him a glimpse of my undergarment.

Bradley's eyes grew wide as I worked my clothing.

"Elizabeth! What are you doing?"

"We're going to be married soon," I said quietly but had no idea what I was actually doing. I knew the result I wanted but had no idea how to be alluring or sensual and everything I did was based off elicit stories that certain girls told when parents weren't around.

He swung his head away so that he could no

longer see me.

"But we aren't yet." He slid down the bench further from me.

"Bradley, either way…"

I moved closer to him, almost giving him no escape, and kissed him the way I'd only kissed Orin.

The way I only wanted to kiss Orin.

He barely responded. Probably out of surprise. But still, I pushed forward. I'd set my mind to make this happen and nothing would change that. He pushed me away gently.

"Elizabeth, what's gotten into you?"

"Please," I begged and I hated that I did. "Trust me."

A small smile crossed my face before I returned my attention to his lips.

I thought I felt him starting to give into me. Just a tiny amount. He had to be. He was a man after all. This is what I'd been told men wanted.

Suddenly, a large hand wrapped around my arm and pulled me violently away from Bradley. I did two full rotations and almost fell to the ground before finding my equilibrium again.

Turning quickly I searched for Bradley and found him being held by the throat against the marble statue.

Orin's knuckles were white against Bradley's neck. Bradley clawed at him but Orin didn't budge.

Orin's acted and looked like holding Bradley off the ground by the throat took little effort whereas Bradley was working up a sweat fighting.

For a brief moment, instead of Bradley, I saw Noah's face lying cold on the ground.

"Orin, Stop!" I ran over, yanking at his arm, the massive bulge of which felt larger than normal. "Let him go! Please, let him go."

Slowly Orin released his fingers and Bradley.

Bradley fell to his knees coughing, struggling for air. My stomach turned at the idea that Orin saw what I'd been trying to do.

"Jesus Christ, man." Bradley finally got back on his feet but his voice still sounded hoarse.

"Orin, what are you doing here?" I asked. He and I locked in a stare-down as if Bradley wasn't even there.

"I think the question is what are *you* doing here?" he asked roughly, anger coating every single word.

I blinked several times not really knowing how to answer. Telling him the truth wasn't something I wanted to do.

Orin's face softened.

"Lizzie…" he started, this time with tenderness.

Heat rose up my face partly out of embarrassment but mostly anger. He'd seen what I was trying to do. Possibly all of it. Me trying to seduce Bradley in the garden before we were married.

My stomach rolled again. No one was supposed to know about this.

"I… I… " The words wouldn't come.

"And you," he turned raging Bradley. "You are more than capable to fight her off."

"I tried," Bradley yelled at Orin though took a big stumble backward when Orin stepped toward him.

"I didn't want him to," I yelled just as loudly, bringing both sets of eyes squarely to me.

"Why would you do this?" he roared at me.

I hadn't seen that side of him yet but somehow I wasn't scared.

Somehow I knew he'd never hurt me. No matter how upset he became but there was something else in with the anger. Regret? Maybe.

"I just… don't want to be passed off to someone else," I finally admitted.

"What?" both men asked at the same time.

"I… figured if I did this, I'd be ruined. If something happened and we," I motioned between myself and my fiancé. "For whatever reason didn't get married then my father wouldn't be able to pass me off to his third choice. I'd be ruined."

I wrapped my fingers around the opening at the top of my dress, suddenly very aware that I was exposing myself to them both at the same time.

Orin's face softened.

Bradley rubbed his forehead but kept his distance from both Orin and me.

"You should still wait until you're actually married," Orin finally said.

"It's only a few weeks," I countered. "What difference does it make? I don't want to be passed off to someone else. I'm sorry if you can't understand that."

"It just does." Orin's voice rose again and he looked like he was about to come unhinged.

He moved toward me roughly, the heat rolling off him in dangerous waves. It would've scared most people. It should've scared me.

"Let's get married," he said as he stopped in front of me.

His words knocked the wind out of me. "What?"

"If you're going to be ruined, I'm going to do the ruining."

Chapter Eleven

"Say yes," Orin urged. "Marry me. We'll go tonight."

I'd never known him to say anything he didn't mean. At first, I thought he was trying to throw me off my axis, get to stop my plan to be with Bradley. But the firm set of his jaw and the intent look on his face meant he was serious.

"I... I... " the words I needed eluded me.

This night didn't feel real. Like I'd wake up in my bed realizing I'd been dreaming all along. I hoped that wouldn't be the case because I'd be devastated.

The idea of a life I wanted desperately being within my reach filled me with fear. My hands shook and my heart thumped hard against my chest. I hoped he couldn't hear it.

Orin grabbed my arm and pulled me away from Bradley who stood watching us with a neutral face and his hands in his pockets.

This wasn't the proposal I dreamed of but I didn't care. He was willing to marry me.

"Wait." I wriggled out of his grip, which had loosened a bit, to run back to Bradley. "Bradley," I said breathlessly. "I have to go with him. I have to."

"I understand. I would have treated you well and we may even have been content but neither of us would've been truly happy." He swallowed roughly. "If this is what you're sure you want, Elizabeth, I'm not going to try to stop you." Bradley dropped his voice. "As long as you're sure he's not going to hurt you."

He said it with such sincerity and I hoped one day he'd find happiness of his own. He deserved it as much as I did.

"He won't," I assured him because Orin had plenty of opportunity to hurt me if he'd wanted to. "I'm sure he thought you were pressuring me."

"I get that. I'd probably react the same way in that situation."

"This is going to cause you problems, too," I said to Bradly because he had to marry someone. If not me, someone else.

And I'd never been able to predict if Father would put any of the blame for me running off on him.

"I'm sure there's someone else lined up. It won't matter who."

I'd known that very thing but hearing him say it made me incredibly sad. I nodded quickly before dropping a kiss to his cheek then ran right back to Orin.

This day turned out much differently than I had expected when I woke that morning.

Moving quickly and precisely, I slipped into my room and stopped short. Orin already waited inside for me.

I grabbed a satchel and stuffed my most prized possessions into it. A photo of my parents in happier times before me and my mother's necklace. Then some clothing. Nightwear, practical, not beautiful, a few dresses that would have to be ironed after being crumpled into a ball and shoved into the bag, and two versatile pairs of shoes.

Then we left.

There was a moment, a very small one, where I realized I'd probably never be welcomed back in that house. Though I'd never been very welcome anyway.

I wasn't going to miss it.

Orin drove us out of town, neither of us speaking. I watched his face for signs that he changed his mind. His jaw remained carved in stone.

He was really doing this. *We* were really doing this. After all the weeks he insisted we couldn't be together, he was whisking me out of town for no other reason than he couldn't stand not to.

Couldn't stand for someone else to have me.

We drove for half an hour if the way the sun drifted further into the horizon indicated passage of time before I gained the courage to ask a question.

"Why now, Orin?" He didn't answer and instead kept his eyes on the road in front of us. "Please." I needed to know. Needed to know what changed.

"I thought I could do it, Lizzie. I thought I could." His hands tightened.

"What?" I touched his arm. The muscle under his skin jumped at the contact.

"Watch you be someone else's wife," he finally said. "Don't misunderstand—this is a terrible idea, but I can't let another man have you."

Someone wanted me.

Orin wanted me.

I'd never been wanted and my heart swelled to twice its size. There was no doubt in my mind that if

I told him I truly wanted Bradley or anyone else, he would've turned us around and taken me back.

I couldn't even think of someone else let alone say it.

"I'm extremely glad you couldn't," I said still grinning like a fool.

I focused on the passing trees to allow myself those few moments of excitement. It all happened so quickly that I hadn't had time to react. I'd just gone with him.

But I was about to marry a man of *my* choosing. Unheard of in Father's circles although if I recall correctly his and my mother's marriage hadn't been prearranged.

"Wait," I snapped, sitting up straight as a board. "How did you know I was there with Bradley."

He wet his lips then held them together tightly. I bounced with every bump in the road. Autos were convenient but not the smoothest ride. We made slow progress but the air around us remained still and thick. Like the weight of what we were about to do pressed down on the both of us.

My brain raced. I wouldn't put it past my father to try to take Orin down. He'd hit me before, in front of other people, what exactly would he do when he learned of *this?*

All the thinking tired me out. My eyes grew heavy although I didn't ever fully fall asleep.

Finally, he spoke, with a voice that startled me half to death. Maybe I did nod off.

"Lizzie, we're here."

My eyes popped open as my body flung straight up. I quickly brushed my fingers through my hair to tame any loose strands.

"Where's here?" I asked. I didn't know where here was.

"Justice of the Peace. Ready?"

A knot tightened in my stomach. Not the kind I'd grown used to. Normally when my muscles tightened it was out of fear, nervousness, or terror of what I'd done wrong and how my father would react.

Not this time. This time I filled with an excitement that I'd never felt before. He really wasn't going to waste any time.

We approached a large Victorian house and I realized I didn't know if we'd left the state or not. I'd been so completely wrapped up in my own thoughts that I hadn't paid any attention but here I was, having run away from home, about to marry a man I'd only known since the beginning of summer.

It was lunacy and yet I didn't pause on the decision for even a moment. No hesitation or second thoughts. Only absolute assurance this was the right thing.

Orin took my hand, enveloping it into his own to lead me up the steps to a large door which he pounded roughly on. The house was completely dark. While not unusually late but its occupants had obviously retired for the night. About to suggest we should come back in the morning but Orin rapped again with a closed fist so hard that it echoed through the foyer inside before I had the chance to get the words out.

Finally, a light-flooded down the stairs, the first sign of life inside. Then came another until an older man, mid-forties with gray hair brushing his temples, stood on the opposite side of the glass staring at us as if he'd seen a ghost.

I tightened my grip on Orin's hand. I didn't know this other man but Orin would keep me safe.

"Orin?" The muffled voice contained the same surprise as his face.

"You know him?" I whispered.

"I know his son very well," Orin said back.

The door opened and the man threw out his arms taking Orin into them for a full twenty seconds in a greeting far different than I'd see in my world. A polite nod maybe, a smile if with someone very familiar. The only person I'd ever hugged before Orin was Olivia.

"We haven't seen you in quite a while," the older man said.

"Sorry about that," Orin said. "I need a favor."

The man's eyes dropped to me, roaming my face as if accessing me. Now, this I was completely used to. Would I meet his standards? How could I when I had no idea what the man looked for?

"I suppose I can guess the favor," the man finally said.

"Will you do it?" Orin asked as I watched them volley words back and forth.

"Ezra?" A woman called from the top of the stairs, her shadow falling on the wall.

"It's Orin, Amy."

She scurried down the stairs then hugged Orin to her tightly. I truly felt like I was intruding on a long-awaited reunion.

"Well, you two better come on in," he said stepping aside for us to pass.

Orin introduced me to Ezra Brown and his wife Amy.

She hugged me. Honestly hugged me and while I wasn't even close to an expert on hugging, it felt very, very real.

After several minutes of polite chatter, while Ezra asked a few questions and the answers on a piece of paper then pulled out his bible, Orin and I stood before him listening to the words of a modified marriage sermon. Orin had asked for the short version.

I had to keep looking away from Orin or I might've melted into the floor. Before we started, Orin looked at me, full of love, full of kindness, and something I didn't recognize. But absolutely like I was all that matter in the world.

All of that might've been true but I couldn't let myself think about it too much or I'd be reduced to tears. My willpower would only last so long.

Each glance sent a shot of electricity through my body. My heart thumped erratically and while I felt as if I would cry anyway with the overwhelming love in my heart, was able to manage to keep my composure.

The only thing left was a kiss.

Chapter Twelve

Orin stroked his thumbs lightly over my cheeks before our lips met. His tongue slid against mine softly as he drew me into him. He snaked a hand up my body where he clasped the back of my neck firmly holding me to him.

As if I had anywhere else I'd rather be.

When Ezra cleared his throat I remembered we weren't alone. Orin kept me right against him until Ezra cleared it again. This time much more forcefully.

"I'll... ah... make sure the paperwork is filed with the appropriate people," Ezra said pointing to the desk where his wife sat. Then he stopped and looked back at us. "Should I be expecting a visit from the police?"

"Not this time," Orin said with a wide smile.

"An angry father, perhaps?"

Orin shrugged the question off without giving a clear answer

"Thank you, Ezra, for everything," he said instead. "You'll make sure it's all taken care of?"

A look passed between them before Ezra responded. "Of course."

At first, it seemed Orin meant gratitude for marrying us in the middle of the night but on second thought, hearing the weight behind his words, it seemed to encompass more.

"We'll be going." Orin folded my hand into his and began leading us back out toward the front door.

"You're welcome to stay," Amy offered and pointed a thumb toward the back of the house, "in the guest house for the night if you like."

Heat crept up my face and I hoped they wouldn't be able to see it in the dim lighting.

I may have been sheltered and innocent but I did know what Orin would expect us to do tonight as a married couple. But I didn't want other people close by when that happened. My nerves took a jagged veer to the left leaving me shaking on the inside but hopefully not on the outside.

"That's very kind of you," Orin answered. "But I think we'll continue on into the city."

I sighed in relief.

Growing up without a mother left certain holes in my education. Things a mother might have explained to her daughter that I had to pick up through conversations with some of the girls that weren't as *good* as me, just to have an idea of what Orin would want to do tonight.

Thinking of us being together made a whole new level of nervousness took over.

My hands began to shake at the idea of intimacy with Orin and I hoped he wouldn't feel it inside his. When he closed his other hand over the top of mine, I knew he'd noticed.

I hadn't been allowed into the city in years and it was like seeing everything for the first time all over again. Lights dotted the skyline, twinkling against the dark blue night sky. While most people back home would have been turning in, the city was still wide awake and alive with activity.

In the lobby of the hotel, people spoke in hushed tones. The thudding of heels on marble flooring echoed from each direction and grabbed my attention.

I stood back admiring the people and the

building while Orin spoke to the distinguished-looking man at the front desk. While I assumed Orin hadn't made a reservation since we'd left so quickly, it still only took him a few minutes before we followed a bellhop to a room.

Every single thing that was new and unusual and exciting only reminded me of how sheltered my father had kept me.

Inside our room, I noticed Orin slip a bill into the boy's hand before he left. Those types of things were not handled in view of the women. At least in my father's world.

"Are you hungry? We could order dinner in." Orin turned on a couple of the lamps as he spoke.

The full moon illuminated most of our room, casting hues of white and blue across everything. And also making Orin's skin glow brightly. It was the weirdest effect, one I'd never seen before him or anyone else but he was beautiful.

"No, thank you."

"Are you feeling all right?" He pulled the curtains open wider and stood to gaze out over the city skyline.

"Yes."

I pulled gently at the waist of my dress. A nervous habit I'd had since I was little.

And I'd never before been so nervous in my life. Then I swallowed hard and began unpacking the small bag I'd brought with me.

As I worked, excitement buzzed right beneath the anxiety of being with Orin. I wanted him touching my body and the mere thought of him making contact quickened my breath as my heart hammered against my breast.

I tried taking a deep, soothing breath but it didn't work.

Orin came to me, took my hand in his, and led me over to the large window where he'd been standing. He slid his arm around my waist and gave a gentle tug so that I'd fall back into his hard chest. He towered over me and his chin resting on the top of my head.

"It's very beautiful," I said, my voice barely a whisper.

Orin swept my hair off my shoulder and dropped several soft kisses onto my neck, almost nibbling on the sensitive spot where my neck meets my shoulder.

I closed my eyes taking a deep breath to calm the waves crashing over me. My heart still took off like a racehorse trying to get out of my chest. He sucked my earlobe into his mouth, his teeth scraping across my skin. When I turned to face him, he seemed even bigger than before. He was always such a strong man but tonight... tonight he seemed absolutely looming.

My gaze locked onto his but I couldn't force any words out of my mouth even though I felt like I should say something. This was completely new territory for us.

His skin acquired an almost luminescent quality in the moonlight, almost matching the glow of the moon.

Orin pressed his lips against mine with a new urgency. I tried to keep up, kiss him back as he kissed me but there was no denying that he was owning me. A full shiver shook my body and then primal instinct kicked in.

As inexperienced as I was, as worried about being with him physically as I had been, none of it mattered once he took over.

Orin slowly undid my dress, one button at a time, as he continued kissing me. Almost as if his mouth could distract my nerves at the prospect of a man seeing me naked.

As he peeled my clothing away, he ran his mouth down my neck and across the tops of my breasts before pushing my dress all the way to the floor. It was hardly fair that once he removed my undergarments I stood naked before him yet he remained fully clothed.

Under a flush of embarrassment, I shifted my weight and folded my arms over my breasts but Orin pulled them down immediately to take a step back and look at me. He just looked at me and I let him. In that moment, I knew I could've never done this with Bradley like I'd convinced myself I could.

I wanted only Orin. It had been Orin since the moment I first met him.

I swallowed hard before taking two steps toward him and reached out to clumsily attempt to undo his shirt. My fingers wouldn't cooperate. Between the adrenaline and the linen of his shirt, I couldn't fit the buttons through the stupid holes.

Then I remembered that one of my friends had said that men didn't want their women to have initiative and I froze. She'd said that men wanted to be in control so I snapped my hands back quickly.

His low chuckle melted every muscle I possessed moments before he yanked his shirt off apart sending the tiny buttons scattering across the floor. We'd never be able to find all of those.

Somehow, Orin managed to kiss me, run his hands up my body, touching me as no one else ever had, remove the rest of his clothing, and move us to the bed seemingly all at the same time. It was like he had extra hands.

"I love you, Orin," I said with a breathless voice. My entire body had come alive and waited, melting from the heat radiating off him.

His cheek brushed against my shoulder as he dropped small kisses down my neck and grazed the sensitive skin with his teeth.

His hot breath tickled my ear. "That's why we're here."

I'd never seen a naked man in my life before him. Yet there Orin was naked before me and I was afraid to look. When I worked up enough nerve, a blush raced up my chest to my face. His... member hung in the air and looked far too large to go where I'd been told it was going. A new fear formed in my chest.

But I knew Orin wouldn't hurt me.

He kissed his way down my body then pushed my legs open wide and kissed me there. I flinched, tightened my legs against his head, and tried to pull away yet it made my body come alive like I'd just been given a jolt of electricity. Orin slid his hands up my legs to the inside of my thighs where he held on strongly, keeping my legs open. I wouldn't be going anywhere. One hand released my thigh and came to rest on my lower stomach where he held tightly.

What I didn't know was how amazing it would feel to have his tongue lap against me.

The sounds coming from my mouth as his tongue worked some kind of voodoo magic on me should have caused me extreme embarrassment. Yet somehow I couldn't make myself feel that way.

The oddest sensation started low in my stomach. A curling, swirling tornado of pleasure tightened my muscles and wracked my body, curling my toes. My body soared and exploded and came alive as it had never been before.

When the explosion of pleasure subsided, Orin made his way back up my body, dropping tiny kisses up my stomach, to my breasts, where he sucked a nipple into his mouth.

This wasn't at all what had been described to me.

He kissed me again then pushed his hard length inside me while whispering in my ear. Sweet words I didn't understand as my breath caught at the invasion. Then he stilled.

Orin didn't move for several long moments. Once the pain subsided, I ran a hand down his back, basking at the fact that I was now allowed to touch him like this, and he thrusted his hips again. This time, is was... uncomfortable but not painful.

Soon my world became full of pleasure and love to the point I thought my heart would shatter from the emotion of it.

He cupped my breast and ran a thumb over the nipple. He kissed me deeply as I pushed my fingers into his hair. All the while, he pulled his hardness from my body then pushed it back it. Over and over then he dropped his forehead to mine. His breath came just as quickly as mine.

As he touched me, I became liberated from the life I was supposed to live and found my place in the one that I wanted. This was the first step to becoming the person I always wanted to be, all I could do was hang on to Orin because he was the one taking me there.

His movements slowed but his breaths did not. A fine sheen of sweat covered both of us when he kissed me once more before pulling his erection out of me. That's what Olivia had called it. An erection.

There was so much I didn't know and I hoped that he'd enjoyed what we did. His breathing said he did. Orin pulled me into his side and kissed my forehead.

"Are you all right?" he asked quietly.

I gave my body a stretch and realized that some

of my muscles were quiet sore. But it was a good kind of sore. "I'm perfect."

In the morning, a sliver of light shined through a small crack in the curtains falling across the room as a loud wake-up call. Forcing my eyes open, I groaned and quietly stretched my stiff neck that knotted as I slept the entire night across Orin's chest. With a small smile that I couldn't wipe away no matter how hard I tried, I positioned myself back against him allowing his body to warm me.

"I'm awake." His voice was quiet, not tired but soft and gentle as his fingers began to trace the length of my bare spine.

"I was trying *not* to wake you."

"I've been awake for a while. I was waiting for you."

I nodded because I had no idea what to say, how a proper wife would act in the morning after making love to her husband. In this moment, I hated just how sheltered I'd been raised. I knew nothing.

"Are you hungry?"

I nodded again.

"We should get dressed and find breakfast."

As I got up from the bed, I pulled the crinkled,

white top sheet with me to cover my nakedness and ran to the bathroom.

Which was silly.

He'd already seen me completely and touched me everywhere. I shouldn't have been worried about him seeing me again. His gaze followed me across the room.

After washing up, putting on a lightweight dress, and twisting my hair tightly into a knot at the base of my head, I returned to the sitting area where my husband already waited. He smiled when he saw me, cupped my cheeks, and gave me a kiss that reminded me of last night. When he stood and hooked my arm through his to leave the suite, my face burned at the memories of what we'd done.

We only had a short walk to a restaurant he said he'd eaten at before. When we entered, Orin asked for us to be seated at a corner table and told me he wanted us to have some privacy. Maybe he'd knew I'd need to talk about last night but how could I do that in such a public place?

We both ordered eggs but he added a steak while I only wanted a couple of strips of bacon and bread with jam. Although once the food came, we hadn't really started talking about anything important and I nibbled small bites while pushing the rest around my plate.

I glanced around the room, looking everywhere except at Orin hoping he wouldn't notice. I should have known better. He noticed everything.

"Lizzie, what's wrong?" He raised an eyebrow at me.

"Nothing," I answered while continuing to stare at my plate.

"You've barely spoken this morning. Something is wrong."

"Of course not," I smiled but already felt a flush burning around my ears. His watchful eyes caught that.

"Tell me."

"I just don't know what's appropriate to say after... " My gaze darted around the room. This conversation was uncomfortable for me and that flush I'd felt earlier turned hotter as it climbed onto my cheeks.

Orin smirked. "You will have to look at me eventually."

Rolling my eyes, something I hadn't done in a very long time since my father's firm hand reminded me that doing so wouldn't be acceptable from a young lady, the corners of my mouth also started turning up.

"Lizzie, you can talk to me about anything. No matter how intimate. Nothing is inappropriate for us." He paused lowering his voice slightly. "Is there... did I hurt you?"

"No." My answer came too quickly and loudly and brought us the attention of those close to us. "I mean everything is fine... there."

He laughed at my reaction.

"Fine?"

I nodded to his frown.

"All right." Orin reached out brushing his hand against mine. For the life of me, I couldn't figure out what I'd said to make him scowl.

"So I can really talk to you about anything? It won't shock you?" For the first time in my life I was beginning to feel like the me I dreamed to be. I'd always wanted to be open and honest, authentic with someone... with Orin.

"It may shock me but it won't upset me. There are things that could come out of that beautiful mouth of yours that would surprise the hell out of me. But I still want you to say them."

Working up the courage to ask the question I wondered about was harder for me than probably most people. I took a deep breath, swallowed, and blurted it out.

"How did you know?"

Again his eyebrows shot up in an unspoken question.

"How did you know what to do to make me feel…"

"Ah." He leaned forward onto his elbows, folding his hands under his chin. "Because I've done it before."

I did my very best to steel my face into having no reaction. I'd suspected he had but suspecting and knowing were two different things.

"The world I grew up in is very different from yours," he said. "We're less formal. I hope that doesn't hurt you."

Did that bother me? No.

Obviously, I didn't love the idea of Orin being with another woman the way we had been together last night. However, he had a life before he met me. It wasn't something I had the right to be angry about. But what a completely foreign idea. If one of my friends had been known to have sex with someone they weren't married to, they'd have been disowned.

"I was raised to expect that our husbands would have some experience before getting married.

Honestly, we aren't really encouraged to expect fidelity after we are married. Men will do what men want to do."

Anger took over his face and I wished I could read his mind.

"Lizzie, that's something you never have to worry about. I love you and I've made promises to you that I fully intend to keep. There could never be anyone else for me."

For some, those may have just been pretty words of reassurance from a new husband but I completely believed him. But Orin had always been honest with me.

"Last night," I began though I pushed my plate further away from me because the anxiety of talking to him this way meant I wouldn't be eating anymore and this gave me a way to lean over the table more. I didn't want to ask him this but there wasn't anyone else that I could. "Last night... there was a point that I felt... something. I don't know."

His brows furrowed. "Something good or something bad?"

I took a nervous breath. "Something good. It was this swirly feeling in my stomach. Maybe pressure..."

"That built until it exploded?" At least he kept his voice down as I had. We really should've talked about this when we were alone in the hotel room. At least the restaurant wasn't very busy. I wet my lips and nodded. "That was your orgasm." When I showed no sign of understanding what he meant, he said, "Your climax." Still nothing. I knew what the word climax meant, it was the pinnacle of the story, but didn't see how it related. "It felt good right?"

"Really good."

Now a satisfied grin replaced whatever had been on his face before. "Good. That's..." He sighed. "I'm not sure how to explain it to you. Women really don't talk about these things do they?"

I shook my head. "Not in my world."

"It's... at the end, I have a realize. I know you know that because there's physical evidence of it." My cheeks heated again. I'd felt that evidence spill out of me last night as I laid beside him. "It's like that."

"Without the evidence."

He shrugged. "Sometimes there's evidence then too."

Now that made absolutely no sense but I felt like I'd already pushed myself too far today and that discussion would have to wait for another time.

"Any other worries?" he asked cutting into his steak again.

"One."

"And that is?"

"My father. I can't believe we did this. Can't believe I did this. I always do whatever he asks of me and this isn't going to end well with him." The words tumbled out of my mouth. "I'm scared of what he'll do when he finds out."

"You don't have to worry about that, Lizzie." He face darkened. "I'll handle your father."

Chapter Thirteen

"I'LL HANDLE YOUR FATHER," Orin said with so much determination, I believed him.

He was well on his way to convincing me that I wouldn't have to worry about my father once we got back home. That he'd take care of me.

Yet it was the how he'd take care of me when it came to my father that began to worry me. Orin had assured me that anything violent he'd done before, including with Noah, was for the protection of others. While I could accept that, I didn't want him to protect me by harming someone else again.

"I don't want you to... I mean my father is difficult but I wouldn't want him... dead."

"I didn't mean... " he said quietly and lowered his

eyes. "The only way I would purposely do that is if someone is hurting you."

I held my hands up in defense. "I just wanted to be clear."

Orin sighed and ran his hand over the back of his head then shifted uncomfortably in his seat. "I'm sorry you ever saw that." He sat back and crossed his arms over his chest "Back to this *fine* business you mentioned earlier. Is that really the best word you could come up with for last night?"

"Is that why you looked grumpy for a minute?"

He nodded.

"What little I've been told about... being with your husband," I said and darted my eyes around him. Looking directly at Orin as I tried to talk about something like this turned out to be more difficult than almost anything else. "Well, I was told that laying with my husband is my duty but a proper lady won't enjoy it."

A war raged inside me. I loved that I could speak my mind with Orin but it would take some getting used to. I had to get used to the idea that I didn't need to worry about the back of my father's hand showing me that what I said was inappropriate.

"And did you?" he asked. "Enjoy it?"

My plate suddenly became very fascinating. I

pushed food around more than eating it, I bit my lips together and gave a small nod. It was so hard to admit.

"That's good. It's kind of my job to make sure you do. And you should Lizzie. This is part of our lives and it should be a good part of our lives because I want you to want to do it again and again. I expect you to tell me if it's ever not a good part of your life. Understand?"

Again I only nodded so he'd know I understood but as I did my heart swelled a little. Yes, this was about sex with him but it showed that he actually cared what I thought and felt.

For the very first time in my life, I knew how it felt to be loved.

"Maybe I should cut my hair." I tried changing the subject to something lighter "Something new and fashionable. Short."

"Don't you dare." He smiled widely. He saw right through me.

Orin told me that he planned for only a few days in Charleston before we had to return to the real world and its consequences. He'd asked me if that was all right with me. Another thing I'd have to get used to. Being asked my opinion and giving it wasn't a normal thing for me.

He took me on a picnic, much like the ones we'd gone on back home, where we sat on the bank of a clear pond with weeping willows stretching toward the water. The shade offered a break from the oppressive summer heat. We lounged and kissed in ways we couldn't before. Away from the watchful eyes of the town and my father.

Just the two of us.

On our last full day in the city, we woke up late in the morning after an even later night of me learning his body and the ways I could make him feel as good as he did me. We ate breakfast in the room and packed most of our things.

When we left home, Orin didn't have any extra clothes with him. He bought whatever he needed on our first day here. That included anything he thought might look nice on me, which seemed to be everything, as well as anything I showed interest in.

We didn't make it out for lunch, instead, we took advantage of the empty room and large bed.

As Orin kissed me, he cradled my hand and guided it down his body until hitting his...

I snapped my head and hand back at the same time.

"I can't touch your... " I was horrified that he'd make me say it let alone do it.

"Cock?"

My face blushed and my breath caught in my chest.

"It's called many things, Lizzie. You can find something else to call it."

I swallowed and wet my lips. I didn't want to call it anything. But I did sort of want to touch him. He'd touched me everywhere already. So I took a deep breath and held my hand back out to him.

Orin guided my hand over his...erection, up and down the entire length. He dropped his head back with a groan. The sound filled me with power. I'd never experienced anything like it. Something I was doing brought him pleasure.

Finally, he groaned, pulled my hand away, and then took back over bringing me to a state of euphoria. A state I hoped he joined me in.

Afterward, I laid on Orin's chest, my hair fanned across my shoulder. He brushed it away to make contact with the soft skin underneath.

"Am I really not allowed to bob my hair?" I asked referring to the brief conversation from days before. I don't know what made me think of that particular thing he'd said and at this of all moments.

"You can if you want," he murmured into the silent room.

When I looked up at him, his eyes were closed yet I would've sworn he was watching me.

"But you said… " I pushed myself up by bracing against a hard sculpted chest.

"*I* love your hair long but *I* am not your father. I'm not going to order you around. You're more fashionable than these half-wits chopping their hair off to prove their independence anyway."

"Right, I've never been independent a day in my life."

Orin propped himself on his elbows, pushing me off him and back onto my own pillow.

"Never been independent?" He chuckled. "You realize that three days ago you left your intended husband to run off with a man you barely know, who your father would never approve of. Then you married him." He brushed his thumb across my cheek. "I don't see Olivia or any of those other girls doing that. They'll all fall in line and marry the men of their father's choosing."

I watched his rant with a smile. For the first time, I filled with pride. I had done all of those things. "I guess you're right. I'm a rebel."

"I'd say so."

After a moment of thought, I told him, "Maybe I'll cut my hair a little. I've never been allowed to and sometimes, I don't want to wear it up."

Orin kissed the tip of my nose. "Whatever you want."

The next morning, Orin treated me to an endless breakfast while the hotel staff loaded our luggage.

The trip into the city had been a frantic race to get away from home before anyone noticed my absence. The ride home was the exact opposite. Orin didn't push the motor of his Packard as hard; his posture stayed relaxed as he shifted. His hand barely gripped the steering wheel as if he was in absolutely no rush to get home.

We meandered along bumpy roads, and country paths worn into grassy fields. I'd bet we both thought about the possible trouble awaiting us back home but neither said it. I couldn't imagine Orin being scared of anything but fear had definitely started to climb up my spine.

Father wouldn't be happy and would react.

I'd been raised to obey the rules and to know that punishment would be handed down if I didn't. I had been raised to feel constant fear.

But Orin... he was too strong for fear.

Then the car hit a hard bump that sent me slamming into the door. The steering wheel shook in Orin's large hands so he gripped it tighter to regain control, the muscles in his arms flexed with the effort.

"What's happening?" I braced myself, one hand on the door, the other on the dashboard.

"Broken tire." Orin guided the vehicle to the side, bringing us to a complete stop. "Are you all right?"

"Yes," I pressed my palm to my chest feeling the rapid heartbeat begin to slow.

"It happens." He took in the look on my face. "You've never been in an automobile when the tire's bent, have you?"

"No," I shook my head. "What do we do?"

He laughed easily. "Change it."

I followed him out of the auto. He walked around the back where the spare tire was kept and began to work.

Halfway through the process, Orin stood and pulled his shirt over his head. His skin glistened in the sun with beads of sweat following the contours of his body. I leaned against the auto, bit my bottom lip, and watched him work.

His muscles tightened as he moved and twisted

creating that feeling I'd quickly started to recognize as arousal.

"What?" Orin squinted into the sun as he looked up at me.

"Nothing," I shook my head.

"You're staring."

"Sorry." I quickly turned my head away from him.

"No, no. Continue. I just wondered if there was a specific reason for the attention."

I sighed. As hard as I tried, I still wasn't totally comfortable blurting out that I wanted him in that way. "I was wondering if I'll ever tire of looking at you."

I did it. My heart raced at my boldness.

"I hope not." Our eyes locked. The heat that had so quickly become familiar meant he wasn't only being playful. "But you probably will."

"I don't think so," I said as I tucked a loose strand of blonde hair behind my ear. "But you will when I'm old and gray and you're still beautiful."

"I'm older than you so I'll be gray first anyway." Orin shook the spare tire to ensure he'd secured it properly then stood and came over to me. "And you'll still be beautiful."

"You're only older by four years."

At twenty-five, Orin was the epitome of a man while I feared I was still too much a girl.

"I could always arrange for you to see more if you like," he said while waving his hand in front of him. He could already read me like a book.

My cheeks burned and not from the summer heat but from the weight of his stare.

His lips were suddenly moving against mine but his fingers had already begun to work on my blouse. Each button popping easier than the last.

"Orin, stop," I said with a smile yet didn't push him away. We were in the middle of a field. Anyone could pass by. "Someone could see us."

"Lizzie," he leaned in closer and wet his lips, "there's a little pond right there across the field... "

"I don't have a suit."

"Neither do I." He grinned and raised an eyebrow until I got his meaning.

"You're not serious. What if someone comes along?"

"Oh, but I am very serious and I promise I'll hear it if anyone comes close."

He wrapped each of his hands around each of my wrists, his fingers overlapping, and began dragging me the short distance to the water.

My shirt was already half-open so it didn't take

long for the rest of my clothes to become forgotten in the grass. I hadn't even put on a girdle this morning because Orin said it was up to me whether I wore one or not. And Orin undressed faster than could have imagined. I loved this side of Orin. The side that seemed to be on a mission to bring me out of the proper, scared little girl world that I hated so much.

When I dove in, the cool water felt amazing against my hot skin.

It probably felt even better for Orin. After all, he'd worked up such a sweat fixing the car.

He splashed me suddenly and I returned the favor. Our laughter hit the trees surrounding us like it was our own private alcove. It wasn't often I could laugh so loudly with such reckless abandon.

Half an hour later, we dragged ourselves out of the pond. My hair laid on my shoulders, unruly and I'm sure quite the mess. I gathered it in my hands and twisted as tightly as I could to wring out the excess water.

Orin... he shook the water off, raining drops all over me. He looked more like a mangy dog after a bath than the vision of perfection he really was.

"Thanks a lot," I said while laughing which made him chuckle again.

Once we got back on the road I said, "I don't recall you being so playful."

Orin sighed and looked over at me with a serious look on his face. "Lizzie, I haven't had a lot to be playful about. We were spending so much time together and I was falling in love with you more each day. We were meant to be yet I knew, in the end, I'd have to let you go have a life with someone else. That didn't bring out the fun side of me."

"I see."

"We were so close, Lizzie," he said keeping his eyes on the road ahead of us as his fist tightened on the steering wheel. "So close, just a breath away from losing each other."

"I'm yours now, Orin, so unless you tire of me, I think we're good."

His hand clasped the back of my neck and pulled me to him for a kiss. He was still driving when his tongue entered my mouth yet he kept the car on the road. When I pulled back, I settled into the seat and watched out the window as we drove until I began recognizing the world passing by as we got closer to home.

So close that the nerves settled back in.

But I wasn't going home. Not to the home I'd known my whole life, the place I'd been born, the place my mother died, at least not permanently. I'd be going to Orin's house but first I needed some of my things.

When we got to my father's house, I inched open the big oak front door. Orin stepped in behind me as I walked through. I paused and listened for any sound of my father inside. I shouldn't have been worried with Orin by my side but after years of conditioning, fear was second nature.

Orin nudged me so I'd start moving. We climbed up the stairs to my room. My movement turned frantic once inside my bedroom as I rummaged through my drawers.

"Only take what you really need to." Orin opened a suitcase on the bed for me. "We can buy whatever you need."

I nodded and pulled a couple of photographs from the bottom drawer of my nightstand. Happy photos of me as a child. The time before I knew that I was a huge disappointment.

With only the things that I couldn't possibly replace packed in that case, Orin and I left my bedroom after one last look around the place I'd spent my entire life.

I wouldn't call what settled in my chest sadness. I desperately wanted a life with Orin. But this house remained the only link I had to my mother. She'd chosen the decorations and set the room up as she carried me in her womb. She'd wanted this environment for me.

We slipped out of the house with the same quiet precision in which we entered.

As soon as Orin pulled the car up to his house, he hopped out to unpack our things and wouldn't let me help. So I leaned against the car with my arms folded across my rumbling stomach.

Orin's house looked far more welcoming than my father's but I knew nothing about the place. I'd been in the kitchen and in the living room but nowhere else.

"Are you coming?" His voice startled me out of my thoughts.

He opened the door and the bags fell to the floor with a thud. I set my handbag on the table next to the door with a more gentle touch. He was big and over-powering while I had been taught to be small and unseen.

"Hungry?" he asked. When I didn't answer, he took my hand softly into his and pulled me behind him toward the kitchen. "Is something wrong?"

"Not at all, but... "

"What is it?" He waited patiently for my answer as I fidgeted with the waist of my shirt.

"I don't know how to cook." Orin laughed loudly making my eyes narrow on him. "Don't laugh at me."

"I'm not. I thought you were going to confess something serious."

"It is. I've never been taught those things. I wasn't supposed to be the kind of wife who cooks."

He nudged into my personal space until I took enough steps back that my legs hit a chair and I sat down.

"You'll learn." He rustled in a few cupboards then held something out to me with a huge grin on his face. "This is bread."

"Not funny."

Orin stood at the counter making us sandwiches, something I'd rarely been allowed to eat. My father thought it was undignified unless served with tea and cut very small. Every meal at Father's house was more elaborate than it needed to be. He came to the table, with two plates and two apples.

"It isn't fancy but it's quick."

"I'm finding that I enjoy sandwiches very much. I've watched Cook spend hours just making lunch and I can't imagine that people have to do that every day."

"I'm sure she's happy for the job."

"True." If there was anything I'd actually miss about living at home it would've been the staff. Being that they actually raised me all while keeping me at arm's length.

"Elizabeth, I can tell you're nervous, and trust me when I say I am, too."

"You are?" I sighed deeply. Just as I couldn't imagine Orin being scared, I'd never imagined he'd be nervous either.

"Of course." He moved closer to me. "If anyone told me a week ago that I would be here in my house with you, alone and married... " He shook his head. "Well, I don't know what I would've said. It's even more boggling that I would've already made love to you and could continue to do so as much as we wanted."

We stared at each other then pushed our empty plates aside at the same time.

He reached out and brushed his thumb across my cheek right before his lips met mine and yanked my chair closer to his. Orin pushed my legs apart and clasped his hands on my hips and pulled me toward him.

Our breaths became ragged by the time his fingers popped two buttons on my top and his fingers crawled up the inside of my thigh. His lips moved down my neck to my chest as I tried to pull at his shirt.

Then he stopped abruptly and his head snapped up.

"Did I do something wrong?" I asked. Maybe Olivia was right and men didn't like their women to be assertive.

"We have company," he said as breathless as me.

I furrowed my brow because I hadn't heard anything.

Suddenly someone banged loudly on the front screen door. We scrambled to make ourselves presentable with Orin tucking his shirt back into his linen pants before heading toward the door.

The pounding resumed, louder and more urgent.

Orin yanked the door open wide to find three men standing on the porch, one leaning lazily against the railing. As I got closer and they came more fully into view, I slapped a hand over my mouth to keep from making any noise and instinctively took a step back.

I knew this very thing would happen eventually but hadn't thought it'd be the day we got back.

My father glared at Orin. "I've come for my daughter."

Chapter Fourteen

My father never once spared me a glance. I swallowed hard and knew Orin would never let these men take me back. Still, my chest grew heavy with fear.

Orin adjusted himself so that I could see his reassuring grin before he took a step forward opening the door just an inch. I grabbed his arm and tugged until he turned and looked at me.

"Don't go out there," I urged him.

My father wasn't alone and never would be during a confrontation, except with me, and I didn't want Orin to get hurt by his goons.

Smiling even wider, Orin placed the palm of his hand on my cheek and gently stroked me with his thumb.

"No worries, Lizzie." He leaned in and touched my lips with his then continued out the door.

"I'm here to collect my daughter," Father said again.

Orin's head shook before he spoke. His posture remained relaxed but the muscles in his arms tensed as he folded them across his chest.

"That not going to happen."

"She's a girl. Very impressionable. You took advantage of that. The girl is promised to someone else and he has agreed to take her even if her reputation is not what it once was."

Father meant if I was no longer a virgin. I couldn't imagine what Bradley had been through since I left. Obviously, he'd told them that I ran off with Orin and that didn't bother me. Our fathers would've made his life quite difficult in the search for information and I never told him to keep it a secret.

"Her reputation is fine and our marriage is legal."

The two younger men with my father, I'd seen but never actually met before, flanked him to let Orin know how this meeting would be ending. But Orin didn't move.

He seemed completely unconcerned with being outnumbered. Bored with it, even.

Father stepped forward which made me move back even though I was inside and Orin stood between us. Years of experience taught me how intimidating he could be, how ruthless.

Orin had several inches on my father and wasn't as easily deterred as me.

Father's jaw tightened, his teeth mashing together. He only did that when truly angry and about to lose his composure. Something he hated more than anything else. He wanted people to jump when he said so and hell would rain down on those who didn't.

"A deal is already in place," he said through his clenched teeth. "This affects my business and I will not stand by—"

"How much?" Orin interrupted him, his voice still low. "How much was the arrangement? Come on. Tell me how much you want. Money, right? Isn't that what this is really about?" His volume dropped. The words came out in a deep growl from his chest. Calm and deadly. "Tell me."

For the first time in my life, I saw my father at a loss for words, not knowing how to handle a given situation.

The men's eyes locked in some kind of game of

chicken that might turn deadly. Orin had killed before he'd do it again if he thought my safety was at stake. He said so.

"Was it stocks?" Orin pushed.

Father didn't answer.

I couldn't imagine what was going through that man's head. I'd always known that my match would be more about what benefitted Father's company than who would be the appropriate choice for me but hearing it said out loud made me feel dirty. Like I was no different than the women in the brothels.

"Ok, would ten thousand cover it?" Orin asked.

He waited for my father to respond. It took longer than I would've liked, making me incredibly uncomfortable but after another long pause he finally said, "That would be adequate."

"I'll speak with my banker on Monday but if at any point you cross paths with my wife, the exchange had better be cordial. Now get off my porch and do not set foot on my property unless you're invited."

Orin turned without waiting for a response and slammed the door behind him once he was inside. We waited until all the footsteps had thudded off the porch and I hoped all three men took the warning to heart.

"Did you... " I swallowed hard. "Did you just buy me?"

"Best money I've ever spent."

A laugh bubbled up from my chest, a nervous laugh that refused to be stopped. Orin crossed the small gap between us, lifted me as if I weighed nothing, and dropped me on the couch only to resume what we'd started in the kitchen.

Orin obviously cared about my pleasure with the way his hands and mouth roamed my body, the way he cared about the sounds I made, the way he whispered in my ear each time telling me again and again just how much he loved me.

Both of our clothes were on the floor next to the couch. Orin took my hand in his and leaned back. I froze.

"I can't..." My face burned. "I can't... I've never..."

He wanted me to touch him. We'd been naked together many times since we got married but I hadn't touched his... cock, as he called it.

"Touch me, Elizabeth," he said against my lips.

My hand trembled as I let him guide me. I almost pulled back. But if this was something he wanted me to do, I was determined to do it.

I wrapped my fingers around him. Air hissed between his teeth. Then he showed me how to move my hand. Orin's eyes fluttered closed as I stroked him up and then back down. I couldn't help but watch with fascination at the way he was so hard yet the skin was so soft. After tightening my fingers around him, Orin wrapped his hand around my wrist and pulled me away.

My gaze locked with his. "Did I do something wrong?"

Orin's dark eyes darkened even more right before he kissed me hard. "No," he told me once he pulled back. "Not wrong at all. But I needed you to stop."

"Why?"

The corners of his mouth turned up right before he pushed that hardness into me causing my breath to catch.

I never dreamed that being with a man would be that way. Intense. Exciting. Enjoyable.

Orin held me like I mattered. He pushed into me like he couldn't stand not to a moment longer. Every time with him got better.

This was the sort of thing that was only done in a bed at night and here I was naked in the middle of the afternoon.

And I couldn't care less.

Afterward, we laid on the couch with nothing covering our naked bodies. Orin tickled his fingers down my arm, barely touching me yet I felt it throughout my body.

"I suppose we need to do some shopping," Orin murmured into my hair interrupting me reliving everything we'd just done.

"I'd rather stay right here."

The summer afternoon passed us by while we laid on that couch but eventually, we forced ourselves up. Orin was right. I needed some more clothes.

We dressed and made ourselves presentable so that every person we saw wouldn't know we'd recently been naked together.

As we strolled from store to store we made several purchases mostly for me.

It didn't take long to find everything from a hairbrush to cosmetics and clothing. Basically, Orin bought me anything and everything he thought would make the house feel more my own. He said having the things I needed would do that.

I tried to talk him out of most of it but he didn't listen. And I tried to pretend not to notice the prying eyes on us the entire time.

Once we finished, he took me to one of the small

restaurants for dinner. This time we actually went inside unlike when we had to sneak around. I asked Orin why he'd turned down every offer to open an account in my name at the store so that I'd be able to make purchases of my own whenever necessary. That's how it usually worked after a woman got married.

"There's no need." Orin took a large bite of his steak.

"What if I need something but you're away?"

"I'll always make sure you have money but we pay with cash, always. It's easier."

A small surge of panic hit me. I'd never handled money before, not really. A few dollars here or there when my father allowed me to do something with friends. Never on a larger scale. I'd have to learn but I was willing to do whatever I had to if it meant we'd be together.

"Now what is it you'd like to do?" he asked after ordering a slice of pie for dessert.

I had no idea how the man ate so much and stayed so trim.

"Go home." And spend our very first night there together.

He smiled and shook his head. "I mean in general. Do you want to go to University?"

The question surprised me right as I'd taken a drink. The cool water stuck in my throat causing me to cough loudly.

"Are you all right?"

"Yes," I barked out. "You surprised me is all. I've never been given school as an option. At least not more school that I needed so I didn't embarrass my future husband." I paused taking his words in. "College?"

He shrugged. "If that's what you want. You're free to make your own decisions, Lizzie. Although I rather hope I will be consulted."

My head bobbed absently back and forth. The shock of everything he said left me speechless. The possibilities were endless but I needed to think about our immediate needs.

"I think I should learn to cook," I finally said. "I wouldn't be a good wife if I let us live off of sandwiches and we can't eat out every single night."

"We could."

I smiled but kept going. "There used to be a woman in town who woould teach some of the... more middle-class girls who grew up without a mother."

"All right. We'll get that arranged."

A few days later, everything was set up for me to take cooking lessons. He worked fast. Maybe we could have eaten out forever but this was important to me. This was something I wanted to do for him.

But first, he showed me the safe in his office on the first floor of our house. He insisted I memorize the combination rather than write it down. The heavy black iron door was harder to open than the number was to remember. Inside laid more money than I'd ever personally seen.

My father rarely dealt with paper money.

"Why do you need so much money?" I asked.

"It's better to have immediate access in an emergency than to have to make a trip to the bank."

"How do you have so much money?" I asked because so far as I knew, he didn't have a job that he worked. He had things to take care of though I didn't know what those were and it wasn't unusual for a wife to be in the dark.

"It's family money." He closed the safe then spin the knob.

"So your family is wealthy then."

His jaw tightened. "You could say that."

But he didn't go into any more detail than that.

The widow Peralta was patient with me and it turned out I'd picked up more in the kitchen than I thought. Apparently, years of watching the staff paid off somewhat. Still, it took two weeks before I was able to prepare a dinner on my own.

The summer heat raged on, oppressive when the sun was at its highest to barely cooler at night.

We slept with fans on in the bedroom and the windows open while wearing the lightest fabrics we could find. Orin even chose to only wear bottoms which I found distracting.

One particularly hot night, I woke up because the heat made it impossible to sleep and I found myself alone in bed. I assumed Orin also had trouble sleeping so I decided to search him out.

The house was empty.

Without any other ideas as to where I could look for him, I poured a glass of lemonade from the icebox then returned to the bedroom. Instead of climbing back onto the bed, I stepped out onto the small balcony. I sipped the glass of cold liquid and let the slight breeze lift my blonde hair off my shoulders.

I shut my eyes to enjoy the moment.

When I looked back out into the darkness, I saw him.

Orin lurked on the edge of the forest. Every muscle in my body froze so I wouldn't alert him that

I was watching. I wanted to see what brought him out in the dead of night and watched until he disappeared back into the forest.

He was naked and alone.

Chapter Fifteen

My husband spent time in the woods naked.

I decided almost immediately not to say anything about Orin's visit to the woods.

He'd proven that there were things in his life that he didn't want to discuss. I assumed that this was one of those things. Though what someone would get out of walking around the woods naked I'd never know.

I saw him go out there the next two nights as well and remembered that the first time I came to his house I'd found him coming from the woods naked.

Orin read the newspaper each morning after finishing breakfast. He'd sit, relaxed with a small smile on his face and I couldn't be sure if his satisfaction was due to his nightly naked visits outside or his nightly naked visits inside with me.

As a proper lady, I wasn't supposed to enjoy our time in bed (or the couch, or the floor) as much as I did. But there was no denying that I wanted him as often as he wanted me.

I pushed food around my plate while thoughts of what he might've been doing in the trees alone at night ran through my head. Deciding not to mention it to him didn't stop my curiosity from taking over sometimes and I refused to consider that any of it was like it'd been with Noah.

"What?" He peered over the paper surprising me.

I'd been so lost in thought and his movements were so quick that I didn't expect it.

"Nothing," I said back.

"Tell me." He continued with the grin on his face.

That look made me wonder how long he'd known I'd been watching him. After all, he seemed to notice everything.

"I was thinking about what I should wear tonight," I said, dropping my gaze back to the table and pretended that my eggs had gotten very interesting. I focused so hard that my vision became tunneled but I couldn't look at him. He'd know that wasn't what had been on my mind.

"Ahhh, yes the wedding. We're going?" He neatly folded the paper then set it on the edge of the table.

"I want to. When I saw Olivia, she was adamant that I was still invited."

"That invitation extends to me?"

"You're my husband," I said quietly.

"Come with me." Orin stood, taking my hand to pull me along behind him.

We climbed the stairs. I moved quickly trying to keep up with his easy movements although I stumbled several times. Grace and athleticism were not my forte. My toe caught a rug threatening to propel me to the ground. Orin steadied me so I didn't hit the floor then he stopped once we were inside one of the bedrooms that we didn't use.

"What are we doing in here?"

The guestroom hadn't been touched and I assumed it would stay that way for the foreseeable future. He went to the closet and pulled out several boxes I'd never seen before as I watched in confusion.

"What is all this?" I asked.

He didn't answer and instead flipped the lids off the boxes until all six were opened. Inside each one laid a beautiful dress or varying colors and level of elegance.

They were all breathtaking.

"Where did all this come from?" I asked.

"The city. I saw a few things and thought you might like them. You'd never ask for anything but wanted to have some on hand for an occasion such as this."

"A few things?" My voice was soft with emotion and my eyes locked with his.

Orin stood there smiling at me. I had to swallow back the lump in my throat. I'd had many beautiful dresses in my life but they'd all been purchased for a specific reason. Not because someone thought I'd like them.

Orin crossed the slight distance between us, kissed my forehead, and said he had things to take care of. I listened to his footsteps go back down the stairs and toward his office where the door closed behind him. All my years of tracking my father's location through sound alone sometimes paid off.

I settled on the red dress. Red. The color of harlots, according to my father. The thought made me smile.

Pulling the dress out of the box, the first thing I noticed was that it did not adhere to the modern style. These days everything was about androgyny. Girls who were thin and flat and resembled boys. Dresses hung from their bodies loosely not showing any discernible shape.

But this one... this would hug my curves in a way that wouldn't have been acceptable in my previous life. Wearing it now would make me feel free and reckless.

The wedding was in the evening with the reception at Olivia's parent's house. Everyone I knew would be there. Yet bold from Orin's support, I decided to leave my hair down on my shoulders in finger waves.

When I finished getting ready, I found Orin handsome as I'd ever seen in a tailored suit waiting at the bottom of the stairs.

"You're absolutely breathtaking," he whispered before kissing my cheek.

The church Olivia and I had attended all of our lives. It had also stood at least a century before we came along. While beautiful, I'd never felt like I belonged there. I knew the vengeful God. He'd taken my mother which left me alone in a house, unloved.

But the opulence of what the church had been transformed into for the night fit Olivia.

Luckily, I didn't see Bradley or my father in

attendance.

As did the reception where Orin and I swayed to the music filling the air. We danced closer to each other than those around us did. As elaborate as the ceremony had been, the reception had more of a romantic tone that I felt in the deepest recesses of my body.

Orin rubbed his thumb on the back of my neck as he held me to him so tightly I couldn't take a deep breath. I didn't mind. If I could've gotten closer, I would have.

"I think we should take a break before things get inappropriate," Orin whispered in my ear, exploding tiny goosebumps over my skin.

"That would be bad?" I cocked my head to the side and watched his face contort with laughter.

"Very," he murmured so his lips brushed mine with the movement.

I closed my eyes, losing myself in the feel of his smooth lips against mine as he kissed me quickly and let his scent surround me. He always smelled like the forest. The aroma of trees and damp moss clung to his skin even if he recently bathed.

"People are beginning to talk," Orin said as he led me off the dance floor.

"How do you know?"

"I can hear them."

"What?" That didn't make sense. No one talked loud enough for us to understand. Certainly not over the music.

"Excellent hearing," he said then grinned. "Come on."

We continued weaving our way through people but stopped several times for a brief conversation. Everyone seemed to already know Orin when I attempted to introduce him. Though most had never spoken to him. It was an odd juxtaposition. They shook hands anyway.

Catching Olivia out of the corner of my eye, I excused myself from the superficial exchanges and crossed the short distance to my best friend. No one would miss me. They didn't know how to make conversation with me before and they certainly didn't try now.

"So you're a wife now," I said with a smile once I got over to her.

"I need to talk to you." Olivia pulled me by the arm to a deserted corner of the room. She squeezed so tightly I'd probably end up with a bruise.

"What's wrong?" I asked.

Olivia bit her bottom lip, chewing back and forth.

"Olivia?"

"Nobody will tell me anything," she finally said. "Even my mother. No details."

"What are you talking about?"

"Lizzie... " her voice trailed off.

She acted as if I should know what she was talking about but her words didn't make any sense. My brows narrowed as I tried to decipher what she meant.

"Lizzie." she snapped, somehow exasperated with *me*.

"I'm trying here, Olivia, but you're not really telling me anything."

She rolled her eyes and lowered her voice, "You're married."

"Yes."

"Is it real?"

"Of course. Yes, he was a way out of that life, a way to not have to marry Bradley, but I love Orin."

"You live as husband and wife... " Olivia's voice trailed off.

Finally what she was getting at hit me.

Sex. She'd have to have sex with her husband tonight. That wasn't a topic that she would've gotten a lot of details about. She knew as much as I did my first night with Orin but it wasn't much. Yes, we knew what went there but there was so much more to it.

"Oh. Oh, I see. You want," I dropped my voice even lower, "details?"

She nodded.

"I'm not sure I can give you those." I glanced at Orin. He stood across the room engrossed in a conversation of his own yet the corner of his mouth turned up slightly like he'd heard what I said.

"Lizzie, I'm begging you. I know some things but don't send me off without more when you have the information." There was honest to goodness fear in her pleading.

"Well, you know what's going to happen, right?"

"Of course, I know the basic idea. How is it?" She dropped her voice even further. "Is it horrible?"

I burst into a laugh before I could stop it.

"Horrible? Olivia, no, it's not horrible. Not for me anyway. The stories we've been told aren't necessarily true for everyone. For me... it's actually kind of great."

She blew out a breath of air.

"It hurt at first," I added. "But that passed quickly."

I wet my lips trying to figure out what else I could tell her without telling her too much about

Orin. I teetered back and forth on whether to decide if I should tell her what surprised me most about being with Orin. But I wouldn't be her best friend if I didn't.

"Olivia—" I took a step closer "—there are things, things nobody would probably ever admit to. Intimate things that surprised me, shocked me even, but go with it. If Charles knows what he's doing, it will be good."

Olivia's shoulders fell as she released all the tension she'd been holding and she sighed deeply in relief. "That puts me at ease. Although it also makes me very, very curious."

I smiled and shrugged my shoulders. That she'd have to discover herself.

Late into the night, after a lot of dances and numerous drinks all I wanted was to be home. All of my drinks were of the non alcoholic kind but still, my head was heavy and it was time to go.

"Did you have fun?" Orin asked as we drove home.

"Yes. I'm surprised there was so much champagne."

"Why is that?"

"Prohibition. It's illegal."

"Somehow I don't think a lot of the laws apply to

people like Olivia's father."

True. I'm not sure the police in town would've dared to interrupt such an event for something like alcohol.

"Did you hear me talking to Olivia?" I asked as we got out of the car.

"How could I?"

"You have great hearing, remember?"

He smiled and took my hand but didn't answer as we approached the house. It was ridiculous to think he'd heard me, he'd been across the room for us the entire time, yet somewhere deep down I honestly thought he had.

The next morning arrived bright and finally mild. The crushing humidity that punctuated summer melted away, at least for that moment.

When I woke, I was once again alone except for the bird chirping a happy tune outside my windows.

I continued with my morning routine, trying not to wonder what Orin was doing. It didn't work. I couldn't help but want to know what he got up to in the woods every day. Especially since the one time I followed him in there, he'd been burying a dead body. Instead, I tried to busy myself by answering a few congratulatory letters we'd received.

At the beginning of my second letter, someone

banged loudly on the front door.

"Orin?" A man's voice boomed around the entry-way, calling in through the screen.

The day was so beautiful that I'd left it open to cool the house. I froze momentarily then found my courage to see who was out there.

"Can I help you?" I approached slowly, my heart hammering against my chest.

The man looked familiar but I couldn't place him. I didn't think I'd seen him before. He was quiet large with dark hair and menacing eyes. The woman beside him was tall as well and while she also had dark hair, hers was lighter.

"I'm looking for Orin."

"He isn't home right now."

"Where is he?" The voice boomed louder, forcing me to take a step back and grip the door so I could slam it in the man's face if he made a move toward me.

"I-I don't know." He legitimately scared me and even more than ever I wished Orin was with me.

"I'm his—" the man dropped the volume of his voice, "—I'm his father, this is his mother."

"Oh," I smiled widely, "Mr. and Mrs. Vilkatas, please come in. I don't know when Orin will be back. I'm Elizabeth."

They both took a step inside but didn't go any further than the front entryway. Something about this made the hair on my arms stand straight up

"What about his wife?" he asked.

Orin's mother hadn't said a word. She watched me with curiosity and didn't try to hide it.

My mouth opened and closed but I said nothing. I knew what I should've said but the words wouldn't climb my throat and come out of my mouth. His mother took a long breath in through her nose.

"Oh my, Anton, *this* girl is his wife. I can smell him on her."

"That's impossible." Orin's father's voice boomed again making me jump back even further and wrap my arms around myself.

"She isn't... she can't be... where's my son, girl?"

The demanding nature of his voice wasn't what scared me. That same tone had come from my own father a thousand times, but this man seemed to grow larger, more intimidating, and inch closer the angrier he became.

"What did he tell you? Where is he? If you're his wife, you ought to know." Mr. Vilkatas kept up the interrogation without giving me a moment to think or answer.

Not that I had one.

"I don't know," I yelled. "I don't know." I tried to yell over him but my voice couldn't match his. Tears pooled in my eyes to go with the brick lying in my stomach. "I think there's been a mistake." I started to shake.

"I demand to know what's going on here."

"Anton, calm yourself," his wife stepped in. "You're scaring this poor girl half to death." Mrs. Vilkatas' voice did what mine could not. She was heard.

"I don't care," he barked to his wife. "I want answers now." He stepped closer.

My legs hit the sofa so I began searching for an escape. Though somehow I knew if I ran, he'd catch me.

"What's your name, girl?" he asked only a breath away.

"Elizabeth."

"Your surname."

"Vilkatas."

His jaw tightened.

"D-Davis before."

Anton began another rant so loudly it became all I could hear. He came closer with each passing word.

I moved to my right slowly to get away from him and closer to the back door.

He didn't stop.

Suddenly Orin blocked me from his father, stepping between us so that his father would have to go through him to get to me.

"Dad, calm down," Orin said firmly, as demanding as his father had. "What are you two doing here?"

"You think we wouldn't come? You've taken a mate. But she's not... " His father stopped short of whatever he was about to say.

"I'll explain."

"Explain?" his father roared.

Orin met rage with rage and the two men stepped toward each other which put them away from me. I worried about Orin but had no power to help the relief that washed over me now that he was there.

Orin would protect me.

They grew so loud I couldn't understand what they said. Then I realized they weren't even speaking English anymore. But I didn't need to understand the language to understand the tone.

Orin and his father pushed each other over and over, moving themselves into the kitchen. I tried to stay within Orin's reach without getting into the argument so I stumbled along with them. His mother followed yet didn't look concerned. More like she was annoyed.

I stood too close. When Anton thumped into Orin, Orin fell into me and I stumbled into the stove. The sharp corner sunk deep into the tender flesh on my forearm then sliced toward my wrist as I fell.

I gasped and bit my lips together to keep from crying.

"Outside." Mrs. Vilkatas' voice boomed loudly.

They followed her direction but gave no sign that they actually heard it or that they knew I'd been hurt. They sprang out of the house then down the steps.

I followed onto the porch and stopped there. A trickle of blood ran down toward my elbow as I held it to my chest.

Even though I knew it was impossible, each man seemed to grow larger as the adrenaline took them over. Ripping material shredded the still afternoon as their clothes were torn from their bodies. I couldn't put together what I was seeing. My heart thumped erratically against my chest.

As I watched, Orin and his father disappeared and two animals rolled into the woods.

Chapter Sixteen

"Wʜᴀᴛ... ᴡʜᴀᴛ ᴡᴀs ᴛʜᴀᴛ?" I didn't look away from where Orin disappeared once I could force myself to speak.

My body trembled so hard that my teeth chattered together.

What happened in front of me made no sense. It was like I didn't really see it at all. The only logical explanation included one where my husband hadn't turned into a large, hairy, beast.

I didn't know tears fell down my cheeks until I felt the wetness.

Something touched my shoulder. A scream erupted from my chest and my entire body recoiled away. That something was Orin's mother and my body rejected the contact. I turned and ran back into the house.

Inside, I scrambled to the other side of the living room to the fireplace and wrapped my hand around the poker.

Pulling it to my chest, I slid to the floor in the corner and waited.

"Stay away from me," I said when his mother started toward me. I tried to sound strong but my voice wavered and I sounded like the terrified little girl I'd actually become.

She stopped advancing toward me and crossed her arms. Her face softened from the stern line it'd been movements before.

"I'm not going to hurt you, Elizabeth."

"What happened?" Tiny beads of sweat dotted my forehead. The makeup I'd taken such time to apply turned into a mask holding in heat. "Where's Orin? What happened to Orin?"

"He'll be back, dear." The woman moved forward.

I jabbed the iron stick in my hand up, ready to defend myself. "Please, don't hurt me."

"I just clearly said I wasn't going to," she snapped. "If it'll make you feel better I'll be in the kitchen. The boys will be hungry once they're back."

She turned on her heel and disappeared from my sight.

Time stood still for me while it kept moving for everyone else.

I stayed on the floor, jammed into that little alcove with my legs tucked under my body. The air was stagnant, thick, and unforgiving. I wiped my face with the inside neckline of my dress several times to remove some sweat. The entire time I kept a death grip on the fire poker. My knuckles turned white and my fingers began to ache.

And I waited.

When I heard Orin and Anton thumping heavy footsteps up the porch, their voices quiet but strained, I pushed myself into the corner as far as I could. Then willed my body to melt into the crevice. A trick I'd learned as a child. If I made myself look small, people usually didn't even notice me.

"Where is she?" Orin asked but I couldn't see him with my eyes squeezed shut so tightly I wasn't entirely sure they'd ever open again. No one answered. He found me anyway. He kneeled right in front of me. His body heat radiated over me before I ever saw him. "Lizzie," he said and my body went rigid as I raised the poker in front of me and swung.

Orin caught my wrist. "Lizzie," he said again as

he gently pried my fingers open, removed the poker, and tossed it aside. "I didn't know they were coming."

"What the hell just happened?" I focused mostly on breathing. In and out to ensure I stayed alive.

"How's your arm?" he asked instead.

I shook my head because until that moment I didn't remember that I'd injured it in the kitchen. It was like my entire body had gone numb.

"Let's get you cleaned up."

Orin helped me to my feet and led me up the stairs to our room. I don't know why I let him bring me along. He guided me to sit on the bed then jogged into the bathroom and filled the sink with water and grabbed a cloth from the small closet in there.

"I'll do it," I said, stopping him as he was about to dip the cloth into the water.

He closed his eyes, the muscle in his jaw tightened then released as his teeth ground against each other.

I couldn't really tell whether he was relieved that I spoke to him or upset that I was going to clean my wound myself thereby not letting him take care of me.

"It's all right, I'd like to... " Obviously the latter.

"Your mother said you'd be hungry. Go down

and eat. I'll clean up." I watched him move around the room but had yet to look directly at him. If he noticed, he didn't say anything and I just wanted him out of the room.

Instead, Orin nodded and walked slowly to the door. He paused but I gave no indication that I wanted him to stay so he left.

Once he left the room, for the first time in my new life, I locked it behind him.

In the bathroom, I locked the door that led to the hall before getting to work on my arm.

The open wound stung when the cold cloth touched it. Once it was clean, I gave it a thorough look and found it wasn't much more than a scratch. I wouldn't need a doctor.

After I took care of my arm, I washed my face and neck and brushed my hair which made me look a little more human. Then I laid on the bed while my mind raced as I stared out the window. Leaves danced in the breeze as if the world was a normal place. That I hadn't seen—whatever I'd just seen. My mind couldn't wrap around it. I didn't intend to fall asleep but those dancing leaves lulled me into a trance until the world darkened around me.

When I opened my eyes, rays of sun streamed through the window at a noticeably different angle. I checked the clock on the nightstand and saw that three hours had passed while my head and heart tried to recover from the emotional exhaustion of what happened. Or of trying to figure out what happened.

Even though I still felt completely off-center, as if my entire world had been thrown off track, I knew I couldn't wait any longer to face my husband.

And his parents.

My fingers trembled as I turned the key still hanging in the lock on the door and twisted the knob. After pulling it open slowly, I paused to listen for any sounds downstairs.

The voices had stopped. An almost eerie calm had settled in the house as I made my way downstairs to find it empty. I began to wonder if I'd imagined it all or if Orin had decided I was too much hassle.

Then I caught a glimpse of dark hair peeking over the window sill. He wasn't moving. Almost too still as I stood watching.

He sat there.

The screen door creaked when I pushed it open then smacked back against the house when I let it go. Slowly, I walked over near him and dropped into the chair beside Orin.

He held a bottle of beer, which was still illegal, with his fingertips turning it in circles on his knee. I didn't remember there being any alcohol in the house so he must've kept it somewhere else. Prohibition may have ended the legal sale of alcohol but it did not end the sale of alcohol.

"Are you all right?" he asked softly, his eyes on me.

"My arm is fine. A scratch." I had to assume he meant my injury. Anything more, I couldn't handle.

"Can I see it?"

I laid my arm on the side of the chair. He ran his fingers around the area, barely touching my skin.

"It's just a scratch," I said again as I pulled it back and clasped my hands in front of me. "Are your parents... "

"Gone," he cut me off, "for a little while, anyway."

"What did I see, Orin?"

"My secret." He put the bottle down on the table between us then slid to the edge of his seat dropping his elbows onto his knees. He looked as exhausted as I felt. And somehow a little older.

"That's what you've been hiding? The reason you didn't want to marry me?"

"I wanted to marry you but I didn't think I

should. I couldn't tell you, Elizabeth." He turned in his chair toward me. "I would have but I don't want you to be part of that world."

"What did I even see?" Because I honestly still didn't know. "Please tell me because I'm not even sure anymore."

He sighed before rubbing his hands down his face twice and taking a deep breath. "My family is different from most. We come from Lithuania—"

"You weren't born in Boston?" Panic filled my body. Maybe I didn't really know him at all. The thought brought my already volatile stomach to the brink.

"I was but my family came here from Lithuania. They adopted the last name Vilkatas because of what they were. What we are."

"You turned into a... a... "

"Vilkatas translates to werewolf."

I sucked in a huge breath like I'd been without for too long and maybe I had been holding it because I started to feel lightheaded. So I blew the air out slowly then took another, somewhat smaller, one.

"Are you all right, Elizabeth? I mean honestly all right? This can't be easy which is why I never wanted to tell you."

"I have about a million questions." I swallowed hard having no idea where I'd even start.

"I'll answer all of them." His dark eyes pled with me. It was the first time since meeting him that he looked anything less than certain. He could be worried that I'd tell someone. I never would but he wouldn't know that. Or maybe he thought learning this about him would send me running back to my father.

It definitely wouldn't. Nothing would do that.

"Is that why you sometimes go into the woods naked?"

"Yes, it's better to get it out of my system on purpose than for something like today to happen."

I took that to mean that anger had filled him and.. turning... that afternoon had been unintentional. Which meant he could control it. He'd been controlling it. For me.

"Your parents hate me." As if that really mattered but I had to say it and it was the most human part of the day.

"They don't. If anything they're angry with me."
"You? Why?"
"I'm supposed to choose a mate like us."
"So, your wife is supposed to be a... "
"Yes."

We fell silent again. I would certainly never fit that requirement.

Once again my mind raced with questions that I didn't really want the answers to. I may not have been able to handle the answers.

He squirmed in his seat the way any man would if he was nervous but Orin didn't get nervous. Or at least I'd never seen it. Orin had always been sure, deliberate, strong, and never worried about anything even when confronted with the direst situations. Nothing unbalanced him.

His confidence made me feel weak and I'd done everything I could not to feel that way since leaving my father's house.

"Lizzie, are you... staying with me?"

"I can't go anywhere else."

He winced. "I don't want you to stay because you have no choice. If you need to leave, I'll take care of you. You'll have money for whatever you need. You can go anywhere you choose. I'd hate it but I won't stop you. I'll always take care of you."

I hadn't meant it like that. No, I didn't have anywhere to go if I left other than my father's house. He'd take me back in because he'd have to but there would be severe consequences. I meant I couldn't go anywhere else because I loved him. Even if none of this made any sense.

We both needed a break from all of this.

"If we have children, will I give birth to puppies?" The words tumbled out of my mouth before I could stop them. I wanted to alleviate some of the stress.

His cheeks rose, his body barked with laughter that refused to be contained. "What?"

"With all our nights together, pregnancy is a very real possibility but if I'll have puppies I think I should know ahead of time."

He rose from his seat and picked me up out of the chair then wrapping his arms tightly around my torso. Air just barely entered my lungs as my feet dangled a foot above the porch.

"You funny girl." His breath caressed my neck sprouting goosebumps over my entire body. "First, we're as careful as we can be so I don't think the chance is as high as you think." Even now I blushed at the way he spoke of our sex life and the precautions we took. Right after we were married, Orin had purchased rubbers for us to use so we would get to decide when we want to start a family. I still got uncomfortable talking about it.

"Secondly," he continued, "If that happens,

you'd have a healthy baby who would likely at some point become very hairy."

We both laughed loudly at the picture he'd created of an extremely hairy human baby.

The front door opened and closed behind us. Orin seemed more relaxed about everything that had happened and he led me into the house where we found his parents standing shoulder to shoulder. They were tall like him with similar coloring—dark hair and eyes. His mother may have been the tallest woman I'd ever seen in person.

"This is my wife, Elizabeth," he said when we stopped before them. "You didn't get a chance to meet her before." He kept my hand tightly in his own.

I hadn't received open-armed hugs or any of the things I'd hoped might happen when I met his parents. They nodded and Orin squeezed my hand to reassure me.

"Perhaps we should talk more over dinner," his mother said. "We have a lot to discuss."

His mother moved to the kitchen and began to set things on the counter as she made dinner. Her words weren't an offer anyone could turn down. She'd seemed used to taking over and I didn't feel strong enough to challenge it.

As soon as she began cooking, a wonderful aroma flowed from the kitchen and drew me in. I set the table, four full place settings, and Orin stayed with me.

"That smells delicious," I said, speaking for the first time since his parents arrived.

"My mother is an amazing cook." He placed a glass on the table, which I automatically moved to the right location. At least all of my training didn't go to waste.

As I headed back to the kitchen for more table settings, I overheard his parents speaking in hushed tones, and I stopped short. I didn't want to interrupt and shouldn't have eavesdropped but curiosity got the best of me and whether their conversation had anything to do with me.

"Anton, we have to get through to him."

"I understand, Emilija, but it's clear he loves the girl. It's not going to be easy."

"Do you want your son to continue the line or not?" she snapped.

"Of course I do."

I turned away quickly. I was wrong. I didn't want to know what they had to say about me. The day already had my head spinning and anything more would have been too much. My shoulders ached, my head hurt, and I wanted to go to bed.

Mrs. Vilkatas brought the food to the table.

I only stomached small bites of the meat flavored with spices I'd never tasted before. The rest I pushed around my plate, a trick I perfected years ago. The Vilkatas' had voracious appetites and cleared more than one plate each yet were trim and muscular. A byproduct of being wolf people perhaps.

Once we finished, Orin and his father cleared the table while I kept staring at the space in front of me. His mother's glare burrowed into me like she was seeing my soul but didn't like what she found.

"Tell me what this is all about," Anton finally said while we had coffee.

"Anton." His mother sighed.

I heard what she'd said when they thought they were alone in the kitchen. She wanted me out of Orin's life as much as Anton did. Maybe she didn't want to say it in front of me. Or maybe she thought they'd have a better chance of convincing their son if I wasn't around.

"No," Anton snapped. "I refuse to hold my tongue. We have a right and a need to know about this situation."

Orin clenched his fists but gave no other reaction. He glared a warning at his father. A warning that would send most people running to safety yet had zero effect on his father.

"What details would you like?" The words spat across the table sounding very unlike the man I'd come to know.

"Orin, you must understand—"

"No." He jumped from the table. His parents followed. "There isn't much I can tell you. I was on the trail. It led to her."

"What?" His mother snapped back as if someone slapped her in the face. "What do mean, it led to her?"

I remained seated and let this entire thing play out before me even though I had no idea what they were talking about.

"That can't be. Have you ever heard of this happening?" his mother asked his father who only shook his head quickly. "We have to look into this. If it led to her then... we must leave immediately."

Mr. and Mrs. Vilkatas hugged their son and left without even a glance at me.

In bed that night, I curled into a tiny ball on my side of the bed while Orin finished getting ready. Once he laid beside me, he wrapped his arm around my body and pulled me to him. He brushed my hair away so that he could kiss the spot where my neck meets my shoulder. I closed my eyes at first and allowed the warmth to course through me then smiled when I felt his erection pressing into my rear. He wanted to make love and if it was any other night, my clothes would've already been off.

"Are you all right?" he asked when I didn't respond the way I usually did.

"I'm tired. Can't I be tired?" I snapped then sighed, annoyed with myself.

"Of course you can." Orin sat up and leaned against the headboard. "I know a lot happened today and I wish I could change that."

"What did you mean?" I asked.

"Which part?"

I sat upright beside him so that we could see each other in the dim light. "You said *it* led to me."

He sighed and swallowed.

"We don't normally fall in love the way regular people do. Somewhere each of us has a perfect mate and it's up to us to find them. My journey led me to you. Imagine my surprise that first night to find that you are not one of us."

"I was supposed to be a... wolf?"

"Yes," he whispered.

"How did you know I wasn't?" I ran over that

first meeting in my head trying to come up with anything unusual but it was completely normal.

"We have a wonderful sense of smell."

"You can smell me?" I yelled out of surprise and disgust.

Orin chuckled. "Yes. Everyone gives off a distinct smell and every species has a certain underlying fragrance."

"So your mother is going to find out why you were drawn to me? Even though I'm not a wolfman?" I tried a new word because *werewolf* didn't really fit neither did *wolf* but what I saw was more wolf than man. Long claws and sharp teeth on a face with a long snout and fur covering every inch of his skin. I had a feeling it was a look that would haunt my nightmares.

He nodded. "Mostly we just say shifter."

"Your parents want to find your match."

He cupped my face in his hands, forcing me to look into his eyes. "I've already found her." He kissed me and I finally understood exactly what I had seen in his eyes on the back porch. The fear that made an appearance was because of me.

And not because he thought I'd tell someone.

He was afraid I'd leave. That he'd lose me.

I melted against his touch, knowing I'd never be

able to resist him because I didn't want to. I lost myself in him. Making me feel as if we were the only two people in the world.

However, it proved too difficult to get all of it out of my mind.

Orin was supposed to marry a shifter. He was supposed to find one of his own kind.

Yet he found me.

I couldn't help but wonder what the hell that meant.

Chapter Seventeen

ORIN BARELY LEFT the house over the next couple of days, which was unusual.

I was always home except when I had my cooking lessons or a rare outing to the market. I received a letter from Olivia while she was on her honeymoon telling me that I'd been right about the things I said at her reception which made me smile. At the very least I knew Charles was being nice to her.

More than nice if I read her letter correctly.

Sometimes I thought about how different things would've been if I had married Noah as intended. I would've been pregnant within the first year and probably the next year then once I produced enough heirs to satisfy his father, he probably would've left me alone.

Instead, I had Orin. A man as beautiful inside with me as he was on the outside. A man who seemed to honestly love me the way I used to think my father probably loved my mother.

Only I had something else altogether hanging over my head.

Something I just didn't understand.

"Hey," he said softly kneeling down beside me as I sat in the chair at his desk. "Are you all right?"

I nodded and tried to give him a little smile.

He didn't believe me.

"What were you thinking about just now?" he asked.

I took a moment before answering him. I knew I'd never lie. I didn't want him to think I wasn't happy with him or in our house.

"How different things would've been if I never met you," I finally admitted.

He swallowed so hard, his Adam's apple pushing out forcefully. "Would it be better?"

"That's not what I meant. If I hadn't met you things would be horrible." Tears burned my eyes as the hard truth hit my heart. "I don't think there was a time in my life I've ever been truly happy. Until you."

"Even though I'm a wild animal?" He smirked up at me which just brought a big smile to my face.

"I especially like that part even if I don't understand it."

Orin laughed at my double entendre then pulled me into a kiss. Soft and slow as if telling me how he felt without words. I'd only spoken the truth.

Yes, I was somewhat freaked out about what he turned into but part of that also made him strong, fierce, and willing to protect me. I couldn't deny that.

"But I do have some questions," I said once he pulled back.

"I've just been waiting for you to be ready to ask."

Orin pulled me to my feet. After a quick stop in the kitchen for lemonade, he led me out to the back porch where we sat next to each other on the swing.

I curled up on there and the wood structure protested against his added weight. We sat sipping our drinks silently for a good long while, enjoying the evening air while I tried to put into words the thoughts in my head.

"Lizzie, if you're trying to drive me insane it's

working," he said while gently running his hand down the back of my head.

"Sorry," I said setting my drink on the small table and turning sideways toward him with my knees pulled to my chest.

Without the worry and pressure that came from living in my father's house, I'd started to become the girl I always wanted to be.

I never would've left the house without shoes on before but here I sat on the porch with bare feet. All in the name of comfort—a word that hadn't been part of my vocabulary in my previous life.

"Did you... I'm not quite sure how to say it. Did you turn into the wolf when... " I looked at him for confirmation which he gave me with a small nod. "When you were with Noah?"

"Yes." He paused and sighed. "My anger took over. Luckily I was able to drag him away before the transformation was complete. That way no one else saw me."

"Is that something you worry about? Someone seeing you?"

He let out a long breath, took his hand and placed it on the back of my foot then pulled gently to straighten my legs across his lap. He ran a hand up and down my calf. It was sweet and soothing, probably the reason he did it.

"I used to only worry about you finding out. I assumed you'd find me hideous and run in the other direction, he confessed. Even before when I knew you'd be someone else's wife, I didn't want you to recoil at the sight of me. That would have broken my heart."

"When you're in your other form, can you control it?"

"What do you mean?"

"Are you still you? If you became a wolf in front of me would you attack me? Would you know it's me?"

The hand on my foot paused.

"I'm still me in every way, Elizabeth," he answered quietly. "I'd know you're you. I wouldn't intentionally hurt you. I know you did get hurt in the kitchen but that was an accident. I swear."

"How is it you're so open with your feelings? Most men aren't in my experience."

"Men who have them are, Lizzie. I don't think you've been around many of those. But my people are much more casual. We love our wives and we let them know by telling them and showing them."

I had to try to keep a smile from taking over my face. He had shown me over and over.

"Why haven't you gone into the woods since I found out?" Unless he did it as I slept, which I didn't think was the case. I hadn't woken to an empty ben once since then.

"Haven't wanted to leave you. I've been worried."

A raised eyebrow kept him talking.

"It's a really big thing you saw and I'm worried that it'll finally sink in and you'll be gone when I get back. And I don't want you to be afraid of me."

"Do I... do I have to worry when you're like that? Am I safe?" I asked. He'd already said he'd know it was me and he wouldn't hurt me but I needed that reassurance.

"You're completely safe. You don't have to worry. When I'm like that I'm still me. I still think like me and that means I think of you."

"I want to see you."

Immediately his head began to shake but I wasn't about to take no for an answer.

"Yes," I insisted. "You want me to be here with you then I have the right to know what this is all about. You shouldn't hide this from me."

The last part convinced him. He hadn't wanted

to keep anything from me even when he had his secret. I watched him wrestle with telling me the truth even then. He wouldn't deny me now.

"Are you sure? Baby, I don't want to scare you."

The pet name caused tiny bumps to break out over my skin making it impossible to speak so I nodded instead.

"Ok. If you get scared, tell me. I'll change back."

Orin stood to his full height and began unbuttoning his shirt. For a moment I forgot that he would have to get naked to make this happen. I'd seen or heard rather, his clothing ripping away from his body when he argued with his father. He tossed his shirt on the end of the swing then popped the button on his pants. My eyes fixated on his fingers.

Not even his deep chuckle distracted me.

"There are other ways we could spend the evening." His voice was low and hungry but not for food.

I snapped my gaze to his face quickly.

He shrugged and said, "Maybe later."

Definitely later.

Orin closed his eyes. His skin darkened but everything happened so quickly that I couldn't be sure what I saw. Did it hurt when he changed forms? My skin prickled with the energy coming from him.

His nails grew, hair formed. Then standing before me was something that looked like the kind of wolf animal you would see in the wild but standing on its hind two legs over six feet just like human Orin. Hair prickled out of every pore of his skin.

I stood and stumbled back two steps.

He looked nothing like my Orin.

Except for the eyes.

Those belonged to the man I loved, my husband. Given the shape of his jaw, I didn't think he could talk so I didn't ask before I moved closer and reached out to him.

My hand touched his… paw then slid up his arm touching the soft fur. Before I got to his shoulder, his fur disappeared and my hand rested against regular human skin again.

Without a word, Orin scooped me up in his arms and carried me back through the screen door. His mouth was hot against mine, scorching his way down my neck as his hand grabbed each side of my blouse and tore it open.

Buttons spilled across the floor at the same time my skirt got hiked up to my waist. In one swift movement, Orin was inside me, my body wedged between him and the wall.

This was a new side of him. I had to assume the

animal side. Normally, we made love tenderly, slowly. Orin liked to take his time to enjoy me, he said, and to teach me when necessary.

Not this time.

He was rough and dirty yet as he pushed into me with so much force my body slammed the wall over and over again, somehow it turned me on more than ever. He wanted me... needed me and I wanted him.

"You feel so good," he whispered close to my ear before working his hand between us to find the spot that brought me to climax. His fingers worked in a circle. His teeth scraped against my neck. How he held me up with only the one arm under my butt, I didn't know.

My world exploded in stars and pleasure. A world that only contained this moment between us. Right as I came down, Orin stopped moving and held me there while I put the pieces of my soul back together.

Good thing too because I didn't think my legs would hold me up.

I dropped my forehead against his as my breath came out in loud embarrassing huffs and I reveled in the fact that he'd wanted me so badly we couldn't make it upstairs to our bedroom.

"You all right?" he asked after dropping small kisses across my forehead.

I nodded because I couldn't speak. Orin let me slide down his body, still holding on to me. I tried to pull my blouse back together then remembered that I'd need to sew all the buttons back on.

"Sorry about your top." But the look on his face said he was anything but sorry. "I couldn't help myself. Lizzie, when you touched me." He blew out a slow breath. "I've never felt anything like that before. I had to have you." Orin didn't care that he stood there talking to me while completely naked.

"Sorry?" The word came out rough and like a question because I still hadn't gotten my sea legs back.

"You have nothing to apologize for." He shook his head. "But we'll need to remember this in case you decide to touch me while I'm like that again."

"Then this will happen?"

He nodded making me smile widely.

"I'll definitely remember that." Looking away from his face for the first time since our encounter, I needed a moment to regain my composure. "Did you want to go out to... run or whatever it is you do out there?"

"You wouldn't mind? It's been a few days so it would feel really good."

I shook my head because I had some clean-up to do anyway starting with a new shirt.

"I'll be back in a bit." He kissed me again, longingly full on the lips then headed outside.

I watched him until he hit the edge of the trees and disappeared inside never turning, at least until he was out of my line of sight. I assumed he did it then.

Trying to work quickly, I picked up as many buttons as I could find then went to my room for a completely new outfit and still didn't put any shoes on. I chose another skirt and a top without buttons because this had become my favorite for comfort. Gone were the restrictive clothing of my father's house, corset included, but that took some getting used to as did the much shorter hemline. It fell right below my knees.

At first, I'd felt exposed.

After all that, I returned back outside to the swing, curled up on it to wait for Orin to return. My eyelids grew heavy but I was powerless to do anything about it.

"Lizzie." Orin's voice broke through the sleepy

haze that had engulfed me. "Lizzie," he said again gently.

I opened my eyes slowly and found it much darker than the last time I'd had a look around. I remembered deciding to wait for Orin to come back from his outing but didn't remember nodding off.

"How long have I been asleep?"

"I don't know." He shook his head. "I've been gone a couple of hours."

When I sat up, I saw that he'd put his pants back on but not his shirt, and I decided that this was how he should always be. Well, he could lose the pants as well.

Then I chastised myself.

I'd turned into the most inappropriate kind of girl in such a short amount of time. The kind of girl that would send my father into a tirade. The kind of girl that I found I liked. And why shouldn't I be that girl as long as Orin didn't mind?

"How about we go out, get dinner."

Sounded perfect to me and my stomach grumbled as if on cue.

The town came alive at night and for the first time, I could witness it. A lot of people my age were out on these 'dates' Orin told me about. Cavorting with a sense of freedom that I didn't even know existed until the day I left my father's house to elope.

They laughed and talked loudly, not seeming to care who heard them as they made their way down the street to the theater or restaurant or speakeasy. I used to envy people like that.

Now I was one of them.

With the night being so beautiful, I convinced Orin we should walk into town. As we made our way down Main Street, Mr. Jackson, someone who didn't exactly run in my father's circles, stopped us to talk to Orin. But I saw Olivia walking toward us. She didn't see me and she was about to turn the corner when I excused myself to catch up with her. It'd been too long since we last talked.

"Olivia!" I called out right before she entered the drug store.

A big smile broke across her face when she saw it was me. We took a step to the side so we wouldn't be in the way.

"It's been too long," she said as she hugged me tightly. "How are you?"

The fact that Olivia never shunned me, regardless of what others thought was why she had always been my best friend.

"Wow. You look so stylish," I said.

She'd cut her hair into a fashionable bob and her clothes had transformed into the drop waist, straight-lined frock that all the girls were wearing. I'd let go of some of the more restrictive items, such as the corset, but had yet to embrace items that didn't follow the natural line of my body even if it meant having new clothes altered.

I was stuck somewhere between the old world and the new without knowing which way I ultimately wanted to go. Orin liked how I looked so I wasn't in a rush to make a change.

"And you're beautiful as always. Life with Orin is agreeing with you," she said with a smile.

We talked and laughed for a few minutes like old times when she said she had to go before she was late meeting Charles. But we promised to meet for lunch soon. I didn't want to lose her friendship because we now had different lives.

When I turned to head back to Orin I smacked into a tall suited man and stumbled several steps so I didn't fall.

My father looked down on me like I was some sort of street urchin that dared approach him. Which was how he'd always regarded me. At that moment I wondered what jaded him so badly. Was it just my mother's death or something else that blackened his spirit? I'd never know and I shouldn't have even cared.

Without saying anything to him, I tried to push past him but his voice stopped me.

"Elizabeth." His words dripped with the same coldness I heard my entire life.

I turned to him slowly.

"At the very least your husband keeps his word." He meant the money Orin had promised.

"I'm glad I was worth something to you. Was my mother?" I almost wished I could swallow those words. Yet this newfound boldness felt good.

"You have no right to speak of your mother." He took a large step closer then looked away from me to something behind me. His jaw tightened and his eyes turned hard.

I knew Orin was standing behind me without looking just from the change in my father's demeanor.

He added, "You're the reason she's dead."

Then he walked away.

Chapter Eighteen

Some days I was almost able to forget that Orin could turn into a werewolf.

A shifter.

A person who shifted into an animal.

While I wanted to convince myself I'd put it to the back of my mind, it wasn't true.

Something about his already strong body morphing into something even stronger warmed me. Even the thought of watching him turn flushed my body with excited anticipation which made me squeeze my legs together that much tighter.

It wasn't a coincidence that each time I witnessed him change, we ended up needing to be with each other so badly that he'd either rip my top open causing buttons to fly everywhere or shred the fabric.

Which led me to need some new items. I'd begun teaching myself to mend the clothing, but I was slow, my fingers not quite nimble enough and I didn't want the seamstress in town to wonder how the buttons on my blouses always seemed to be ripped off.

My cheeks blushed at the thought of him tearing the dress in my hands off my body. I immediately put it back on the rack.

"Elizabeth, there you are." Orin came toward me breathlessly.

There was something wrong. Very wrong. He tipped his hand by the way he held himself taut and on alert as well as the tone of his voice.

"What are you doing here?"

I'd only been gone a couple of hours. What could've happened to put him on edge in that time, I didn't know. Didn't think I wanted to.

As he came closer, I noticed the small beads of sweat dotting his forehead and worry creasing his brows. The only time I'd seen him perspire was when we had sex and since that couldn't be the reason now, I swallowed hard, steeled myself, and waited.

"We have to go," he said as he roughly grabbed my elbow.

Two of the items in my hands dropped with his roughness.

"I just need to—"

"Now."

Orin snatched everything from my arms and dropped them on the nearest table then took my arm again and dragged me from the store.

He moved so quickly that all protest got trapped in my throat.

Something happened but his lack of explanation scared me. He wanted me home. I could deal with that because I felt safest there. Yet still, I wanted to know.

We burst through the front door, not bothering to shut it behind us, and climbed the stairs two at a time. I tripped, banging my shins against the wood. It stung then ached and he still didn't stop. Once in our bedroom, he had a suitcase flayed open and was tossing everything from intimates to shoes inside without folding them.

"What are you doing?" I asked.

"You're leaving," he said without looking at me.

My stomach dropped and my heart ached.

"Where are we going?"

"*We* aren't going anywhere." Satisfied with his packing job, he finally stopped to look at me. "*You* are."

I heard him wrong. I must have. Orin wouldn't be sending me away. "What?"

"You have to go home."

"This is my home."

His jaw set hard, those teeth grinding together as he stood there looking at me.

My eyes burned with tears ready to fall. He couldn't be sending me away. I hadn't done anything wrong and he loved me. And he loved me.

I took a hard swallow so I'd be able to speak but barely caught my breath as if I'd been punched in the stomach.

"To my father's?"

He nodded.

"I can't do that, Orin." I blinked rapidly trying to figure out what I'd done to make him want me to leave. Yet nothing stood out. "Did I do something wrong?"

"No. I did."

"What?"

Orin approached me taking both my hands in his. "My—" he sighed, "—My brothers are on their way here."

"Why does that mean I have to leave?"

"I need to protect you. They're strong."

"You're strong," I yelled.

This was my worst fear. Going home to a father that I'd disobeyed on the highest scale wasn't going to be pretty.

He gave me that sideways smile that I loved.

Having the strongest person I knew protecting me meant there was no chance his brothers would get close enough to hurt me.

"Together, they're stronger." He took a deep breath. "Once we find our mate and bond, we are the strongest. But that's when our mate is one of us."

"Are you saying that I... that I make you weak?"

"No," he said then took a deep breath. "I guess technically, yes but I'd rather—"

"Why do they care?" I dropped onto the bed feeling more like a petulant child than the married woman I really was. But I didn't want to leave the only place that truly felt like home. Or the one person I trusted and loved more than anyone else.

"Our family would be unstoppable if we all have our mates. Mates like us." He meant wolfmen. Women. Whichever.

I thought about what he'd said. That they'd be

strongest if the entire family was mated. That they were coming here.

That he may not be able to protect me.

"Do they want to kill me?"

Orin pinched his lips together and stared at me then crossed his arms over his chest.

That silence answered what his words wouldn't. The reality hung heavily on my shoulders. We stood there as I tried to come to terms with the idea that four werewolves wanted me dead and one would die to keep it from happening.

We were there for a very long time not speaking but searching each other for an answer.

The shrill sound of the telephone downstairs broke us out of the showdown. I'd never answered the thing so I wasn't going to now and Orin made no move for it either.

"It's not going to be easy," I whispered, "going home."

Understatement of the century. Returning to my father would be as close to Hell on Earth as one could get. Not to mention humiliating.

I wouldn't try to talk Orin out of sending me because it never would've worked. And I didn't want him to get hurt.

The mere fact that he wanted to send me away

meant he wasn't sure he could protect me from them. And I trusted his instinct.

"If there was any other way," he said. "I don't know what else to do. We have to get my smell off you. I can't send you any further away. If they find you... I want to be close."

My lips trembled as reality set it. The reality of what crawling back to my father would mean.

"He won't let you in," I whispered. "He may not even let me in but he really won't let you in. Ever."

Orin's gaze slid over my face as he ran his hand up and down the back of his head. He already knew that.

"So we won't see each other," I said even though I clearly didn't need to.

We stared again. Tears filled my eyes at the thought of leaving him. I also didn't want to run home with my tail between my legs like a lost puppy. I wanted to stay with him. Wanted my husband. I thought I saw his eyes glistening but when I looked again, the moisture was gone.

"Lizzie, we have to go. They'll be here soon. The longer you're away from me the better."

I wet my lips, took another breath, and walked past him out the door.

We rode in silence like strangers at first but then

as if to make me or himself feel better, he quickly told me his mother was the one to alert him that his brothers were coming. Their wives had kept it from his parents at first but Phillip's wife finally broke down and told them everything.

She only warned him because she knew that if they did something to me, it would fracture their pack forever. It wasn't me she cared about.

He didn't look over at me as he spoke or touch my hand the way he sometimes did when we were driving.

When he turned into my father's drive, he stopped the car halfway to the house.

Orin didn't want my father to know he was there, that he'd dropped me off.

He would want everyone to think he'd abandoned me.

I couldn't move until he got out of the car and came to my side then pulled me out by the hand.

As he walked me up the drive, I looked at the house I'd grown up in. It was past dinner, not yet dark, but a few lights shone from the windows. Father would be in his study for whatever he did in there at night.

Finally, we stopped outside the front door where Orin set my suitcase down.

"I'm sorry, Lizzie," he said so softly that I almost missed it.

He turned to leave but I couldn't let him go like that.

"When will I see you?"

"I'm not sure." He kept his back turned to me. "When it's safe."

I watched him walk away without so much as a glance at me until I couldn't see him anymore. He hadn't even kissed me good-bye.

Then I knocked on the door.

Mrs. Atherton opened the door and furrowed her brows. Still, she moved aside so I could step in.

"Miss Elizabeth..." But she couldn't finish her sentence which I was pretty sure was going to be a question before my father came walking through.

He stopped suddenly when he saw me. This was going to be worse than I'd imagined given the hard set to jaw and the ticking of the muscle by his ear.

That cold mask I'd seen my entire childhood appeared on his face. His eyes flit down to my suitcase then back to me. Nervous tension curled in the pit of my stomach and I started fidgeting with the hem of my shirt. Something I hadn't done in months.

Maybe he'd been happier without me here, too. That was something we could have in common.

"Elizabeth," he said with a tone meant to get me talking.

"I need to come home," I responded hoping he wouldn't ask for more of an explanation.

The words tasted like vinegar on my tongue. My only plan was for him to fill in the blanks himself so I wouldn't have to lie or tell him the truth.

"What makes you think you're welcome here?" He stared out over my head refusing to look at me.

"I don't have anywhere else to go." I hated the begging tone my voice had taken on. I was begging to come back to a house that I'd hated my entire life.

"What about that husband of yours? The one you were keen to run off with? Shouldn't you be his burden?"

"Things are complicated right now. May I please stay here? Temporarily, of course." I waited for his answer not sure if I hoped for a yes or a no.

"There are rules in this house, Elizabeth."

I nodded because I knew what was coming. I'd memorized every rule of that house by the time I turned three and I tried so hard not to break even one of them.

"He's not allowed here. You are to have no contact while under this roof. Is that understood?"

"Yes, Father." My voice came out barely a whisper. I don't know why. I fully expected him to say that about Orin which with how angry I was at my husband for sending me here, I didn't think it would be an issue.

Stepping out of my way, he finally let me inside although every muscle in my body screamed at me to run in the other direction. Instead, I held my breath as my left foot crossed the threshold. The echo of the closing door behind me sent shivers up my spine almost as if I really thought I'd never walk back out.

Deep down, I worried that I wouldn't.

Being back in my old room again was exactly as uncomfortable as I thought it'd be. Father had taken me in but not without consequences. So far it hadn't moved past the *I told you so* lecture I endured for an hour after I arrived.

Father believed I hadn't been a proper wife which caused Orin to stray and put me out of his house.

The truth sat perched on the end of my tongue but I couldn't say it no matter how badly I wanted to. I just had to endure it.

Alone in my room that night, I missed Orin's lips, longed for the feel of his body against mine. It'd only been hours, not even a full day, yet the linger of Orin's touch on my skin began to fade.

The next morning, my rules reverted back to when I lived at home before which meant I'd be expected to be dressed and seated at the table with my father for breakfast. Luckily my old clothes were still in the closet because he wouldn't approve of my new wardrobe.

The silence hung heavily with the exception of forks scraped across the plates. This was even more uncomfortable than it'd been before.

"Thank you for letting me stay here," I said to break the awkward quiet.

If I was in his house, I had to play the part.

He didn't look away from his paper.

"What else could I do? Can't have my abandoned daughter on the street. How would that look?"

"I wasn't abandoned," I said quietly planting my eyes back on the plate.

The newspaper rustled and I felt the heaviness of my father's stare on me.

"Where is your husband then?"

"I don't know." It was the honest answer, and I didn't see the harm in it. Plus I got to pat myself on the back for keeping things civil and continued to eat in silence until I could hide away in my bedroom.

My room looked exactly the same as it had when I left it months before. Likely my father hadn't set foot inside. He'd have no reason to. Yet I was no longer comfortable in there. This had been the one place I could be without the pressure of my father. Now when I returned to my room there was a large envelope sitting in the middle of my bed. That hadn't been there when I went down to dinner.

I tore the envelope open and dumped out the contents.

Three thick stacks of banded money landed on the bedspread.

Only Orin could've left this here. He'd been in this room while I was downstairs.

I ran to the window and searched the landscape for any signs of him. He'd come and gone without anyone knowing. I knew how he slipped in and out quickly but I really wished he'd do it when I was in the room.

After finding a safe place to hide the money and still not hearing from Orin, I tried to do the few things I used to love. None of my books kept my attention. The garden seemed drab and boring, although I still walked it several times a day to escape the oppressive air of the house.

Two full weeks without seeing Orin made me crazy and left me with an overwhelming need of a different sort. I didn't bother to fight that either.

Touching myself to provide the release that Orin normally did was something else that I didn't know about. Often I wondered if he tired of my naivety though he assured me that he loved every second of teaching me anything I needed or wanted to know. My fingers weren't nearly as magical as his but it did get the job done even if I felt odd doing it without him watching which was how he normally preferred it, too.

I sent Olivia a note asking her to meet me for lunch in town because I needed out of my house. She sent back a time and place and was already there when I arrived.

"Did I hear right?" Olivia asked the moment I sat in the chair across from her in the diner. "Are you back at your father's?"

I grimaced but nodded then hoped she'd take the hint not to ask any questions.

"What happened?" she asked anyway. "The way you and Orin were together I never thought... it was like a dream."

"It's temporary." It had to be. It better be.

"How long has it been?"

"Two weeks."

"Have you talked?"

We ordered before I had to come up with an

answer. Saying that I hadn't spoken to my husband in weeks brought a lump the size of an apple to my throat like I couldn't breathe.

I shook my head instead. "What's new with you?"

Her face exploded with happiness. "Things are so much better than I ever imagined it'd be. Charles is very kind. We hope to be expecting soon."

"Really?" I hadn't even started to consider children. Then again I didn't think Olivia would be able to bring herself to prevent a pregnancy the way Orin and I did. Even she wasn't as brazen. Most of the girls I'd gone to school with were either already starting families or wanting to. But I thought part of this new world the flappers were helping us to create meant we could take time for ourselves first. Time to enjoy our husbands, if you were lucky enough to be in a love matched marriage.

"We want a family as soon as possible." The dreamy quality in her voice told me that she meant it too.

Talking the way we hadn't in months, lunch turned into a two-hour event after which we hugged tightly before going our own ways. I couldn't let so much time pass before seeing her again.

In no rush to get back to my father's, I walked

slowly down the street pretending to window shop. Glancing in the windows used to be something fun I did with Olivia. Now, there was nothing I wanted anyway.

Then I saw him and stopped in my tracks.

Orin stood across the street, three doors down, with four men who looked remarkably like him. I finally got a glimpse of my husband and he was with the men who wanted me dead.

Chapter Nineteen

Orin's brothers stood beside him on the sidewalk, large and intimidating. Their laughter and a playful slap on his shoulder was a direct contradiction to the fact that if given the chance, they'd kill me where I stood.

My husband smiled back at them but knowing him as I did, it took great effort to put that on his face. It never quite reached his eyes the way I knew it could. The way it had all the times he smiled at me.

He was as heartbroken over being apart as me. After swallowing hard and steeling my nerves, I forced myself to keep moving.

The closer to their group I became, the harder it was to keep from looking at Orin. If I let my gaze fall on him, I wouldn't be able to tear myself away. The smart idea probably would've been to turn the other direction to avoid them altogether.

Instead, I kept the lot of them in my peripheral as they moved to my side of the street and put themselves directly in my path. Their massive frames took up all the space on the sidewalk in front of me and I had to stop.

They towered over me as Orin did and I knew I should've been scared or at the very least worried they'd figure out who I was and attack. I quickly decided that would be unlikely since we were in public. There had to be some sort of rules of conduct even among shifters.

"Pardon me," I said quieter than I'd meant to be.

The four burly men intimidated me as they turned their very dark eyes to me. They looked so similar yet different prominent features set them apart when I got close enough.

"We're sorry, Miss," the one on the left said. "Didn't mean to take up the entire walkway. We're just brothers who haven't seen each other in a long time."

They parted for me to pass.

I smiled and dipped my head then pushed forward through the pack.

I tried to keep my eyes off Orin and could see

him doing the same though we were both failing miserably. When I was almost in front of him, I kicked one foot with the other, purposely tripping myself so that I would fall into him.

Orin caught me easily and held on for an extra second then gave my elbow an extra squeeze and ran his thumb over my skin quickly.

"So clumsy of me," I said looking at my husband, trying to convey everything I'd thought and felt over the past two weeks in that one hard look.

"That's quite all right," he said back holding my gaze.

I pushed off him to right myself then hurried away. Without knowing how his world worked, I didn't want to chance hanging around too long.

But I had to see him.

Seeing him was so much better and worse than I could have imagined.

He was such a sight for sore eyes but did nothing for the need that had been building inside me. Yet I hated that I couldn't talk to him, touch him with any meaning, or love him. I had to act like that man who knew me so intimately was a stranger.

Doing so hurt. Turned my stomach to the point I had to swallow my lunch down again.

"Now," one of the deep voices behind me said. "Let's go talk about this marriage business again."

My body tightened as I tried not to visibly flinch at those words.

Without looking back, I walked the town from one end to another, took two laps around the park, then started for home. Yet somehow, my legs took me to Orin's home instead of my father's.

My husband's house was my home now, even if I'd been exiled to the bowels of hell. As I got close, tense voices and strained words came from the back-yard. I should've turned and gone the other way as fast as my feet would carry me. Nothing good could be happening back there.

There was a spot, a tiny spot I could stand, peer around the corner, and not be seen, though I worried that they'd hear me or... smell me. They were outside which meant people would be walking by and I had to hope that they'd chalk it up to that.

"Where is she, Orin?" One of them, I'd call him the biggest but not by much. "This'll be easier if you just tell us."

Orin stood glaring at the other four. I couldn't see his face, his back was to me, but I could imagine it. Stern and serious, ready to pounce if the need arose. His arms hung limply at his sides, fists opening and closing tightly. He was ready for a fight.

My heart rate skyrocketed. I didn't know exactly what was happening but these were his brothers. They wouldn't hurt him, right? If they did, I didn't know if I could just stand there and watch.

"A human, Orin?" The next one in line spat. "You're going to kill our parents. They don't like it any more than we do."

"I'm not going to stand here and listen to this," my husband's voice came out calm yet lethal. "Do what you need to do."

If I hadn't seen it with my own eyes, I wouldn't have believed it.

That biggest one drew back then slammed his fist into Orin's jaw.

Orin barely took a step back at the impact.

Then the next did the same.

The third one landed on his stomach.

The last brother didn't have much force behind his punch but they kept going.

Again and again, his brothers hit him, kneed him in the stomach, elbowed his back while spitting questions about me at him.

Orin never spoke.

He took the beating with barely a sound.

I watched only because I couldn't look away. My hand wrapped around my mouth so my own squeaks wouldn't escape. It was horrible to see the man I loved being hurt.

Tears pooled above my hand but I didn't remember starting to cry.

Why were they doing this? Why wouldn't Orin answer them already?

"Is she really worth all of this, Orin?"

Orin was down on his knees when he snorted then spat blood into the grass. He clutched his stomach where they'd hit him again and again. Pain laced his words when he spoke.

"Is Aras?" he finally got out.

The brother that had asked the question blanched. His eyes widened and his mouth fell open.

"It's not the same thing," he replied once he turned his jaw back to stone.

"It is the same thing." Orin pushed up onto his feet. It took him a few seconds. He swiped a hand across his bottom lip. When he pulled it away, it was smeared with blood. "You love your wife. I love mine. You guys can do whatever you need to, I know how this works, knew when I married her. But you will have to kill me because I won't tell you where she is."

I gasped at his offer to die and squeezed my eyes closed. I wanted him to tell his brothers I wasn't worth his life because I absolutely wasn't.

The group stood there as seconds ticked by, heaving chests as they tried to catch their breaths. Two of them stomped away into the house while the other two and Orin still stood there.

"Sorry Brother," one said before clapping Orin on the back and walking away. A move that caused Orin to wince.

Then my husband was alone. He took two painful-looking breaths before he walked toward the back porch and out of my line of sight.

As quickly as my legs would carry me, I got away from them, from that house, the only place I'd been comfortable in my entire life. That wasn't true anymore. With his brothers staying there, I would no longer be welcome.

I had no true home.

Back in the park, I dropped onto the first bench I came to and let my brain take me places I didn't even want to acknowledge existed. And I let the tears flow freely. Watching Orin being battered that way was one of the worst things I'd ever seen and I didn't want to see it again.

Even if it meant not being with him.

When I noticed the sun dropping low in the sky, I pushed to my feet, dried my face, and put one foot in front of the other until I was back at my father's. My feet ached from all the walking as I slowly climbed the stairs to my bedroom. The room remained dark with only a sliver of the evening sky peeking through but I saw his outline immediately.

Orin was there in the shadows in the corner.

I dropped my bag and ran to him, throwing myself into his arms and somehow forgetting that he'd been badly beaten just hours before.

He caught me and held me tightly before lifting me off the floor and nuzzling into my hair.

I wanted to ask if he was all right but then I'd be admitting to being at the house in the first place. Asking would've told him I was there to witness whatever happened with his brothers.

"I couldn't stay away," he finally growled in a soft and tender way.

Orin lifted me off the ground then carried me over to the bed.

I'd wanted to talk to him but it'd have to wait. I wanted him first.

His lips crashed into mine like a man who'd die if he didn't taste me. At the same time, he let his hands roam over my body. My less than sturdy summer dress was no match for his strong hands.

We kissed and pulled at our clothing until nothing was left between us but air.

Sometimes Orin took his time. Others were like this. When raw need and desire took us over.

The feel of his skin sliding against mine, the taste of his tongue on mine, and the way his hands knew how to touch me was all I needed. His erection pushed against me.

"Orin," I begged because I wanted him inside me now not later.

Orin pushed inside me, stretching me until I didn't think I could stretch any more. I bit my lips together to keep from making even the slightest sound. He felt so good but my father was in the house and I didn't want any interruption. Then he began to move. He kissed me while his hands cupped my breasts before sliding between us, touching a spot so sensitive I almost bolted out from beneath him.

Biting my lips no longer worked so I slapped a hand over my mouth as he pushed me higher. So high I wasn't going to be able to hold on much longer.

I wasn't going to worry about any of it. Not his brothers, not my father, not the fact that we weren't currently living together. I wanted to let Orin take me, own me in the way only he could. The only way I wanted to be owned.

Orin took me to that special place where only he and I existed. But that didn't last long enough and we were soon both still and exhausted. He rolled onto his back and pulled me to him.

"It's a full moon tonight?" I asked quietly instead.

"You're keeping track?" His voice low and tired.

"No." I blushed although he couldn't see it. Then kissed him on the chest and added, "You get... bigger when it's a full moon."

"Yes but... "

"You're... You get *bigger*..."

I couldn't believe I said that. Orin assured me when we eloped that I could tell him anything but I never thought I'd talk to him about the size of his... cock. But I blushed again at thinking the word.

He chuckled low in his chest. From his reaction, I didn't think anyone else had spoken this particular truth.

"I miss you," he whispered kissing the top of my head. "How are things here?"

My husband was letting me off the hook. Yet another reason I loved him. He knew when to push and when to let things slide.

"My father doesn't speak to me unless it's absolutely necessary. Barely looks at me. I disappointed him by marrying you and coming back proves that I can't be trusted to make my own decisions. It's not like I can tell him why I've come back."

"How much did you see today?" he asked taking me by surprise.

He couldn't mean what his brothers did to him, I hoped.

Even in the dimness of the room, though, I could see the remnants of bruising across his chest. Though his injuries weren't as bad as I thought they'd be. Instead of answering right away, I leaned down to kiss each one I could reach.

"At the house, Elizabeth. You weren't supposed to be there. How much did you see?"

"I'm not sure. I saw them ask where I was. I saw them... " I said quietly. "Why did they do that to you?"

He shook his head. "It's how the pack works. I don't want you to worry. They won't get to you." Orin sighed deeply. "I expect they'll leave soon so we can get back to normal but you can't come around. If I could smell you so could they. They just don't know your scent or rather that it belongs to my wife.."

"And next time?" I sat up crossing my legs under me keeping the blanket pulled to my breast. "The next time they come, will you hide me again? Like a dirty secret?"

"I'm trying to get them on my side. My brother, Phillip, the one who spoke to you today, he already is. He understands but the others are more concerned about the strength of the family."

"Did you tell him who I was? Phillip."

"Yes. He's keeping them busy so I can be here right now."

"I won't do this again, Orin."

I defied my father, married a man I loved though hadn't known very long, changed the way I dressed and how I behaved.

I wasn't now going to be pushed aside.

"What does that mean?" He shot up beside me, standing next to my bed completely naked and not caring a bit.

"I won't hide from them again. Once they leave, I'm coming home. If they return, I'm staying. If they kill me then they kill me but I hate being away from you and I'm miserable here."

A new sense of confidence and determination manifested. It was completely his fault that I now felt like I could speak my mind. He'd promised me I could always do but this was the first time I was speaking against him. Still, I wasn't scared of how he'd react.

What I did know was that I liked the feeling, liked knowing that I could fight for what I wanted instead of accepting what others were willing to give me.

"If one of them hurts you, I have to kill him. My own brothers. Is that what you want?" He stomped over to grab up his clothing then roughly yanked his pants back on as I spoke.

He finally turned toward me while buttoning his shirt.

"Of course not," I said. "But... "

"No buts, Elizabeth. I'm your husband. You'll do as I say."

Orin jumped down from the balcony and looked up at me.

I'll do as he says?

He may as well have slapped me in the face himself. He sounded like my father. Orin must've forgotten that I wasn't the same girl he met months ago. I wasn't going to sit back and be told what I could do without having a say.

My Orin had never spoken to me that way.

I narrowed my eyes at him, ready to lay into him

and let him know he had another think coming. But his expression gave me pause.

He looked nothing like my father. There were no anger lines marring his face. No veins bulging in his neck or forehead. Orin didn't look nearly as demanding as his words made him sound. Instead, he looked... afraid.

Orin didn't want to tell me what I could and could not do. He wanted to keep me safe. And that scared me—because he was a strong, capable were-wolf, and yet, he was afraid something terrible was going to happen to me.

I stood in my room, naked, as cold fear made moving impossible. This wasn't some passive fear as I'd originally thought. The idea that he was overre-acting had crossed my mind. That wasn't what was happening. Orin was actually afraid his brothers would kill me, and there was a real possibility this situation could end in my death.

Chapter Twenty

I just wanted to talk to Orin. Or see him for a few moments. It didn't sit well with me that our last words to each other had been in anger.

Whenever I went into town, which became every day, I searched for him so that we could "accidentally" bump into each other.

Most of all, I wanted to apologize for not seeing his side of our situation. As well as, hopefully, get an apology for him acting like my father. I spent hours drinking coffee watching out the window for any sign of Orin or his brothers. I figured where one was the others couldn't be far behind.

Alas, he never appeared.

I even took the risk of walking past Orin's house but there was no sign of life inside.

No idea when I started thinking of it as *his* house again.

My days became routine. I woke, dressed, walked around town, spend hours at the diner, spend hours at the library then returned home as late as possible without drawing my father's wrath.

He tolerated my presence but wouldn't do the same with anyone he deemed inappropriate. A girl out late unsupervised was definitely inappropriate. It didn't matter if she was technically married or not.

Also, I used as little of Orin's money as I could and only bought necessities as I needed them. As much as I didn't want to use his money, I certainly wouldn't ask my father for anything more than room and board because I had to.

What I didn't understand was how Orin, who professed his love for me every chance he got, could go so long without even a visit.

If I had a choice, I wouldn't have chosen this.

After another two weeks passed, I finally hit my limit of being ignored by my husband and marched over to his house, if for no other reason than I would've liked more than three dresses to change into.

I'd been back at my father's for a month and the

weather had slightly shifted. I needed a few warmer things for the evening.

"Where are you going?" my father asked as I got to the entryway.

I'd almost slipped out without him noticing during a time when he was relentless about knowing where I would be.

"For a walk," I lied to his face. Technically, it wasn't a lie. Technically, I was walking... to Orin's house.

My father moved close to me, too close for my liking but I couldn't step back. That would just make it worse.

His gaze looked me up and then down. "You're not sneaking off to your husband are you?"

All of the things I wanted to say needed to stay locked away. It wouldn't do any good. Or that was what I tried to tell myself. "Of course not." Well, that barely worked. The underlying tone of my words wasn't going to sit well with him. I took a long, steadying breath.

"Don't use that tone with me, Elizabeth. I don't know why he sent you away so I couldn't possibly guess if he'd want to see you." He looked at me with disdain. "I wouldn't think so."

"He didn't want to send me away," I snapped

then fought the urge to cover my mouth. "He had no choice."

Father took a step closer. "Men always have choices." That was a stark reminder that women didn't. Women had few choices.

"That means you have the choice not to treat me the way you do."

His hand lashed out quickly, connecting with my cheek and sending my head snapping backward.

"Don't you dare," was all he said before walking away.

I'd brought that on myself. Living with Orin, the freedom that had brought, was harder to suppress than all the years with my father before that.

Refusing to cry, I hurried out of the house.

Now, I was a pit of staunch determination until I reached the door to Orin's house. Then the nerves set in.

My stomach turned over itself several times but I took a few deep breaths before realizing I didn't know if I should knock or not. Which pissed me off. I shouldn't feel like I have to knock at my own house. I steeled my will and yanked the door open.

Where I found the house silent and empty.

"Well, that was all for nothing." I laughed at myself.

With the eerie quiet in the house, I decided to get the clothes I'd told myself I was there for.

When I pushed open our bedroom door, it felt as if it'd been untouched, like the room had been empty since I left it.

Instead of dwelling on that, I grabbed a suitcase and packed up some of my clothes, then forced the bag shut because admittedly I'd taken a lot. It was heavy but not so much that I couldn't carry it myself.

Then I left again, wondering when or if I'd be back.

The weight of the bag started to wear on my shoulder when I finally got back up to my room. It clanked against the stairs several times but I kept moving. When I dropped it to the hardwood floor, the bag fell over. I pushed away blond pieces of hair that had fallen into my face away.

"You went there?" Orin raged at me before I saw him. He took up most of the space in my room and had his back to the balcony doors.

I hadn't even seen him.

"I needed clothes," I said simply giving him half of the truth.

"Buy what you need," he said through clenched teeth. "They were going to leave. I'd convinced them to go. Now they know you've been there and decided to stay. Do you have any idea what you've done?"

His eyes raged with fire as he glared at me. He didn't try to hide the anger.

"I want *my* clothes. I don't want to buy new ones with *your* money." I don't know when I decided to become so obstinate but it wasn't going away.

Orin had no idea what my life was like now or that staying with my father instead of running off with him in the first place would've been easier. Then I wouldn't know what I'd been missing.

"It's isn't *my* money." His teeth were clamped down so tightly that his words made it past his lips.

"Quiet down," I snapped. "My father will hear you."

"I don't care," he growled.

"Well, I do. If he finds you here he'll kick *me* out. He's already had his lawyers over to advise us on how to file for divorce on my behalf for abandonment. Where would I go then?"

Orin's eyes widened and his face softened.

He sighed but the anger didn't go away. It just became more controlled.

"I'm sorry all right?" I walked over to him and laid my hands on his muscular arms.

His muscles relaxed at my touch.

"Why did you do it? Why did you go there?" He sounded down, defeated even. Sad.

"I was hoping you'd all be there and—"

He charged forward forcing me to drop my hands as I fell onto my bed. He paced back and forth in front of me.

"You wanted them to find you?"

"At first but then I was relieved when you weren't home."

"We didn't miss you by much. You can't go back there. No matter what, Elizabeth." His eye blazed brighter the closer he came to me.

I understood why he told me this. If his brother's found me they'd probably kill me first and ask questions later. Questions I wouldn't be around to answer.

"I need to see you once in a while."

That was all I really wanted anyway. To not have to go weeks without even laying eyes on him. To not have to waste away in the hell that had become my life once again.

"I wish that were possible," he said back.

Now *my* temper flared. It almost never did but that was more than I could take.

"So you'll come here, come to my bed, make love to me and then ignore me as if I don't exist? Orin, I deserve better than this."

"I shouldn't have done that. It wasn't fair and for that I am sorry. Do you think this is easy for me?"

"It seems to be," I countered as I threw my hands out in front of me. "You're all over town enjoying time with your brothers, doing whatever men do when they're with other men."

"I can't even sleep in our bed, can't stand to be in our room," his voice grew louder again. "This is almost harder than watching you try to fuck the man you were supposed to marry. At least then I didn't know what I was missing."

I smiled and snorted because he'd spoken out loud exactly what I'd thought on the inside. The argument had gone far enough for one night.

"I am pretty fantastic aren't I?"

"You have no idea." He leaned over placing his forehead on mine.

I couldn't close my eyes to enjoy the moment. It was like I didn't want to miss seeing him for even a moment given I got to so rarely.

"You really aren't sleeping in bed?" I asked quietly.

"I am. Just not our bed."

"Come here." I sighed, pulling him with me as I laid back so I could nuzzle in next to him with my arm across his chest and my head on his shoulder. This is where I truly wanted to be.

I never intended to fall asleep yet with his warm comfort beside me, I couldn't stay awake.

In the morning, Orin was still there, exactly as he had been when my eyes closed, watching me sleep.

"Good morning." I yawned while stretching my arms and legs.

He must've moved me in the night because when I fell asleep my legs had been hanging off the end of the bed but when I woke, I was on my comfortable pillow under the blanket.

"I have to go." He didn't take his eyes off me, didn't even blink.

"I know," I whispered back but had to turn my face away to keep my composure. The mere thought of him leaving was crushing, but now that it was actually happening again... I didn't think I could make it without crying.

"What is this?" Orin's fingers grazed my cheek. The very spot I'd covered for days with the smallest brush of rouge.

"Nothing," I turned back to him so he wouldn't be able to see it anymore.

"Elizabeth." He made his demand with only a word.

"I spoke too freely." That was the best explanation I could give and it was the truth.

Orin's teeth ground together so hard that I could hear it.

"I don't know what to do," he finally said. "If I take you home, this will become violent. If I leave you here..."

"I'm fine here, Orin." It was a sacrifice I was willing to make. "It really was my fault. I knew as I spoke that it wouldn't turn out well."

"He hit you, Elizabeth. He marked your skin with his hand. I want to go to his bedroom right now and end him while he sleeps."

"He'd be in his office at this hour," I said without thinking about it.

My eyes bulged when I realized what I said but he used his thumb to remove the worried wrinkle between my eyes.

"You should be able to speak your mind," he said. "Even when it angers someone. You shouldn't have to pretend."

"But I do have to, Orin. It's the only way I'll survive this house again."

"I'll try to come back soon." He finally gave in, kissed my lips softly then headed for the balcony. Suddenly, he stopped. "Lizzie." He paused, looking back on me with eyes that were much more vulnerable than a minute before. "Please don't let your father file... "

"I wouldn't sign for it even if he did."

Then he was gone again.

With the summer season ending, the onslaught of closing parties became oppressive. The first two I received permission to skip. Since I'd been living with Orin, Father said I had nothing appropriate to wear. By the third party, I had to have that matter resolved.

I did as instructed even though I had zero desire to attend any of the parties. The last one I attended without Orin since meeting him was the ill fated night with Bradley. It wouldn't be the same.

But I'd grown very adept, once again, at following all of Father's rules. I didn't even blink when he handed me the divorce document, meant to show my desire to divorce which was the first step to a divorce trail, that had been drawn up by his lawyer. I took it, said nothing, and went to my room.

They still sat on my nightstand because I hadn't lied to Orin. There was no intention, on my part, to sign those papers.

Instead, our housekeeper, Mrs. Atherton, helped me lace my corset, something I had not missed. The gold dress had been cinched and tucked snug to my body the way it would have in the last decade. There was nothing modern about this.

That was how my father preferred it.

The new dresses that hung from a women's body were not acceptable in Father's circles. They all hoped this shapeless era was just a passing fad. Truth be told, I preferred certain aspects of the old world. I liked clothes to fit my body but would've loved to lose the corset that made breathing difficult.

"Elizabeth," Father called up the stairs as my cue to leave.

I'd put a small smattering of cosmetics on to enhance my face but nothing like some of the girls would be wearing. He'd never let me out of the house if I tried that.

Most of my life we walked wherever we were going if it was reasonable to do so. If the destination was further than walking distance, I usually stayed home.

Before Orin, I'd only been in Father's automobile a handful of times for parties further away that for whatever reason he didn't want me to miss. Since I'd come back, that rule had relaxed. I thought he figured I'd already been compromised.

When I'd asked him before why I wasn't allowed

he'd said that he heard what young people did in cars. His daughter wouldn't be that sort of girl.

I had no idea what he meant until Orin showed me in such detail that I had a semi-permanent blush for hours.

I guessed my father didn't want me to think being in a car was normal.

We arrived fashionably last at the Halstead's. Olivia's parents' house was usually the last we attended each year. This time, as soon as we entered, Father left me to greet his friends and business associates and I gave my wrap and purse to the right person. Olivia's parents would have set up storage in one of the rooms down here.

When I found Olivia, I realized that there would be no spinning at this party.

It was stupid really, but something we'd done at every party since we were eight. Olivia looked far too grown up to do something so juvenile. She'd cropped her hair short so the finger waves made her look very adult and her dress, while beautiful, hung loosely from her body in a pretty shade of rose that offset her dark hair and eyes.

"Lizzie," she squealed in a voice I didn't exactly recognize. When she got close enough to me to give me a squeeze, I could smell the reason for the unusually high squeak in her words. As a married lady, what she did fell onto her husband and it seemed that Charles was quite liberal at the idea of women and alcohol. "I was worried you wouldn't come."

"As if I had a choice."

"Let's go outside and spin. I could use some air."

I smiled at her suggestion and wasn't about to pass up the opportunity to be alone. All the eyes in the room had fallen on me as soon as I arrived.

Out in the night air, Olivia took my hands and we started to twirl.

Faster and faster until I teetered on the verge of tears from laughter. It seemed my entire life had become about longing and missing those I loved. And I had missed this with her. I never wanted to lose this feeling or her or Orin.

Or myself. I'd just found myself but living with my father I could feel the new me drifting away.

"Oh." She stopped abruptly and clasped her stomach. "I think I might be sick."

We both dropped onto the cool grass, on our backs looking up at the evening sky, the sliver of a moon casting its light down over us.

"That's better," she said with a sigh.

"How much have you had to drink?"

"Just two glasses but I'm not used to it." There'd

be no reason for her to have gotten used to alcohol. "What's wrong, Lizzie?" she asked quietly.

I didn't realize until then that my eyes were watering and apparently, I'd even sniffed a little.

"And don't say nothing. I know you better than that."

"Nothing is as it should be, I guess." In best friend spirit, she waited until I was ready to continue. "I thought I was going to marry Noah and be miserable until I died. Then Orin came along... "

"And you fell in love." She gave my shoulder a playful bump.

"I fell in love and things were better than I'd ever imagined. But now I'm back right where I was before only worse because now Father looks at me as if I'm a whore."

"What happened?" She rolled on her side to look at me which took me by surprise.

I'd expected her to worry about getting dirty and being proper. I should've known better than that with Olivia.

"I wish I could tell you."

"You can tell me anything, Lizzie, you know this."

I sighed and decided to tell her without telling her. I needed someone to talk to, someone to understand. "There's something different about Orin and his family. They don't approve of our marriage—"

"Neither does King Davis." We both giggled at the nickname we'd given my father when we were children, but rarely ever used now.

"But with Father, I'm not worried about my safety. Orin has four brothers. They came to visit so he sent me back home. Once they leave I can return but they haven't left and I'm beginning to wonder if they ever will." Swallowing the lump in my throat turned out to be harder than I thought it would be.

"No one has heard from Noah," she said, watching me closely for a reaction. "I don't think he's ever stayed away this long."

My gaze popped open at the same time my body shot up. Olivia sat up too.

"Did Orin have something to do with that?" she asked.

"Of course not," I snapped. "Liv, you know Noah. He'll show up eventually. Remember when he disappeared for a month during school? He does this." I prayed that any hint of guilt would remain hidden because I did feel guilty. Noah was dead because of me not that he didn't put himself in whatever predicament Orin found him in. But Orin wouldn't have been there if not for me. This was what I'd told myself over and over and was the only reason I'd been able to move on. "Let's go back to the party."

We stood and brushed the grass off our dresses. We locked arms then turned back inside where the music played, the dancing had commenced and champagne, still illegal, flowed freely.

Almost an hour later, I took a break from all the fun we were supposed to be having and stepped out onto the veranda.

Olivia's parents' house was among the largest in town. They'd raised five girls there, Olivia being the youngest. The older four had already married with three moved to other states. They came to visit once a year. The one that lived in town, Sadie, had a baby two months ago so she was sitting the entire season out.

Memories of the night I met Orin invaded no matter how hard I tried to keep them away. It'd been too long, again, since I'd seen him and the heaviness that lived in my heart brought with it a physical ache. I walked around the side of the house, almost to the front, and took a seat in the shadows. It was unlikely anyone would see me there unless they were purposely looking. I liked feeling invisible.

Invisible was better.

I watched as two young couples took an evening walk around the property, the girls giggling in an obvious attempt at flirting. A few older attendees left into waiting automobiles, leaving early as they tended to. A late arrival made their way up the path.

Or five late arrivals.

Orin and his brothers came toward me. My breath caught in my chest and my heart took off like it was in a race with their footsteps. He lagged behind, more beautiful than the rest and more reluctant to join the party.

Why were they even here?

My body remained completely frozen. I closed my eyes and prayed they wouldn't see me. I had no idea where he stood with his brothers or where I stood with them. Whether they'd just cause a scene or rip my throat out the moment they saw me.

Then they passed right by me but didn't seem to see me sitting there. I peeked in the window to watch as the group made the rounds with Orin introducing each brother.

I watched as they smiled and seemed personable. Almost normal. No one would be able to tell what they really were. I finally went in to retrieve my wrap and purse to leave before they saw me.

I was almost out the front door, only feet from

the Vilkatas'. My fingers were clenching the knob. So close to my escape when Father jumped in front of me, blocking my way and his voice boomed through the foyer.

"You'll go directly home, Elizabeth?" My entire body clenched when I saw Orin's head snap up and felt his eyes on me in an instant.

"O-o-of course. I'm... I'm not feeling well." It took everything inside me to get those few words out.

He stepped aside to finish his brandy with several business associates and before I could do anything else, Orin had me by the elbow, dragging me out the door.

Chapter Twenty-One

My FEET barely hit the ground before they sprung up again. Orin gripped me mercilessly on my wrist as he moved at a faster than human pace.

A pace I'd never be able to keep up with.

His movements were unnaturally fluid until we reached his Packard. Then he tossed me inside and folded himself in behind the wheel.

I glanced back over my shoulder and saw his four brothers turn back toward the forest instead of following us.

"What's happening?" I asked after the car jerked forward but Orin didn't answer.

He concentrated on driving much faster than I'd ever been and maneuvering the machine around the tight corners.

"Orin, please, I'm scared." The vehicle lurched again then swerved to the left but the hum of the engine lowered which meant Orin slowed down.

"We need someplace private where we can talk," he finally ground out.

"Can we go home?"

"That's where they're headed."

That made sense. I told him to go to my Father's.

There was an old shed behind the garden that no one used anymore. Actually, Father had wanted it torn down this summer but no one had gotten to it. Directing him the back way, we were almost on top of the building before it came into view which meant good things as far as being discovered. Orin pulled the lock and got us inside with very little effort.

A shiver skittered across my skin. The nights got cooler but the air inside the shed burst out with an unnatural coldness. Orin noticed and rushed out the door then came back in flash with a blanket he must've gotten from the car.

"Better?" he asked standing very close to me. So close that his own body heat rolled off him warming me as much as the blanket.

"What happened?" I pulled the blanket tighter around me when he started pacing in front of me. I missed his presence around me.

"It's my fault," he said quietly. "I honestly thought your father would be keeping you under lock and key. Then I heard him say your name and I reacted." His gaze landed on me heavily. "I haven't seen you in such a long time." Orin sighed then dropped down to the floor, leaning his back against the wall.

I did the same, bringing my knees up to my chest. Orin swept an arm across my back then pulled me into his body.

"Now my brothers know exactly who they're looking for which means you're no longer safe at your father's."

"You really think they'd kill me? It's not just you being overprotective?"

The way his eyes sliced slowly across my face like he wanted to remember every single detail was enough of an answer.

"Even... um... Phillip?" The brother he said had been on Orin's side.

"He doesn't want to but I can't be sure if he'll fight the others if it comes to that."

"Then we need to go talk to them." Slapping my hands against my covered thighs, I pushed up at the same time until I stood over him. "Orin, we can't hide out here forever. I'm done with this. Either they kill me or they don't but I can't be separated from you any longer."

He rose to his full height beside me, cupped my cheeks then kissed me like he hadn't in weeks.

Which he hadn't.

The fact that his tongue swiped mine almost immediately didn't surprise me anymore. Actually, I'd begun to welcome it, crave it even. He had a way of making everything seem like the right thing to do. He pulled away but I felt the reluctance in his fingers because they tried to pull me with him.

"I will die protecting you. You can't try to stop me," he said softly causing waves of emotion to crash over me.

Fear took over. It would've been stupid not to be scared but the thought of Orin getting hurt in the process terrified me. Yet hiding was no longer an option.

"Isn't there something I could use to protect myself?"

He looked at me, his face scrunched up in confusion.

"Silver bullets, maybe?" I'd heard the urban legends about werewolves.

"That is just part of the fairy tale, Lizzie. Any

bullets could kill us. We just heal at a very fast rate so it's hard to do."

We left the shed quietly even though no one would be around to hear us. I insisted on changing my clothes first. I had no desire to deal with his brothers in an evening gown and shoes that ensured I wouldn't be able to attempt a getaway without breaking my neck. Not to mention the corset.

Slipping inside the house was easy since Father wouldn't be home for hours but I also didn't want any of the help to tell him that Orin was with me. Once in my room, Orin assisted me in undoing the small buttons that ran down the back of the gold dress. He took his time doing it too. My body exploded in goosebumps as he did it.

Absolute relief, along with fresh air, flooded my body as soon as he yanked the lace on my corset. I wished he'd been undressing me for a very different reason.

"I've never understood those contraptions," he mumbled. "Why would women want to be so constrained?"

With my back still turned to him, I yanked at the jewelry I'd chosen for the night.

"We don't want to be. Corsets have been a

requirement for generations. Some of us don't have a choice." I said the last sentence softly.

I didn't want to make him feel guilty over me staying with my father. His fingertips slid down my spine stopping just above my covered bottom.

He didn't say anything but I felt his tension as if he had.

Choosing to ignore it, I quickly slipped on an older dress, grabbed a pair of sensible shoes with a very low heel not because I thought I could outrun a pack of werewolves but at least this way I'd have a fighting chance. I also quickly removed all the pins holding my hair close to my head letting the silky gold locks flow past my shoulders.

I still hadn't brought myself to bob my hair and the twist I'd taken so much time to prepare earlier resulted in long waves down my back.

Then we slipped out the way we'd slipped in.

Orin drove back to his house slowly. Slower than normal for sure but inevitably we were almost there.

I missed his house, my real home, and hoped to one day return fully.

"They'll hear us coming," Orin said quietly while we were still inside his auto about a block away from his house. "I love you, Elizabeth."

I took a very deep breath, on the verge of

speaking words like I'd never had the courage to before. I needed the oxygen and the moment.

"I could say I love you, Orin. I could do that. But I'd rather wait until we're in our bedroom and you're ravaging my body in ways you never have all because we're happy to be alive and you're happy to have me in your bed again."

I have no idea where that came from. That was a new level of boldness I'm not sure existed outside of brothels. Part of me worried he'd think less of me and part just didn't care anymore.

If I was going to die, I'd die as the person I chose to be not the person I'd been forced all my life to become.

The fire in Orin's eyes told me he didn't mind at all.

"Keep talking like that and we'll never make it out of this car."

A quiet giggle slipped from my lips at a time when laughing like a school girl was wholly inappropriate but it couldn't be helped, really.

Outside, Orin pulled me to him as we walked slowly to the house. He didn't lead me inside. Instead, we rounded the house to the backyard where we found the four brothers standing in a tight huddle talking quietly. There was only a low hum from them until one of their heads snapped up and a growl released into the night.

"Stay back," Orin let me go and pushed me behind him. The menace in his voice the exact opposite of how he sounded when he spoke to me in the car.

His brothers formed a line, shoulder to shoulder with bulging biceps crossed over their chests. It was a sight to see. And if those intimidating men didn't put the fear of God into someone then nothing would.

"Have you gone mad, Orin?" One of them stepped toward us.

"Phillip, we won't hide anymore. I won't hide her. She's my wife. Let's get this over with."

So that was the brother who supported Orin's decision to marry a lowly human and risk their family's strength and dominance over their pack. He did his best to take in every one of my features.

Phillip searched for something in me that I didn't know if he'd find. When his eyes softened as he scanned me, it gave me a little relief in this very tense situation. However, every muscle tightened and his posture snapped up rigidly as the other three also stepped forward.

Before my mind registered what happened, the five of them stood in a circle, though Orin was careful to keep himself between me and all of the others, and they were yelling in what I assumed was Lithuanian. The same language Orin had argued with his father for the first time I met his parents.

Their voices grew as did their bodies. Muscles bulged and popped, their faces started to morph. I took several large steps back until I hit the railing at the corner of the porch. This time I knew what was about to happen. Suddenly, Orin turned to me, his teeth large and pointed in a jaw that was much bigger than before.

"Stay back," he growled.

I didn't need his warning. I wouldn't get any closer than I had to.

Brother number one shoved at Orin who didn't budge. Phillip grabbed number one by the shoulder, wrenching him away when brother number two stepped forward with brother number three.

Words flew, then claws.

Orin swiped across number three's neck and cheek.

Blood spurted from the open wounds and a full-out fight was about to break out when I heard another voice from behind me.

"*Užteks!*" Anton bellowed appearing out of

nowhere. He hadn't been standing there moments before. *"Viduje. Visi tave išgirs."*

I wasn't sure if my brain just wouldn't absorb any more information or if Anton actually spoke another language but that's what he said. Surprisingly, all five boys snapped back to their full human selves and walked toward the house. Except for Orin who came for me. They hadn't fully transformed so at least their trousers remained still in place. Ripped but in place.

"You still with me?" Orin asked leaning down to be at my eye level.

I nodded quickly but didn't say anything. My eyes were so wide they almost hurt.

"Oh... uh... Dad said 'enough. Inside. Everyone will hear you.' We aren't supposed to let the humans know what we are." Orin actually smirked at me. "I didn't know my parents were here."

"I'm ok. Are you ok? You made one of your brother's bleed."

"Yes, I'm fine. And that was Daniel, he's the oldest. Next is Phillip. Roman on Daniel's left and on his right Ivan. I'm the youngest. We have to go in there but I promise you'll be safe for now."

I nodded because he'd given me a lot of information to take in all at once.

Although what stood out was that Orin promised I'd be safe at least right now. He hadn't made such a promise before we'd come here so I had to assume this new sense of security has something to do with the arrival of his parents.

Inside our kitchen, the four older brothers had already arranged themselves around our small table with his parents taking up space in the middle of the room. Orin led me to lean against the nearby wall so that he'd be between me and them.

"*Jūs, berniukai, dabar apsigyvensite,*" his mother began.

"English, please, Mother," Orin interrupted. Some very curious glances came at him from the table. "My house. Lizzie doesn't speak Lithuanian."

Sighing, his mother then started over. "You boys need to calm yourselves. And figure out a way to work together. From this point forward, Elizabeth is protected not only by Orin but by your father and me."

What? Last I knew, they wanted me out of Orin's life, if not dead, as much as the brothers did. Since they'd left to try to figure out why Orin had been led to me even though I wasn't a shifter, I assumed it had something to do with that and anxiously waited for them to tell us what they'd found.

"There are bigger things to consider now than the power you boys crave."

"She's dividing us." Daniel jumped up from the table. The chair slammed into the wall and fell over with a loud smack making me jump. "Making us weak."

Orin placed a calming hand on my arm.

"There are bigger things to be concerned about right now, Daniel," their mother said again.

"I highly doubt that, Mother."

"Even the Balodis?" She folded her arms under her breasts like she was waiting for a response.

I didn't know what a Balodis was but just the word changed the atmosphere in the room. Everyone became alert and the attention shifted from me.

"Orin," I whispered even though no matter how low I spoke, they'd all hear me. "Orin, what's a Balodis?"

"Not what but who," he said back without looking at me. Much louder he asked, "Where do they fit into this?"

"When Anton and I left to find out why you'd—"

"Wait," he cut in then turned to me. "Lizzie,

could you go wait in our room while we figure this out?"

"I don't want to leave you." What I meant was I didn't trust his brothers not to gang up on him then come for me although I didn't think one of them would go against their parents.

"Everything is fine right now, Lizzie. But it will be easier if we figure out what's going on first. Then I can fill you in. I promise I'll tell you everything. I swear it."

After a hard swallow, I nodded.

Before I could walk away, his hands came to my face and mine latched on to his wrists when his lips gently touched me. He gave me two good ones before pulling and quietly saying, "I love you."

On my way up the stairs with only my thoughts to comfort me, I realized that Orin had made that display of affection and declaration very publicly. Likely as a way of making sure his family knew this wasn't a game he was playing. Every eye in the room had been on us.

I'd felt them more than seen them.

With nothing else to do, I found myself on the balcony outside our bedroom staring off into the horizon. My attention snapped back twice when the voices in the kitchen raised several levels but not enough for me to understand what they were saying if it was even English.

A harsh-sounding word from Anton and everything calmed back down. I was back to staring off into the night with that same sliver of moonlight from earlier as the only light in the sky. It was too cloudy to see the stars.

My head fell to the side and hit something hard and warm. When I forced my eyes open I saw the curve of Orin's neck. The spot where his neck met his shoulder where my head still laid.

My lips touched his silky skin sucking just enough to make him moan and whisper my name. He had me in his arms, carrying me back into our room.

He laid me gently on our bed then began unbuttoning my top. Slowly. One at a time.

"What happened?" I asked.

His gaze jumped to mine but his fingers kept working until he completely remove my shirt.

"The Balodis' are another family. Another pack."

He continued lower until my skirt slid sliding down my legs where he paused only to remove my shoes.

"Another, not as well evolved pack."

He sighed looking down at me as I lie there in only my underthings.

"They are more of what people envision when you say werewolf. They aren't as civilized."

He said it in a way that meant he wouldn't elaborate on what he meant by not as civilized.

I didn't think I wanted him to.

Chapter Twenty-Two

"Why is this other... pack a problem? Why are your brothers so calm right now? And what took your parents so long to come back?"

"If they find out about you they'll come for you. My parents know I'll die to protect you which means they all need to protect you as well." Orin sighed. "My brothers aren't calm but they have to listen to my father. He's our alpha and wouldn't have known that my brothers were here. My parents took so long because it took that time to find what they were looking for. There's so much I need to tell you but can I do that in the morning?"

"You said you'd explain everything." I wasn't about to let him out of that promise.

"And I will. Can it be in the morning? You've been gone weeks, Lizzie. There are other things I'd like to do right now instead."

I smiled because I couldn't help and I wanted him at least as much as he wanted me. Orin only needed that smile as confirmation I'd allow him to remove what little I still wore. Then he yanked the sheet out from under me and climbed on top, pushing my legs apart with his. His erection pressed against that sensitive spot and threatened to make me come undone right away.

Orin began by kissing me softly on the lips, licking the seam until I opened and let him in. Then he turned my head away from him and licked down my neck. My mouth watered at the idea of what was to come. He knew I loved it when he tasted my skin. Then he moved lower and lower quickly and I had to bite my lips together to keep from audibly groaning as he slid his hands over my curves, firmly grasping my hips as his mouth worked over me.

Then he stopped, pushed up onto his arms, and whispered just inches from my face.

"Say it, Lizzie. Earlier you said you'd say it when I was happy to have you back in bed. And I couldn't be happier than to be between your legs right now."

"I love you, Orin," I said without further reminder of what he was referring to. He pushed into me causing my eyes to close. I whispered again, "I love you."

His lips claimed mine again as he pushed inside me. I missed this with him. My body tingled with the anticipation of what he'd do next. We'd been apart far too long.

I just wanted to touch and explore him, remind myself of every muscle, and dip on his body. He moved in a way that created space between us and I immediately missed his presence so I pulled him back to me.

The next time he pulled out, I whimpered which made him smile. Then he laid on his back and pulled me on top of him.

"Orin," I said surprised. We'd been together many times before I went back to my father's house but not like this. Was this something people do. "What..."

"Trust me, Elizabeth." Which I did.

Orin nudged me up and held his cock in his hand then wrapped an arm around my waist and pulled me down. This time when he filled me, it was completely different. It felt different. I braced myself against his chest and allowed my eyes to flutter closed. It was like he was the deepest he could be.

At his urging, I moved my hips. He groaned and wrapped his hands around me, squeezing tightly. The muscles in my legs burned but I didn't care. This felt too good.

Soon, though, he flipped us over so that he was on top slamming into me as I came undone and he followed right after.

It'd been too long.

Once he recovered, we spent the next couple of hours trying to remember that there were other people in our house.

People with very acute, long-range hearing.

As I fell asleep in my husband's arms, honestly happy for the first time in weeks, I tried not to think about what Orin meant about this other group of *less civilized* werewolves and how I would factor into it. Anytime I let my thoughts drift to the Balodis, it was like Orin knew and he did everything in his power to make sure I was otherwise occupied.

The morning bloomed brightly through the curtains I'd forgotten to draw. When I turned over to see if my husband had woken, his side of the bed was empty. I laid there staring at the ceiling when the sounds of a much happier group burst loudly from the kitchen. I glanced at the clock next to the bed and couldn't remember the last time I'd slept that late without being sick or heartbroken.

Before I could swing my legs off the bed, the door creaked open then Orin slid inside.

"I was just coming to wake you up," he said making his way to the bed to sit beside me. "Thought you might be hungry."

"Why did you let me sleep so late? You're mother's going to think I'm lazy."

"They all know you needed to sleep." The satisfied smirk he wore confirmed my worst fear. They'd known exactly what we were doing last night.

"Oh man... " I said covering the blush of my face by dropping my head into my hands. "I can't go down there. Your parents heard us last night?"

"Lizzie." The smile in his voice only made it worse. "It's all right."

"Can they hear us right now?" I whispered.

Shaking his head, he answered, "I asked them not to listen so I assume they'll respect our privacy."

"Orin, what haven't you told me?"

I let out a long sigh before speaking he scratched his fingers through his hair. "Because I've mated with someone who can't protect themselves, the Balodis family might decide to eliminate you once they find out you exist. It puts you at risk."

I cringed at the word *mated*. That's not exactly how I'd characterize what we did. "I don't understand. If they killed me wouldn't you eventually marry one of your own?"

He shook his head before I finished speaking. "That's not how it works. I could technically do that, marry someone else but you only truly mate once. I guess it's what humans would call a soul mate. Besides that, there isn't anyone else for me, Elizabeth. You're it."

Orin took that moment to kiss me good morning. His lips were soft against mine. I wondered if mine were sore from the battering they took last night. He'd kissed me until I couldn't breathe and then kissed me some more.

"So you're saying soul mates as if you don't have a choice."

"We have a choice. It's really hard to explain." He sighed. "When the search for my mate led me to you, I could have walked away and I would have been on another path. However, once we decide to be with this person that's our mate... that's it."

"Let me see if I have this right. Fate led you here but you chose me?"

He nodded.

"Why would you do that? You had to know this would cause you trouble."

"I fell in love with you, Lizzie. I knew I would the night I met you on the balcony. I'd had my eye on you for a few days before but once you spoke... I wanted to protect you."

"Which is why you tried to keep me away from you."

"I didn't care about the trouble it would cause me. I cared about the trouble it would cause you and even if I hadn't been in love with you that night, I was completely drawn to you. Once I did fall in love with you there was no going back." He took in my reaction before continuing. "Then I saw you with the man you were supposed to marry, trying very hard to remove your clothes and I knew. I knew I couldn't let you go. I couldn't watch you with another man."

We sat silently while I tried to make sense of all of that in my head. No one had ever chosen me before. Not even my own father. My heart grew with love for my husband to the point it might have turned painful.

"But there's more," he said suddenly. "How much do you know about your mother?"

"Next to nothing really. She died giving birth to me and my father wouldn't talk about her. Why?" An uneasy feeling settled in the lowest part of my stomach. I felt as if I was sliding down a hill and might throw up.

"My parents think... " He blew out a breath. "I don't know the details, my parents don't know the details, but they think your mother may have been from the Balodis pack."

I heard him wrong. "Are you saying my mother was a werewolf? An uncivilized werewolf? My father would never have married someone like that."

He leaned in and kissed me softly. When he pulled back, he took a deep breath and closed his eyes. When he opened them again, he said, "A long time ago our elders heard that full-blooded females were dying off in the Balodis, pack. No one knew why but the men were outnumbering the women by a lot. Because of that, the men had no choice but to marry humans. This didn't pose a problem because the babies were born healthy and eventually made the shift when they were still children."

"I don't understand what this has to do with my mother."

"The women knew that their husbands were werewolves. It didn't matter. Then one of the Balodis men who'd married a full-blooded shifter had a daughter who never shifted. She was full-blooded and never shifted. Some chalked it up to the pack being too closely related, though this female's parents were not related at all."

I could hide the unintentional cringe when he said they weren't related at all. Meaning some of them were.

"Then another female never shifted. Then another and another. Four non-shifting full-blooded werewolves were born before the pack gave up on breeding with the full-blooded females once the mothers began dying in childbirth. Those four non-shifting females decided to leave the pack. No man would have them if they didn't shift and they'd just die in birth anyway."

"And?" I asked, not realizing I'd been holding my breath. "What happened to the women who left?"

"Two were killed soon after they left. No one would say how. The other two were never heard from again." He took my hand in his and waited until I looked at him again. "One of their names was Thora. We don't' know the other."

I froze at the sound of his deep voice saying the name I recognized.

"What was your mother's name before she got married, Lizzie?" Orin asked.

"My father never told me."

Orin pulled me to him. I didn't know how to react to that news. His family had to be wrong. My mother wasn't a shifter.

"Are you hungry?" Orin asked. "How about we get you something to eat then figure out our next step?"

I got out of bed, was able to dress, and put myself together for the two of us to head downstairs where the entire family was waiting. They were all uncharacteristically quiet and watching me.

"Everyone can stop staring," I said finally when I couldn't take it another minute.

"We're all just surprised you can walk this morning," Phillip snickered just before his mother slapped him on the back of the head.

"Inappropriate," she said with an authoritative tone.

"Sorry," he mumbled.

"I think my boys all have something to apologize for." Emmie waited a moment before sighing. "This is where you apologize for trying to kill the girl. She's your brother's mate. You should at least wait until you have all the information."

A mumbled round of "Sorry" spread like a wave over the room but it didn't sound like any of them actually were.

A plate of eggs and bacon appeared in front of me. I ate while they planned the day. Anton said there were a few things they still needed to look into and wanted Orin to go out with them. My husband refused. Said he wasn't leaving me alone.

"You can't expect us to go out there and put our necks on the line," Roman scoffed, "while you relax at home with the little wife. We all have wives, Orin. Wives we aren't with right now."

"He's right," I said softly because I just didn't have the energy right then to be more forceful. "You have to help them."

"That's not going to happen," he snapped.

"I'll stay here with her, Orin," his mother offered. "No one will get through me, I promise. You have to do your share."

"Do we all have to go or can one of them stay." He waved over at his brothers.

None of them volunteered which didn't surprise me. I didn't think any of them wanted the responsibility of me on their shoulders nor did they want to spend the day with me.

"It's fine, Orin. I'm going to my father's house today anyway."

He snapped his head toward me. "Out of the question. You're not going back there. Certainly not alone."

"When did little Orin turn into a Neanderthal?" Roman snorted.

"You don't know what the hell you're talking about, Roman."

"I have the solution," Anton cut in before things really got out of hand. "Roman was injured by his brother recently." A pointed look fell on Orin who didn't seem to notice. "So he'll stay back to make sure everything here is taken care of. He has healed but let's make sure he has his strength up. The rest of us will leave in twenty minutes."

They all groaned. None of them seemed particularly happy with this arrangement, me included, but nobody argued with their father.

In the short time I'd spent with this family together I'd learned that Anton presided over everything. They all may have listened to Emmie but Anton's word wouldn't be disregarded when it came to pack matters even with his completely grown adult children. To look at him, I wouldn't go against him either. As large as Orin and the others were, their father's mass still outshined them all.

In my life, it had been stressed that I shouldn't grow too large, as if that was something I controlled. For fear, he'd have a harder time finding me a husband. I was to stay thin, but sturdy and learn to keep my tongue. When I stopped growing at five feet and three inches, he'd been pleased. I dwarfed Orin's family. Almost disappeared, within this group.

Orin snapped his fingers in front of my face to bring me out of my own thoughts. Everyone else had moved away from the table leaving him and me some privacy even if not completely.

"Does this all sit well with you?" he asked me quietly.

"If you have to go, you have to go. I'll just go to my father's quickly then come back to wait for you."

"No. I don't want you going there alone."

"Christ, Orin," Roman called from the other side of the room. "I'll go with her."

Orin kept his attention on me, his jaw was tight and unyielding. "Please don't go without him." He dropped a kiss to my forehead, stood to his full height then looked over at his brother. "I swear, Roman, every hair on her head had better be in place when I get back."

"Calm down, brother." Roman popped a cookie in his mouth. A cookie that I had no idea where it came from. "Your precious human will be intact upon your return."

Without further conversation, the four brothers and Anton were walking through the backyard and I'd been left alone with two werewolves, one of whom would really rather see me dead. It was late morning by that point, most people would have been eating lunch by then but I'd just had breakfast. I wasn't sure what to do with myself.

Roman insisted we wait to get my things at my father's until he was sure the family was far enough away, whatever that meant. For several reasons, I suggested we walk to my father's house. I had questions and I thought that since Roman already didn't like me, he'd at least be truthful.

"So tell me, Elizabeth, why is Orin against you going home?" Roman asked after we got a block from home.

When looked over at him, it hit me just how much he looked like Orin. They both—or all—had that very dark hair and eyes and toned muscles that could've been sculpted by Michelangelo himself.

"He doesn't like my father and only sent me there to protect me from you all," I answered but was rewarded with that Vilkatas look that said he wanted more. "My father isn't very nice to me. Actually, he's never nice to me and he's not that nice to a lot of other people."

"Did he deny you your one true wish?" he asked mockingly. "Why wouldn't he be nice to you?"

"I killed my mother."

The almighty Roman in his tracks.

"She died giving birth to me," I clarified.

"How is that your fault?" he asked but I only shrugged.

It wasn't always easy to explain that you didn't blame someone for hating you for something that happened out of your control.

"You're married, right?"

He nodded while watching me out of the corner of his eye. That's one thing I'd begun to notice. The Vilkatas family were always watching me whether because they were trying to figure me out or if it was because I was the only human in the room.

"What is your wife's name?" I asked.

"Karina."

"And she's a... " I twirled my finger in the air of saying the word werewolf.

Roman nodded the confirmation.

"What's she like?"

He didn't answer right away. We walked an entire block before I decided to prod him along.

"You may as well answer me. I'm not going anywhere, Roman."

He cracked a smile. "She's beautiful and funny. I think she'd like you. That last thing you said sounds like her."

I wasn't sure what to do with that. It almost sounded like a compliment but Roman didn't like me and had recently wanted me dead. I only trusted him now because Anton and Emmi put me under their protection and Orin trusted that. Luckily I didn't have too long to worry about it because we were walking up the drive to Father's house. Roman waited patiently while I stood staring at the large brown door before I finally decided to knock.

"Miss Elizabeth," Mrs. Atherton greeted me in surprise before moving aside to allow us both in.

Roman followed me up the stairs to my room and even helped me pack the few things I wanted to take with me which included most of the stack of money Orin had left me before. I was beginning to think that we were going to get out of the house without a confrontation with my father. I was wrong.

"Elizabeth Davis you stop right there," his voice boomed into the room long before his body made it over the threshold making me snap to stand pin straight. "Do you think you can come crawling back to this house then disappear without a word?" He came to a stop when he noticed I wasn't alone. "I guess I should add and bring a man with you. A man that is not your husband. Elizabeth this is not how I raised you."

"This is Roman Vilkatas. Orin's brother. My father Henry Davis." I couldn't believe I was actually introducing them. "I came to get the rest of my things. I'm going home."

"This is your home, Elizabeth. I opened my door to you when your husband abandoned you."

"This has never been my home." I should've kept my mouth shut. Having Roman with me and Orin always backing me up, made me reckless.

"How dare you," he roared moving toward me. Before he got two steps closer, Roman stepped in front of me blocking my father's path. I could only imagine what Roman looked like standing there with his arms crossed looking dangerous.

"How dare I?" Suddenly I no longer felt I had to rein in what I was thinking and feeling. Whether Roman had wanted me dead or not, right now he was protecting me. "How dare *you*, Father? You've never even told me my mother's full name? Where did she come from? How did you meet? Nothing other than she's dead and I'm to blame." A lump formed in my chest. A result of years of fear of this man. I pushed it down and would deal with it later. Moving forward, I stepped in front of Roman to face my father alone.

"Just as surly as always right, Elizabeth? No wonder Noah ran off rather than marry you. You've brought nothing but shame to me. You're one job was to marry well and instead you run off into the night with a man no one knows anything about."

"Orin loves me and couldn't stand the thought of me being with someone else."

"Poor excuse for a man, I'd say."

Roman growled behind me. For all his bravado, he loved his brother, which made me feel even worse for coming between them.

"He's a wonderful man and will be a much better father one day."

I knew that those words would set off an explosion like none I'd ever seen but I was beyond the point of caring. Father charged me. I wouldn't be quick enough to avoid him, I never had been. I didn't need to be.

Roman jumped in front of me, grabbed my father by the throat, and held him against the nearest wall.

"Elizabeth?" Roman growled.

"Don't hurt him." My words weren't to save my father because he'd never tried to save me. I didn't want one of the Vilkatas to live with another death because of me. Even if Noah deserved it, I didn't want to be the cause of another life being taken. "I'll be right back."

I didn't know where the idea came from but I ran down the hall to Father's office. In the bottom drawer of Father's desk, all the way to the back, there was a book that my mother wrote in while she was pregnant with me. Mrs. Atherton told me about it when I was thirteen thinking that Father would one day give it to me. She said my mother wanted me to know how happy she was that I was on my way. I'd pushed it out of my mind until now because my father was never going to give me anything.

Of course, he'd never given it to me at all. I pulled the drawer out slowly. And found it hidden under a pile of other papers and snatched it right up.

I'd only been gone a minute but it felt like a lifetime and the ledger was heavy in my hands. Roman still had Father by the throat and while I couldn't know what passed between the two of them, I could guess. I knew just how sharp my father's tongue could be. The tension had ratcheted up three notches since I'd left the room.

"We can go now, Roman," I said as I lifted the satchel that was stuffed with the things I cared to take with me.

The muscle in the arm holding my father's throat tensed before he finally let go.

"That is not yours to take, Elizabeth," my father said.

It really wasn't. I was stealing it. "I'll bring it back when I'm finished." And I would, too because it wasn't mine to take. My mother didn't leave it to me in a will.

When I was little I used to try to imagine what he'd been like before she died. Or what he might've been like if she had lived. I was never able to come up with a clear picture of that in my head since I'd never seen a softer side of him. I used to hate him. After meeting Orin and discovering what love was really like, I pitied him.

"If you leave here tonight, Elizabeth, you will not be welcomed back. No matter what that husband of yours does to you." His words stopped both Roman and me at the door.

"She won't need to come back," Roman said with

a low, dangerous tone. "She has a family to take care of her."

"We'll see."

Roman had effectively just claimed me as their. As part of their family. I didn't know what caused the change of heart but I was glad for it.

This meant that I'd never be without family again.

Chapter Twenty-Three

As we stepped off the front steps of my father's house, Roman grabbed the satchel from my hand aggressively. A move of chivalry that took me by surprise though I thought the anger rolling off him had more to do with the aggression than anything else. He'd held my father back to protect me but this was more personal. Something he did not because Orin told him to but because he wanted to.

"So this is why Orin didn't want you going there alone?" Roman finally asked when we were halfway back home. "Orin feared your father would hurt you if one of us wasn't there."

"Because my father has before and now I've left for a second time. There was no telling how he'd react if he saw me again."

Roman shook his head then looked away from me. All of his muscles tightened the same way Orin's did when he was trying to hold himself back. Yet, I didn't fear him. He'd proven to me that he'd stand by his word and not hurt me.

"And Noah is the boy Orin..."

"You say that so easily," I countered.

"Because there's nothing we can do about it now, Lizzie." Using my nickname for the first time surprised me and gave me a small sense of satisfaction that maybe, just maybe I'd won over one of Orin's brothers on my own. "As a general rule we don't go around killing the humans but from the sounds of it, that couldn't be helped. I'm surprised Orin has allowed your father to live. Believe it or not, Orin has a worse temper than the rest of us."

Saying that about Orin just made me laugh. I'd rarely seen a temper on him other than when someone or something threatened me. Orin had even seen Bradley as a threat to me.

"I asked him to."

Roman gave me a questioning raised eyebrow.

"I asked him not to harm my father. He promised he wouldn't." My answer seemed to be enough because he didn't bring it up again the rest of the way home.

"Do you want to do something fun?" Roman asked after I sat the satchel near the back door. Emmie was filling the house with the most delicious smell of chocolate as she worked in the kitchen. The aroma came out the windows.

"Roman," his mother warned from inside.

"Ma, it's fine. They're not going to be back for a while. So, Lizzie, are you up for it?"

"Am I dressed appropriately?"

He nodded.

"Okay then."

The only spontaneous thing I'd done in my life was Orin. I liked the feeling that gave me, the freedom I'd never known before. Going off with Roman without knowing what would be in store would be the second thing I'd done. It was a whole new me.

He led me out through the woods behind the house. We were in pretty deep when I remembered that he was one of the brothers who'd come to kill me. Disposing of me out here would made that desire a reality. Yet, I felt safe with Roman. Maybe because he'd given his word and I knew how seriously their family took that. His mother had made the decree and Roman had just protected me from my father.

After twenty minutes of avoiding overgrowth

and underbrush, we arrived at a small waterfall. Clear, sparkling water rushed over what looked to be about a thirty-foot cliff. We stood at the top looking down.

"I didn't even know this was here," I said.

"I found it on our way to town."

"On your way to kill me?" I asked and that came from nowhere. Inciting him should be the last thing I did.

Roman stilled beside me, keeping his eyes firmly on the scenery so he could see the small grin on my face. The old Elizabeth would never have been comfortable joking about someone wanting her dead. But this Lizzie, me, somehow I was.

"Yes," he said finally.

"I'd do anything so that Orin isn't hurt," I confessed and it was the truth. that man had given me more in mere months than I'd had in the previous twenty-one years. More than I'd ever allowed myself to dream or hope for.

"What do you say we jump?"

My eyebrows shot up. "Uh… "

"It's fun. The water's deep enough. I'll go first to prove it."

I still wasn't convinced. This wasn't something I

ever thought of doing. Yet, that's what made it so intriguing.

"You've barely lived, Lizzie. There are so many things out there to experience and this is one of them. I guarantee that while you were locked up in that prison your father calls a house, your schoolmates were doing this very thing."

That wasn't something I would have been privy to but I didn't think he was wrong. Even Olivia who'd also known what her future held was allowed some freedom. The idea that she may have already done this sealed the deal for me.

Without waiting for an answer, Roman stepped to the edge and jumped without a second thought. I watched, partly in horror, as his body hit the surface, a giant spray of water shot toward me. The wave fell short of hitting me. I held my breath until Roman finally came up for air. He smiled widely up at me and waited to see if I was going to jump or not. At some point, I decided I was going to.

Stepping to the edge then pulling my skirt into a ball in my fist so that the rest hugged me tightly which would keep me from exposing myself to him. I didn't give myself too much time to think about it. Then, I just stepped off.

I fell so fast and felt completely free like I was a bird leaving the nest for the very first time. The crisp chill of the evening water hit my toes and as if in slow motion, rose to my knees, backside, waist, breast then I was completely engulfed. As soon as I was under, my arms and legs worked against the flow of water to get me back to the surface. It was on instinct.

"Well?" Roman asked with a playful voice as I gasped for air.

"That was amazing."

His boyish excitement, a side of him I hadn't yet seen, made me burst out in such a laugh that he had no choice to join in. We only spent a few minutes swimming and splashing before he said we needed to go home to beat the rest of the guys.

We leisurely made our way to the shore even though I knew he could make it so much faster than I could, he still waited for me. Back on solid ground, Roman shook off in a way that reminded me of a dog and of Orin at the pond on our way back from the city. I laughed loudly but didn't tell him about it. I didn't think he'd find it as funny as I did.

We talked quite a bit on the way back. Him mostly about his wife who he clearly missed. When I asked why they didn't bring the women with them, he said they hadn't known if it would be safe given how Orin was likely to react. Seemed to me someone should've gone to get them now.

I'd paid attention when we left the house so I knew we were getting close.

"Shit," Roman muttered just before a large mass hit him with bone-crushing intensity.

I stumbled back into a large tree because I had no idea what was happening. The bark scraped down my arm. My heart thudded against my chest at the deep growls filling the air. Branches and twigs snapped and the ground shook each time as the bodies hit. It all happened so quickly that I didn't even realize it was Orin who had attacked until Anton, Phillip, and Daniel were there pulling the brothers apart. With my wrist firmly in his grasp, Orin pulled me the rest of the way home, up the back stairs, and into the house.

"Orin, calm down," I pled through gasps of air. He could move so much quicker than I could and it took everything I had to even keep up. He was seething. I'd seen him angry before but not like this. Or maybe it was fear. I hadn't ever seen him scared but I was starting to think that was the problem. "I'm ok. I'm ok." My hands cupped his face to bring his eyes to mine. Before that, he was wild and unseeing but he needed to focus. "I'm ok."

"Where did he take you?" he asked as the others came through the door.

"To a waterfall."

"Why are you all wet?"

"We jumped from the top."

While to normal people that statement may not have been enough to elicit violence, to Orin it seemed to be. He lunged at Roman going for the throat. Luckily his brothers were able to hold him back so he never made contact.

"Orin, calm down." Roman stood behind the other two with his arms crossed over his chest like he didn't have a care in the world. He ran a hand up through his hair to rub the back of his neck. "We went to her father's house. Things didn't go well. I thought she could use some fun. Give me some credit please."

Orin's head snapped to me. "Did he hurt you?"

I didn't know if he meant Roman or my father. Either way, the answer was the same. "No." But I knew I needed to elaborate to ease some of the tension in the room. "I said some things my father didn't like but Roman handled him."

Orin's dark gaze bounced from me to his brother then back again.

"I'm getting cold so I'm going to go dry off."

Turning on my heel, I didn't quite make it out the door before I turned back, my gaze dropping on Roman. "Thank you, Roman."

He only gave one quick nod in return before glaring back at Orin.

The brothers would have things to work out. I didn't expect Orin to join me but he was suddenly back at my side, my elbow in his grasp as I stood in the bathroom. I slowly began unbuttoning my blouse but my fingers shook so violently both from the chill I was catching and the adrenalin from the confrontation that it became a difficult task.

"Here." Orin stepped closer. "I'll run you a bath then help you with that."

As the tub behind me filled with steaming hot water, my husband began to work on my clothing. Standing before him completely naked warmed my skin. His smirk meant he knew exactly what I was thinking.

"Get in." He gestured toward the claw foot tub.

The first touch of the steaming water caused a full-body shiver to take over. But as soon as I was in up to my chest the cold from the waterfall receded. Orin dropped to his knees beside me, his arms rested on the side of the tub with his chin on top.

"I have half a mind to join you." He dipped one

hand in then dragged fingers pulled through the water.

My head dropped back against the cast iron with a small grin. "Don't you have family things to deal with?"

"I do." He nodded. "But I think in there with you would be more fun."

"It would absolutely be more fun. However, your brothers miss their wives, you know. I feel sort of selfish enjoying... us while they're apart. It doesn't look like they're leaving soon because of the new information right?"

I was grateful to be in water hot enough to have flushed my skin otherwise the blush of embarrassment would have been palpable. I loved this new side of me. The side that wasn't afraid to say that I enjoyed the time Orin and I spent alone, sometimes in bed, sometimes not but I was still getting used to being that person.

"I don't mind being selfish."

The low, raw sound of his voice told me he was already three steps ahead of me, and as much as I would have like to lock the world out to get lost in my husband, instead, I narrowed my eyes so he'd know I didn't think that was a good idea. If he would have continued, I wouldn't have denied him. I was weak when it comes to Orin Vilkatas.

"You're right," he said then sighed. "I know you're right."

"Before you run off, I haven't had a chance to read my mother's journal but I took it from my father's desk and her name is written on the inside cover." Our eyes locked and there was no way either of us would look away. I didn't even know what any of this really meant but I did know that nothing good was headed our way. "I only found out about this when I was thirteen and even once I knew where he kept it, I was too... scared to read it. Inside the cover read Thora Balodis Davis."

Orin closed his eyes and swallowed so hard his Adam's apple jerked violently.

"She was one of them," I added which we both clearly knew. "What does that mean?"

"That means you need to finish up so we can get downstairs."

Before that revelation, Orin was going to leave me alone in the bathtub. Now he wasn't. His presence didn't make the apprehension or the constant feeling that danger loomed just outside of my protective bubble, leave my body. I had wanted to stay right there in the warmth of that water until my fingers pruned.

Dressing in a simple skirt and top, I threw my hair into a messy Gibson tuck. Orin insisted I was fine to leave it down, his family was my family after all and Emilija left hers down all the time but I just couldn't do it. There were some things about my upbringing that would be hard to overcome no matter how different Orin's beliefs were.

When we joined the others back in the kitchen it looked like we'd entered the sacred den of a secrets. His father sat at the table, very much in charge, with his mother standing just behind him in a clear stance that screamed 'second in command' with the other brothers scattered around the table. Orin sat down on the only empty chair.

I had no idea what to do with this awkward and uncomfortable grouping. Mostly because I didn't know what was going on. As I tried to slink back to the corner on the other side of the room, Orin's hand shot out, wrapped my wrist firmly in his grip, and yanked until I fell into his lap.

"Really?" Ivan growled.

Looking from the angry brother to Orin, I thought my husband was about to bring out his famous temper. Or what Roman had said was the worst temper of them all.

Instead, Orin smirked and one eyebrow lifted infinitesimally.

"*Palikite ji,*" Emmie snapped which made Ivan slump back into his chair.

I made a mental note to ask Orin later what his mother had said. For now, it was time for me to find out what exactly was going on and how I figured into it.

At first, no one spoke. I got the feeling that me being in their private group made them as uncomfortable as me. Whatever they were going to say had to do with me directly and with my mother.

"Lizzie took her mother's journal while at her father's house." Orin's eyes looked from me to his father. "Her mother was a Balodis."

Dead silence filled the room as all of them looked directly at me. I'd never felt that amount of scrutiny including in all the years I spent under my father's watchful eye.

Ivan sat back with his large arms crossed over his mountain of a chest and glared at Orin then said, "Then wouldn't it be easier to give her to them. Or dispose of her?"

Chapter Twenty-Four

"If we hand Elizabeth over to them, it would keep the peace for a while. They'd be too preoccupied to be a bother to us," Ivan said.

The brothers obviously hadn't gotten on board with the plan that included not killing me.

Orin gently lifted me off him. I took two steps back and held onto the edge of the counter to keep from falling. My knees weren't cooperating and threatened to buckle. Given the climate of our kitchen and the anger rolling off my husband, I was surprised I was able to stand at all.

"Say that again, Brother," Orin spat. "And we're going to have a serious problem. You will get to her over my dead body."

"And mine," Roman agreed, sliding in next to Orin.

"And mine," Phillip joined them as well.

"We don't need her," Ivan yelled.

"I need her," Orin yelled even louder.

The room erupted in chaos, words in a language I couldn't possibly know. As a group, they fell into Lithuanian without realizing it sometimes and I hated not knowing what was being said. Especially since it was clearly about me.

I couldn't take the arguing so I took the one giant step toward the table, putting myself in the middle of very angry werewolves. Swallowing down any fear that I had because, honestly, you couldn't be in the middle of that group and not have some fear, I took a deep breath.

"Before we start with the "Kill her" part of this scenario may I ask a question?" I made sure to enunciate loudly so they'd hear me.

The group fell silent and while I could feel them all looking at me, I couldn't focus on any of them. Orin tucked my hand inside his for support.

"If the Balodis... pack?"

Emmie nodded at my word choice. I saw her out of the corner of my eye.

"Ok, if their pack were to get me, what would

they do? I mean why would they even want me? I just want to understand."

"Elizabeth," Emmie spoke before anyone else had the opportunity. Her voice was so soft and gentle that I knew I wouldn't want to hear what she had to say. "From what we know so far, you are the last of the purest bloodline for them. Your mother was the only child of their oldest branch of the family. Her parents had been brought together with the specific purpose of continuing the bloodline. Your grandfather was pure and important. Your grandmother healthy and chosen. Your mother was the hope for the future. When she left, hope left with it. We don't know why the four women chose to leave their pack but half-human babies are working but they aren't nearly as strong. The hope would be that if one of them mated with you, your offspring would be stronger and shift even though neither you nor she have."

"And not being strong is the real problem?"

"Yes. It's why *some* of the Vilkatas' were not ecstatic about you pairing with Orin." She shot the brothers a scathing look. "With strength comes power. With power comes greed." This time she glared at Ivan then Roman. Roman put his hands up in surrender. He'd offered his life to protect mine just moments before. He wasn't on the other side anymore.

"So if they get me, they'll want to... " I wasn't sure how to say it in front of everyone. I didn't even want to think it. I'd only been with Orin and I only wanted to be with Orin. The thought of someone touching me against my will brought on a physical sickness that was extremely hard to control. "They would want to impregnate me?"

Emmie nodded softly but Orin pinched my chin between his thumb and finger to turn my head toward him.

"I will not let that happen, Lizzie. If you trust anything, trust that." The intensity with which he spoke along with the look in his eyes made me believe completely that if the Balodis got their paws on me, it was because Orin was dead. I hated the thought. Yet it made me feel safe at the same time.

"On a much lighter note," Phillip interrupted. "I called and the women will leave in the morning to arrive around dinner time. We need to figure out where we'll all stay because I am not having my wife sleep on the floor in a room with you three."

What he said lightened the tone of the room and brought on a bout of laughter. Their wives could not sleep on the floor. That would make me a terrible hostess and made me even more nervous. I would once again be the only human in a pack of werewolves. Only now there would be more of them.

Orin sighed then said, "I own the house next door."

"What?" He'd never told me that.

"I had to buy it. It was the only way that I could ensure total privacy. The other houses are either far enough away or blocked by the trees. So I could... "

"Frolic naked in the woods?" I couldn't keep the small smile from crossing my lips as I remembered the first time I came to Orin's house and he'd come out of the tree line without clothes on. It was also the first time I'd seen him naked or any man for that matter. No matter how hard I tried, I couldn't keep curiosity from taking over and taking a peek.

"Exactly." He laughed.

Ivan immediately said he wanted to stay in the other house. Not surprising considering how he felt about me. We had three bedrooms in our house. We had one, of course, Roman said he'd be staying in one, and the third Phillip claimed. Leaving their parents and Daniel to the other house with Ivan. Emmie assured me that they were still close enough should anything happen.

Sitting on our bed that night, I asked Orin to give

me the rundown of his brothers and their wives. I had a good memory and wanted to know who was who before they arrived. To be prepared. Orin said I'd get along quite well with Phillip's wife, Diana, and Roman's wife, Karina. Ivan's wife Nell would be an obstacle considering that she usually chose whatever side Ivan was on. Which wasn't mine.

Lastly, Daniel's wife, Aras, and Nell had been best friends before they married into the family and tended to stick together.

I slept better that night with the Vilkatas who hated me the most away in a different house.

The next morning, everyone was restless while waiting for their wives to arrive. I helped Emmie properly open the house next door, making sure that each bed had fresh linens and clean towels. Orin must've bought it completely furnished because it looked like the family who lived there was about to return at any moment.

We washed the towels that were there so everything would be clean and ready for the new visitors. Emmie snuck a few things from my house just so we wouldn't have to go to the market right then.

Around dinnertime, a dinner that I helped Emmie prepare, Daniel and Ivan returned with their wives and a toddler while Phillip and Roman returned with their wives and a small baby.

Karina and Diana hugged me when introductions were made. Karina had dark blonde hair and was tall. It seemed I was destined to be the shortest person in every room. Diana was tall and strong with what I would've called strawberry blonde hair and they all had dark eyes. Aras shook my hand strongly and had the most beautiful chestnut hair but Nell just gave a slight nod, her dark hair moving with her. Then I got to meet Daniel junior, a two-year-old cherub of a boy that hid behind his mother. And Phillip brought the baby over to me. She was six months old, he said and her name was Ruby. Her chubby cheeks and big dark eyes were precious. When he said, to Ruby, that I was her Aunt Elizabeth, I almost burst into tears. It wasn't logical but I knew it was his way of making it clear to everyone that I was part of the family and I was permanent.

Emmie and I had figured out how to extend the table so that we could all sit together but it was still close quarters at dinner. Yet it didn't feel close. We were side by side and it was the exact opposite of every dinner of my life.

"So, I hear you're a member of the Balodis pack,"

Karina said breaking the awkward silence. "How come your hair is so light?"

"I got it from my father."

"Your mother was dark then?"

"I think so. I've only seen one photo of her and that was several years ago. I think I remember her hair being dark."

Karina scrunched up her face at me. "What do you mean you only saw one photo?"

I figured it was as good a time as any to just get my life story out there. Well, not all of it but the part about my mother. They listened quietly, not asking me to elaborate on the parts that I skimmed over, and held all questions or comments until the end. Even then they didn't have many.

The next morning the brothers were gone before I woke up.

The Vilkatas women were already in the kitchen when I arrived which earned me a snide glare from Nell, who'd barely spoken last night at dinner. Karina, on the other hand, bounced over and pulled me into a tight hug.

"Good morning, Lizzie," Emmie said over her shoulder as she worked with some beef on the countertop.

"I'm sorry I'm late. I think Orin turned my alarm off."

"That sounds like him," Diana said with a laugh.

I didn't know what she meant and I didn't ask. If her comment was regarding a past sweetheart, I really didn't want to know.

"What can I do?" I asked pulling an apron over my head.

"Why don't you cut up these vegetables? We're making stew. The guys will be starving when they get back." Diana pointed a knife at a stack of carrots and potatoes.

Wrapping my hand around the knife, I worked slowly, starting with the carrots and cutting them into bite-sized pieces. The others talked amongst themselves but for the most part, we just kept working. It was easy and normal.

"Where's the closest market?" Karina asked. "We need a few more things."

"I can go," I offered.

She was already shaking her head. "Sorry. Orin said you weren't to leave the house alone."

"He isn't my father. I can go to the market."

"Why don't we both go?" Karina asked instead. "You can show me where it is and Orin won't have a fit at the thought of you being out there alone. I promise I can hold my own."

"Didn't doubt that for a minute," I said back smiling.

Karina was tall and thin, not to mention absolutely beautiful. Not someone to normally fear.

But if I'd learned one thing, it was not to judge a werewolf by their human form. With my father out there in the world and would no doubt cause problems for me if given the chance; Orin's werewolf brothers, some of who still wanted me dead; and now the Balodis' out to get me so that I could help them repopulate their pack with what they saw as purer blood... I'd keep Karina as close to my side as humanly possible.

Chapter Twenty-Five

Karina walked beside me, talking fast like the girls in school used to, about nothing in particular. It was like she was going out of her way to make me feel comfortable being around her. What she didn't know, couldn't know, was that I was more at ease *because* of her. We were halfway to the market when she finally asked questions.

"I have to know how you and Orin met."

It wasn't exactly a question but more an excited demand.

"A party at my father's house."

"Aww." She folded her hands under her chest. "Did you see each other across a crowded room and immediately fall in love?"

I smiled at the memory she was bringing up.

Love, at first sight, wasn't the exact description that I would've used but still the basic idea.

"Something like that."

I told her as much as I thought appropriate, leaving out the parts that should've remained between Orin and me or the ones that were too embarrassing to say out loud. Katrina shared with me that she knew in third grade that she'd marry Roman. It wasn't arranged or determined by their families but still, she knew. She loved him even then.

We were all giggles when we got to the grocer where she went in one direction and I the other to gather everything we needed. I put a small sack of flour in the crook of my arm then continued on for the other items. Turning the corner at the end of the aisle a man bumped into my shoulder. Hard. It would probably bruise.

"Excuse me," I said with a smile.

He turned back grinning like that cat that caught the canary. Dark hair in his face, eyes narrow. I looked at him then away and slowly turned my back his way.

"Not a problem, Mrs. Vilkatas."

I swung back toward him, already knowing I'd never seen that man before but there was something familiar about him. Something I did know. No idea how I could be sure, but this man was a werewolf. I was sure of it.

Spinning around, I tried to run, to get away from him, to the other side of the store and Karina's protection. But he was quicker. He roped an arm around my waist and slapped a hand over my mouth as I kicked and struggled to get out of his grasp.

"Keep fighting and you're going to get hurt," he growled.

I had the feeling I was going to get hurt either way so I didn't stop.

"Do you want me to kill the bitch with you?" he said into my ear after I got in a good kick to his shin.

I couldn't let that happen. Forcing myself to give in and stop fighting took every bit of willpower I had. But, I wouldn't allow Karina to be hurt for me if I could help it. She may have been strong but she was outnumbered.

"So, we're going to walk out and you're not going to say a fucking word or I'll tear the throat out of every person in here."

Right then a child of maybe six skipped by us and I closed my eyes.

"Understand?"

After I nodded, he slowly removed his hand from my mouth like he was just waiting for me to scream for help. But I didn't. I wouldn't. We walked out of the market and were met by two other large men outside. These were my mother's people. They had to be.

Dead would be better.

Because the thought of someone other than Orin touching me so intimately made me sick to my stomach. He nudged me around the side of the building before I heard Karina calling my name into the void. The big guy who had his hand wrapped around my upper arm yanked hard to keep me moving.

But I kept hoping and praying that they wouldn't kill her. She couldn't see me but I heard her screaming. Then two more large men turned the corner and came toward us.

They stuffed me into the front of a truck with the original man driving, one of the others on the other side, and the third in the back. The truck jerked to attention and jerked every single time he shifted. By the time we stopped almost an hour later, my neck was sore from the sudden movements. We stopped so deeply into the woods, next to a run-down house, that no one would even know it was there.

Apparently, the Balodis pack was used to manhandling their women because the big guy yanked me out of the truck with one pull and pushed me roughly toward the house. My feet stepped and stumbled along the dirt.

"I came here willingly. You don't have to be so rough," I said over my shoulder.

"You haven't seen rough yet," he spat back. Something in his voice told me that I would not like the kind of rough he was alluding to. "Now keep moving."

Inside, the house barely had any furniture and what little of it there was, was old in need of repair. There were five men inside the house with me which set my stomach on fire. All the horrible thoughts in my head sure didn't help.

"This is her?" The older man nodded at me. He was large like the others but his face was wrinkled with time. Not the way a human's would have been but enough for me to know that he'd seen many years. His hair was dark and pulled back away from his face and there was a hint of gray near the temples. "This is Thora's daughter?"

"Yes, sir," the one who grabbed me said.

The way everyone stood around this older man, the looks on their faces, and the way in which they held their bodies made it clear that he was the one in charge. If anyone was in fact in charge. His dark eyes took inventory seeming to stall on my light hair and again on my blue eyes. I was the exact opposite of every other person in the room.

"Do you know who I am?" The older man asked me, coming down to my eye level and much too close for my liking. I shook my head. "What did your mother tell you about her family?"

"Nothing." The voice that came out of my mouth didn't sound like mine.

He nodded slowly as if that was the answer he'd been expecting.

"Is someone retrieving Thora?" he asked glancing around at each of the men who would not meet his eyes. None of them said a word so I decided to fill him in.

"She's dead."

He snapped his head back around to me.

"She died giving birth to me," I said.

"Impossible," he snapped. "She mated with a human."

"Sir, the men have mated with humans," the first large one countered but looked extremely uncomfortable doing it. "Our women have never mated with a human before. We don't know what would happen."

The one in charge gave me a hard look like I was supposed to hold all the answers.

"I don't know." Fear took over again. "My father said she died in childbirth."

He leered at me intensely. "Well that's neither here nor there, now is it? We have you now."

"Who are you?" I asked.

"Thora was my daughter."

My mouth went dry. I'd never had another family member other than my father until Orin and now this man was standing there saying we were blood-related. Yet he didn't pull me close the way a grandfather would. Instead, he was going to allow his pack to do unspeakable things in the name of producing a full-blooded werewolf.

The murmuring started small, quiet and the words were inaudible. Until they weren't. They got louder and they were talking about me.

"Who's going to get her?" One of them called out.

Get me? My stomach clenched and acid rose in my throat. None of them were going to get me, I told myself. Orin will find me. Orin will save me.

"Not you," another threw back. A ripple of laughter spread like a wave.

"I'd like a chance," a man, probably a good ten years older than me stepped forward. "My family's line has been strong. We could make it stronger."

"I think it's obvious who will get the opportunity." Another stepped to the front of this small group. Of the two, I'd take the first one. He at least looked a little kind. The second one scared me immediately. But neither was overly appealing.

Each time one of them came closer, I moved away until my back hit the wall and I had no escape.

"Not a chance, Gunther," the first one said.

"Who's going to stop me, Mitchell?"

"Maybe I will."

They stepped closer and closer as they argued reminding me of the argument Orin had with members of his family when they then broke into their other form. I pressed into that wall even harder and prayed that I didn't escape one arranged marriage to be forced into another.

The one called Gunther drew back then his fist connected with Mitchell's jaw and a full-out brawl started right in front of me. But none of them shifted. They fought. Punches were thrown. A person was tossed onto the table. That's when it became too much.

"Enough!" Their leader, my grandfather, bellowed and all activity stopped. He pushed his way in between the instigators.

"All interested parties may submit said interest to me. We will decide who she belongs to."

Belongs to? That was almost too much.

"Take her to her room."

The one they called Gunther, yanked me to him hard once again. I knew I'd have bruises on my arms from the battering yet still I struggled against it. I didn't care it wouldn't make a difference. For a brief moment, I imagined all the ways Orin would make him pay for every single one of them.

Hours passed with me sitting on the edge of a disgusting mattress that lay on the floor in the small room I'd been taken into. That room, up the stairs, first door on the right, I contemplated the idea of belonging to one of them.

I'd been my father's until Orin came along, then I was his. Orin didn't make me feel owned, though, and he was who I wanted to get back to.

There was a window. I tried to pull it open but it was sealed shut.

I searched the room and the closet for something to break the glass with. Even if I did, they'd be on me so fast that I'd never get away. There were a couple of chairs in the corner but they were too heavy and the lap next to the bed wasn't heavy enough to do any damage.

I was stuck.

I really wished I'd seen Orin that morning. Kissed him goodbye possibly for the last time.

Before I could linger on memories of Orin, the key in the door lock turned and the door was flung open. One of the three who'd taken me entered, with a tray.

"My name is Peter," he said quietly. "I'm not going to hurt you. I'm just bringing you something to eat."

I watched him but didn't respond. He said nothing else then left, locking the door behind him. Looking at the plate, it smelled a little like heaven since I hadn't eaten that morning but the aroma also made my stomach turn. There would be no choking that food down.

But I took the glass of water and drank all of it as the room had gotten hotter since I'd entered it.

No one came back that I saw and at some point, I fell asleep.

The sun was up when my eyes opened again. It wasn't bright and oppressive which meant it was still early. Someone had come in to take the tray of food away because when I glanced around, it was gone. The thought of one of them being near me while I was asleep causing a chill up my spine and I became acutely aware of the fact that I needed to use a restroom.

Listening by the door, I could hear movement in the other room. Without any other options, I had to get their attention otherwise I was going to have another, wetter problem. So, I pounded on the door three times then waited for the footsteps to get closer before stepping back. The face that peeked through was Peter again.

"Do you need something?"

"I need to use a restroom." It was embarrassing to have to say that to him but I had no other choice.

"Right." Peter dropped his head then stepped aside so that I could slide in front of him. Then he led me down the stairs to another area of the house, off the kitchen, until I was finally in the bathroom. "You can't lock the door. I can break it down anyway so please don't."

"I won't."

And I wouldn't. The last thing I wanted to do was give them a reason to kill me before Orin even had the chance to come get me. Though that thought brought a lot of conflicted emotions with it. Someone else could get hurt trying to get to me. But in the end, I knew Orin would never let me go without a fight.

After I was done, I took an extra second to splash

some cool water on my face and neck. That room really was becoming unbearable and with the rising heat of the day, it was about to get even worse. Apparently, I was taking too long because Peter rapped on the door roughly.

Worst of all I had to pass a group of them on my way back to my room. They leered. One licked his lips. It was like they'd never seen a woman before. Or maybe it was that they all knew what they'd get to do to me if they were chosen. Whatever it was, they didn't speak as Peter escorted me through the room, putting his body between me and the group of horny werewolves. And I felt myself blush just thinking the lewd word but I didn't have anything better to describe them.

Then I was back in the stifling room that I was starting to think I was going to die in.

"Um... is there any way to open that window? Even a crack? It's hard to breathe in here."

Peter thought about that a moment then walked over and undid the latch, which of course was so easy for him, then pushed the thing up. A slight breeze blew the curtain and I knew at least I wouldn't suffocate.

"We have people all over outside. And I assume

you know that we can hear everything you do so don't bother trying to escape. You won't make it."

"I know. Could I also please have a glass of water?"

Without answering he left, closing but not locking the door behind him. I thought about smashing the lamp against his head but I needed to know my move after that. It was my only move. Moments later, he came back with a pitcher of ice water and a glass.

"Anything else?" he asked.

I shook my head and this time when he left, he did lock the door behind him. It was the first time I wished I actually was a werewolf. Then I could hear what was happening and I'd stand a chance of getting away.

Alas, I was just a human surrounded by an angry pack of werewolves in heat.

Chapter Twenty-Six

WITH NO CHANCE OF ESCAPE, I curled up next to the window and folded my arms on the sill to rest my head. The leaves on the trees outside danced on their branches.

The ability to move around for no other reason than I wanted to was a luxury I'd taken for granted now that I was restricted in this locked room. But those leaves weren't totally free either. They were at the mercy of the wind and I was at the mercy of my mother's family after spending most of my life at the mercy of my father.

Then the lock disengaged and the door creaked open slowly. Peter appeared and dropped another tray on the floor beside me. His hair was too long and disheveled and I realized that the shifters I'd met so far were all dark and mysterious. My gaze jumped from the tray to look back out the window. It'd been over twenty-four hours since I'd eaten anything. But I didn't trust their food.

"Eat," he said roughly.

I didn't even spare the food a glance. Out of the corner of my eye, I watched his jaw clench and his eyes narrow before he stalked over.

Peter squatted down beside me and forced my head to turn him until I was looking into his dark eyes. "If we wanted you dead, you'd already be dead," he said.

I didn't doubt that a bit yet still didn't trust the food they brought me.

"You're here to help repopulate the pack with fuller-blooded werewolves. If you're dead you can't do that," he explained as if I hadn't thought about that very thing. Then he walked away.

After contemplating what he'd said, and realizing he was right that I was important to them, the pain in my stomach won out. I ate the chicken sandwich and apple that sat on that tray without tasting them. As soon as a bit went in my mouth, it went down my throat. I ate so fast that nausea knocked me off my knees. Nausea from putting too much in my stomach too quickly.

Then I waited.

What I was waiting for I had no idea. For something, anything to happen. Then the voices on the other side of the door grew louder. Something slammed against wood loudly making me jump to my feet and wrap my arms around my stomach. I hated being in there alone not knowing what was happening on the other side. It gave me too much time to think. Too much time to imagine what Orin was going through.

He had to have been losing his mind.

Roman had told me that Orin had the worst temper out of all of the brothers. If it was true, with me gone, things could get very, very bad. Longing crushed my heart.

I wondered if he knew he'd never see me again. He'd never admit it even if he did. Instead, he'd spend the rest of his life searching for me. He'd never give up so I couldn't either.

I was still new to this world and had no idea how the werewolves worked as far as tracking each other down.

When the door finally opened again, I thought it'd be Peter coming through. He was the only one I'd had any real contact with. But the footsteps that crossed the room were heavier, louder, more menacing.

Gunther.

Scrambling to my feet, I didn't know what I thought I'd accomplish but I knew I didn't want to be on the ground while alone in a room with Gunther. I couldn't be vulnerable when his eyes were on me.

He was large and intimidating. His dark hair was clipped short somehow making him look even meaner.

"Elizabeth Balodis... " he sneered as his dark eyes looked me up then down.

"My last name is Vilkatas."

He smirked at my words. "Not for long." He took another step toward me, a menacing glint in his eyes causing me to step away until my back his the wall.

His hand wrapped around the back of my neck, squeezing as he led me roughly over to the bed and pushed until I fell.

My head hit the wall hard enough to make me cry out.

Then his hands were everywhere. He was everywhere as he hovered over me switching between almost crushing me under his weight and barely touching me. His fingers scraped against my skin, trying to pull my shirt up. I kicked my legs to push him away.

He was bigger. He was stronger.

I wasn't going to win.

His face was so close I could feel his breath against my cheek, smell alcohol all around me. My stomach churned. That food I ate earlier had been a mistake. But that was my chance. I dug my fingernails into his skin until I drew blood. He snapped back but not far enough for me to get away.

"You're just a bitch like the rest," he spat then slapped the back of his hand across my face.

I guess I should have thanked my father for all the times he'd done the same thing because this one hardly registered even though it was much harder. I'd gotten good at blocking out the pain.

"This is what you're here for." He collapsed back onto me using his knees to push my legs apart causing my skirt to tip.

I hated the way he was touching me, what it was he wanted to do to me.

I slammed my elbow into his nose but that just made him even angrier. I would've rather they kill me than put their disgusting seed inside me.

I was supposed to have Orin's babies. Not a man I didn't know but allegedly belonged to.

"Get off of her," Peter's voice boomed into the room then Gunther was no longer on top of me. "What do you think you're doing?" Peter released the back of Gunther's shirt so my attacker could stand on his own feet.

"She needs to get pregnant."

I wanted to throw up.

"The alpha hasn't decided who is going to mate her. She is not yours to take."

"And you think she's going to be yours?" Gunther took a large step toward Peter.

Peter being the smaller of the two, though still large enough to rival a mountain, didn't look scared in the least when he shrugged. "Maybe. Maybe not. But I know she's not *yours*. If they find out you tried this... " He shook his head. "You'll regret it."

It took a minute for that to sink into Gunther's head but when it did, his skin paled and he scurried out of the room.

"Are you all right?" Peter asked without looking at me.

I nodded because there was no way I could speak while still trying to catch my breath. Somehow he saw my answer and left, locking the door behind him.

I collapsed onto the bed and curled into a ball to

let myself cry for the first time. That had been too close and I knew I had to try something to escape but didn't know what. Whatever I decided needed to happen soon because I really would've rather be dead than with one of them.

Blood trickled from the corner of my mouth. I used hem of my shirt to wipe it away, Gunther had torn my skirt and my shirt, I found when doing an inventory of myself.

That night I didn't eat the food Peter brought. Not because I was worried they were poisoning me now but because any appetite I'd had disappeared the moment Gunther put his hands on me. I stayed there on the horrible mattress and cried until there was nothing left.

I cried until I was no longer scared.

I cried until I fell asleep.

In the morning, the sound of the lock disengaging put me on full alert.

"Breakfast," Gunther grunted before dropping a tray on the dresser next to the poor excuse for a bed.

I refused to acknowledge him in any way. I wished he was Peter.

As much as they all scared me, something in Gunther's eyes made me fear him the most. There wasn't an ounce of humanity in those dark eyes.

Absolutely nothing soft. Something feral. He then turned and went back out the door without another word.

A full glass of water slid down my throat but did nothing to quench my thirst. I refilled it from the pitcher Gunther set beside the tray but couldn't bring myself to eat any more than the toast.

Hours later, another large man came through the door. One I hadn't remembered seeing. Without a word, he grabbed my arm and dragged me from the room.

"Where are you taking me?" I asked.

He didn't answer. We stopped inside another room with a bed in the corner, very similar to the one where they'd been keeping me. He shut the door. Fear and acid rose in my throat.

"I'm sick of the fighting. We're getting this done," he said. As he unbuttoned his pants, I knew what he meant by "this." He was going to make me his.

"Please don't," I begged. "I don't want this."

"It doesn't matter what you want. This is about what I want and what the pack needs."

I wasn't just going to lie down and take it. I charged him. Digging my nails into the flesh covering his face. It took him almost no effort to toss me to the ground. When I hit, my head bounced off the wood. I groaned at the pain.

I hadn't caught my breath before he was on top of me, pushing my shirt up, causing a few of the buttons to pop and I just wanted to pass out so I wouldn't remember any of it. His fingers were rough on my arms. He smelled of sweat and something else that made me want to vomit. My head felt too heavy to lift, my arms too tired to use.

There was a loud crash from outside that made him jump off me. Still, he pulled me with him as he stormed out of the room. My feet refused to cooperate as I struggled to keep up. I didn't know what had made the sound but I was grateful for it. At least for now, it had stopped me from being raped. That man tossed me roughly back into "my" room and locked the door behind him.

I shuffled to the window and tried to pry it open but couldn't get it to budge.

Standing there watching, fear skittered up my spine. The Balodis' were running. Not away from something but toward. One thing I'd learned about werewolves was that they never gave up. Never ran in fear. Something was coming to them and they were going to protect what was theirs. And now that included me.

I ran to the door and tried to turn the knob but it wouldn't budge either. Not knowing what was happening wasn't what scared me. Not being able to get away from whatever it was did.

The door to the house crashed open. I'd listened long enough and had been out of the room several times so I'd gotten a pretty good layout of the place. That crash was the door in the kitchen. The one everyone used. There was yelling from all sides of the house but I couldn't make out the words.

Grunting and the sound of something wet, came from the other side of my door. Possibilities were endless. Gunther could be making his move and within moments I was going to be used and defiled without a second thought. Growling cut through the thick air. There was definitely a fight out there.

Something large slammed against the door as if whatever was out there would break through at any moment. The door rattled on its hinges. Then whatever it was thudded down the stairs. I couldn't just stand there and wait for them to get inside to me.

The pitcher of water still sat on the dresser. I grabbed it. The heavy glass pitcher might do some damage. I lifted it back above my head the swung it forward and let it crash into the window. The pitcher shattered but the window cracked a spider web pattern across the surface. Then I pulled the drawer out of the dresser and repeated. Finally, the window broke open so I could push the remaining shards out. It'd be a two-story drop but I would've rather break my neck than be raped by Gunther.

When the doorknob jiggled again, I acted.

I leaned down to carefully get through the opening but a large, strong arm grabbed me around my waist and pulled me back inside. I kicked and fought with everything I had, throwing my elbows and struck my feet to the man's shins.

"Elizabeth... stop... it's... Phillip. You're safe." Phillip's voice was like coming home. The only thing that would've made this better was if it had been Orin.

"Phillip?" I spun around. When I saw it was actually him, I threw my arms around him and squeezed with what little strength I had left.

"Are you all right?" he asked, his eyes scanning over me to see for himself. His thumb brushed the corner of my mouth that had been bleeding before.

"I'm... I'm all right now." I tried to keep tears of relief from falling. I couldn't come apart. We still had to make it out of this mess.

"Stay close to me." Phillip grabbed my wrist and pulled me along behind him. We took the steps one at a time in quick succession like we were sneaking but very quickly. "Watch your step," he said when we entered the kitchen.

My breath caught in my throat, which burned with the acidic preview of vomit that wanted out to mingle with the coppery smell of blood. Three very large, very bloody bodies laid out in unnatural positions around the room.

The body closest to me was Peter. I shouldn't have felt too bad. He did help kidnap me after all but he'd been the most decent of them all and had saved me from some of the ugly. Now he was dead. He'd earned that death but I thought in another world he would've been a man worth knowing.

Phillip glanced back at me and his jaw tightened.

"I had to get you out," Phillip said like he was trying to explain the deaths to me. Which he didn't need to do.

He rescued me. I wasn't about to question how. I'd learned that with Orin and his family killing sometimes happened and if that person was a threat to one of the members, it wouldn't even be mourned.

It was how they survived.

"He was... " I swallowed hard. "Less barbaric than the others." I didn't want to tell him what that meant. I didn't want to tell any of them that I'd almost been raped. Twice.

With one quick nod, Phillip was back to dragging me out of that godforsaken house and into the woods around it. We'd be less noticeable among the trees.

"Where are the others?" I asked as we made our way through the woods trying not to make a sound.

The Balodis had enough people around and I wanted to avoid any further confrontation. I just wanted to go home. But I also needed to know where everyone else is. His large hand was still wrapped around my wrist like an iron shackle as if nothing could make him let go. It hurt a little but also made me feel safer.

He stopped so suddenly that I ran into his back. He held his hand up to quiet me before I had a chance to ask why we'd stopped.

Then I didn't need to ask.

Three large masses blocked our path and stalked toward us. There were very few times that I'd wished to have the heightened hearing and vision that the werewolves had but this was one of them. I would have heard them coming the way Phillip had.

"I think you're trying to make off with something that belongs to us," the largest of the three snarled. I didn't recognize him but his voice was familiar. He'd been on the other side of my door at one point or another. "We'll let you walk away if you go now. But leave her."

"That's not going to happen," Phillip growled back as he pushed me further behind him.

There are moments when you know something bad is going to happen. I'd honed that skill living with my father. An odd feeling usually filled the air before he went off on me so I'd know when to back away, try to isolate myself in my room. It wasn't an exact science but it did sometimes help me avoid the back of his hand.

The three Balodis' leapt at Phillip from all sides. They hit so hard, I was sent flying into the tree behind me. The contact knocked the wind out of me as I fell to the ground scraping my arm against the bark along the way. I laid there, gasping, trying to get even the smallest amount of oxygen in. My head pounded against my rib cage and black spots edged into my vision. I thought I was going to pass completely out. Finally, the pounding began to subside and I was able to suck in a large breath that made my lungs burn.

I couldn't see Phillip, he was on the bottom of the werewolf pile in front of me and I didn't know what to do. I was no match for them. I needed a weapon so I searched for one. The only things I could find were tiny switches that wouldn't make a difference.

"They're coming. Grab the girl," a different man said but I didn't recognize him at all.

While I was scared of the ones I knew, I was terrified of the ones I didn't.

Another hand, this one much rougher, yanked my arm almost completely off my body. I was definitely going to have finger-shaped bruises on my forearm not to mention a sore shoulder. I scrambled to my feet. The other two Balodis' had their backs to us but somehow I just knew one of them was Gunther.

Orin's voice surfed the air like a dream. He wasn't talking to me, wasn't even close but instead called out to his brothers. My entire body came alive regardless of the throbbing pain and exhaustion. Orin was coming for me. He was so close.

Everything happened so fast that I couldn't take it all in. I couldn't get a good look at Phillip, where he was, what was happening to him. He'd been outnumbered and I was useless against werewolves.

But the one I didn't know still had a hold of me. He tightened his grip as Gunther hissed. He suddenly released his grip making me fall to the ground again and the air filled with growls. I readied myself to run as I'd never run before but I didn't have the chance. As I was about to leap into action, the Balodis pack took off running back toward the house.

I didn't know what scared them off and I didn't care.

My body relaxed and took a deep breath before searching for Phillip. He had to be close.

When I didn't see him, cold fear crawled up my body, straightening my spine. I didn't want to be alone in those woods for even a moment not to mention what his disappearance could mean. Something on the other side of one of the large trees groaned.

That was the sound of pain.

I couldn't move fast enough. It was like my legs were trudging through mud, slowing me down. Finally, I got to Phillip laying on the ground and dropped to my knees beside him.

"Phillip. Phillip, are you okay?" It was a stupid question. I touched his chest and my hands were immediately covered by something warm and sticky.

When I pulled my hands back, there was enough sun splitting through the trees to let me see the dark crimson running out of Phillip's body. Something wet gurgled in his throat. My eyes filled with tears. Ones that I had no hope of containing. "Phillip. They're coming. Orin will be here soon. Hold on. They're coming."

Werewolves healed faster than normal humans. Phillip needed to heal fast before...

I yanked his shirt apart where it was already ripped to find the very large, extremely gaping, slice from his collarbone to the ribs. I'd never seen anything like it.

My stomach lurched. I wanted to cry. Wanted to vomit and wanted to recoil but I refused. I wouldn't leave him alone. I wouldn't leave him to die alone in the woods.

"Phillip, tell me what to do." I sobbed loudly because I couldn't keep it in. "Tell me what to do. I'll do it. I'll do anything. Please," I begged. He needed to tell me what to do to make him better.

He'd promised to protect me. Now he was dying on the ground and I wasn't any more important than him. He had a wife, a child. I wouldn't let little Ruby be raised without a father.

Something heavy settled on my chest. Something I'd never felt before. I'd never had a family so I'd never lost one of them. Now... now I was losing a brother.

"Please, Phillip. Please," I begged again but my voice no longer had any energy behind it.

His eyes rolled slowly toward me, his breathing uneven and labored.

"Please just tell me what to do. I'll do it. Just tell me." I begged him to give me whatever would magically repair his wound. And I would've done anything. Anything at all.

"Diana…"

"No. Phillip, stay with me. Tell her yourself, please." I sobbed again, this time louder. "You should've let them have me," I screamed as more tears choked my words. I meant it, too. Being used to breed would've been better than this.

Phillip tried to swallow. His throat contorted and he couldn't get it down. Instead, blood spilled from his mouth. His body trembled, sputtered against me then stopped as I cried louder.

"Phillip." I shook his body. "Phillip." I sobbed and begged. I didn't know what I was begging for. Logically I knew he couldn't come back to life but I wanted to trade places with him. I would've done anything for that. "Phillip, please," I whispered before collapsing onto his still chest.

How was I going to tell Orin?

And what about Diana?

Chapter Twenty-Seven

My body shut down. Right there lying half on top of Phillip, my brain refused to function. The side of my face was right against the gaping wound, his body warmth fading. Cooling unnaturally.

"Elizabeth," Orin called out. He sounded like he was at one end of a tunnel while I was at the other. "Lizzie." The relief in his voice was momentary. His footsteps faltered just on the other side of his brother. "Phillip?" He dropped to his knees beside me.

I didn't look up at him, didn't want to see the pain in his eyes as he figured out what I already knew. That I'd gotten his brother killed.

"What... happened?" I think it was Ivan who asked. "What the fuck happened here, Elizabeth?"

Definitely Ivan. He pushed me off Phillip with so much force that I fell back onto my bottom. My hands took the brunt of the impact. I tried to focus on the stinging because if I felt pain it meant this wasn't all a dream.

I wanted to it be a nightmare.

Somewhere in the periphery, I vaguely acknowledged Daniel, Roman, and Anton. I hadn't had time to consider that Anton would arrive and find his son dead. Because of me. I was waiting for their reaction. For their anger to be directed at me and I would welcome it. My only hope was that Orin wouldn't be injured too badly in the process when he put himself between me and them. He didn't deserve that. I did.

They were talking all around me. Mostly in whispers though Ivan sometimes was louder. I wanted to burrow into the ground below me. Maybe not loving anyone would have been easier. Phillip would certainly still be alive if I hadn't come along. Orin wouldn't have been beaten by his own brothers. Their world would have been the same, balanced. Not whatever it was now.

"Lizzie... Lizzie." Orin gently coaxed me to look at him.

My head only lifted because he lifted it. The blood began to dry on the side of my face, tightening my skin. Orin's hair was a mess, his face dirty and sweaty with a small trickle of blood running down his cheek.

"I'm going to get you home now. Can you stand?"

I didn't know. Could I? Orin used his strong hands to lift me and somehow my knees locked and I didn't tumble to the ground no matter how much I didn't want to move or how weak my legs felt. With his arm securely around my shoulder, we moved slowly away from the rest of his family. Branches snapped behind me. Anton barked out orders that didn't make any sense to me.

"What are they doing?" My voice didn't sound like mine. The volume was barely audible but Orin had above average hearing so he'd hear me.

"Making a cot to carry Phillip home on."

It made sense but the numbness that had taken over wouldn't let me acknowledge it. Take him home... Sadness consumed me, turned my stomach. I had to stop to vomit. Couldn't help it. Orin stood beside me, holding my hair back, not caring about the disgusting thing I was doing. He rubbed my back while whispering soft words. I didn't deserve his kindness.

"What do you guys do with... " I didn't know if death was handled the same for them.

"We will bury him, Lizzie, just like you would." His voice didn't betray anything he was feeling.

That was all I had in me. It could have taken hours or minutes, time had no meaning to me but everyone around me was absolutely frantic. I knew we had made it to through the back door into the house when Orin's mother gasped and asked what had happened. I thought that was what she asked but she sounded as if she was under water.

Orin carried my weight up the stairs and then I was vaguely aware of standing in the bathroom, Orin turned the water in the tub on.

"What are you doing?"

"I need to get you cleaned up," he said starting to push the buttons on my shirt through the holes. He was focused on the job, working quickly but stopping before he was done.

"What about... " Phillip, I wanted to say.

"My brothers have it under control. I need to take care of you right now."

As guilty as it made me feel, I was glad to have him there with me, thinking about what I would need because, to be honest, I couldn't think about it myself.

He moved around the room, grabbing a washcloth, making sure the water wouldn't be too hot. I tried to focus on those things. Those things were normal. Unfortunately, I caught a glimpse of myself in the mirror. The image made my stomach lurch again. The blood alone... I couldn't look for more than a second.

Being more careful, gentler than he'd ever been, Orin slowly worked the rest of the buttons on my shirt until he could peel it off. It felt like he was taking a layer of skin with it. Next was the skirt I'd been wearing the day I was taken. Everything came off but before I could think about the fact that I was standing in front of my husband dirty, bloody, and naked, he swept me off my feet and set me in the bath.

I didn't feel the heat of the water when Orin climbed into the other end. Our bathtub was large enough to accommodate the both of us but I hadn't expected him to join me. Taking the washcloth, he then soaked it with water, soaped it up, and went to work on my face. I just sat there staring at nothing as he swiped the cloth down my cheek, rinsed it in the water, and repeated the movement. Without a word, he used a small bucket to dump hot water over my head. I didn't even blink as he began washing my hair. When he was done, he went back to work on my skin.

I could have sat there quietly for hours until I heard a howling roar from outside. My eyes popped wide as fear gripped my body that the Balodis family followed us back. Everyone would be in danger then.

"My mother," Orin said quietly.

His mother? It was a full thirty seconds before the memory of what would cause her to make that kind of sound took me back over and filled my eyes with tears again.

I didn't know how much more I had in me but these were more like teasers because they did not fall. And at that moment I realized how selfish I'd been since he got to me in the woods. I'd been worried about me, thinking about how everything was affecting me. But Phillip was Orin's brother, they'd grown up together and Orin was taking care of me. Only concerned with me.

"Orin?" I didn't know how else to ask him if he needed to cry or scream or rant over the death of his brother.

"You absolutely do not worry about me right now." The sincerity in his eyes almost made me cry all over again. I knew he wasn't done though. His jaw hardened and he had a hard time lifting his eyes back to my face. I still hadn't looked directly at him, much preferring the view from my periphery. It felt safer. Like seeing his grief head-on would completely crush me. "Did they hurt you, Elizabeth?" He asked this quietly as he wiped the cloth down my cheek and neck.

I knew what he meant. He could see the small bruises, scrapes, and scratches. He wasn't talking about that. He wanted to know if they'd raped me.

My gaze finally snapped to catch his eyes which made his concern even more obvious.

Biting my bottom lip, I shook my head quickly. The movement felt odd to me because it was the first deliberate movement I'd made since I'd been thrown to the ground in the woods. He searched my eyes as if trying to decipher whether I was telling the truth or not. I shook it again and looked away.

"They hadn't decided... who... yet." Thankfully the Balodis family was quite unorganized and he didn't need to know that a few had tried. "Two tried anyway though."

He nodded. "That means I don't have to make them die slowly and painfully unless you can tell me who put their hands on you."

"What?" I asked feeling confused. My mouth was dry and my tongue felt too big.

"The ones that touched you that way, I have to make them pay for that."

I swallowed hard. I wanted to tell him to take the high road, not to kill the other pack but deep down, I wanted them all dead. They'd just keep coming for me, that much was clear. I didn't want to go back to living my life in fear.

We finished the bath in silence, staying right there after I was clean until the water was cold. The water, darkened with dirt and blood, emptied while I sat there watching all remnants of Phillip go down the drain. Orin tucked a towel around his waist then wrapped one around me, went into our bedroom then came back with a nightgown. He dried me then dressed me. I was so grateful because I was feeling weak and shaky but hating that I couldn't care for myself.

As Orin led me to the bed, he grabbed some bottoms for himself and pulled them on roughly just in time for the bedroom door to fly open and smack the wall behind it. Diana stood just inside the door with Nell right behind her. Once again, I couldn't look at her and see the pain. I wanted to be of some comfort but needed to shield myself. The way she'd burst in I knew she was there to lash out. She deserved the right to lash out. Orin quickly slid between her and me.

"Not now, Diana."

"Yes, now, Orin. I need to know what happened. How is it my husband is the one lying dead?" Her voice broke on the word 'dead.'

My heart went with it and my eyes filled with tears.

"Elizabeth can't answer your questions right now," Orin said as gently as he could. "Tomorrow."

"Not tomorrow! She owes me the truth!"

I recoiled away from them when Emmie come through the door. It was too much. My skin was crawling again, anger and sadness buzzed in the room creating an air that was so thick I almost couldn't breathe.

"Mother," Orin said softly but stepped forward folding his arms across his chest.

I thought Emmie would want at me like Diana did but instead, she wrapped her arms around her daughter-in-law, whispered in her ear quickly. Everyone else could probably hear what was being said but I was too exhausted to even try. Whatever it was worked because Diana let Emmie lead her from the room. When they were all gone, Orin shut the door tightly then came back to me.

He led me back to the bed, pulled the covers out enough so I could climb in. The tightness of his jaw and the way his eyes took in every mark and bruise made me aware of the fact that he was controlling his temper. Then he climbed in beside me and wrapped me in his arms.

"He saved me," I said quietly after we'd laid there long enough for the sun to fully set. I felt like I hadn't had a good night's sleep in a month instead of days. The small burst of exhaustion that I'd had in that house didn't count as sleep. That was more falling unconscious but it wasn't restful. "He wouldn't let them have me. He should've let them have me."

Orin's body tightened beside me. "No, Lizzie, Phillip did what needed to be done."

"How can you say that?" I wet my bottom lip with my tongue. "He's your brother."

"And you're my wife." He sighed. "Lizzie, if the situation were reversed... it would have been me dead on the ground to make sure Diana returned to him. That's how this works. Do I wish I could've been there instead of him? Yes. But that isn't what happened. He just got there before I did."

"I'm sorry, Orin. I'm sorry about your brother."

Orin pushed back and slid down so that we were eye to eye.

"I know, sweetheart. I know." He searched my eyes for signs of something but what I didn't know. "Can I... Lizzie, can I please kiss you?"

Instead of answering, I leaned over to him and pushed my lips against his. I felt him sigh against my mouth. With his hand fastened against the back of my neck, he held me there while his tongue pushed into my mouth softly caressing mine.

I was home.

"Sorry," he pulled back.

"It's all right."

"I'm just so relieved to have you back. I can't tell you... " he said softly which just about melted my heart then and there. "I need to know, Elizabeth." He kissed my forehead. "You said they didn't hurt you but I see the bruises."

Nodding I knew I had to tell him. "They were rough and I mark up easily. They didn't succeed in touching me the way you fear. A couple tried but were unsuccessful."

"Tried?" Air seethed out of his flared nostrils.

"Orin, he didn't get very far. At most he scared me but I'm fine now because I'm with you." I leaned in to kiss him again which released a little more of his tension. "Are you all right?" I asked again.

"He was my brother. I'm sad. I feel horrible but I know he wouldn't regret his sacrifice for a minute." He eyed me again. "I need to focus on you."

"I'm fine," I insisted again. More aggressive than I'd ever been, I leaned in, initiating a long slow kiss in which our tongues found each other's again and again like they were dancing. "Let me show you that I'm fine."

His eyes changed from that of concern to a look of heat, still tinged with sadness but I needed him. Needed him close and loving me while I showed him just how much I loved him. Showed him that I was still me and not damaged. And it was the only way I could think of to make him feel better even if only for a few minutes.

Orin pulled back to watch me but I could already feel his arousal against my leg. "Are you sure, Lizzie? I... don't... "

"Orin. Please make love to me."

He didn't need any more convincing. He took control, rolling on top of me so he could settle between my legs, kissing me slowly, and letting his hands move up my nightgown until he had to lean back to pull it over my head. Any former embarrassment at being completely naked in front of him was long gone as I laid there letting him look as long as he wanted. I knew there were some bumps and bruises but nothing severe enough to stop him.

Normally when we were together, Orin took his time, using his hands, tongue, and mouth to drive me to a release I'd never known, or hoped, possible. But our situation wouldn't allow it. He had to be one with me and I with him. When he pushed inside me slowly, my heart broke and mended all at the same time. I pushed the lingering guilt out of my mind. A part of me thought we shouldn't be doing this when Diana would never be with her husband again but we were both still alive and that wasn't fair either.

Orin held me tightly and moved against me softly burying his face into my neck. His breath, even as it began coming faster and faster, feathered against my skin causing goose bumps to break out across my body.

I clung to him just as hard and I never wanted to let go.

I'd do just about anything to not have to face tomorrow.

Chapter Twenty-Eight

I HONESTLY HADN'T THOUGHT it possible that I'd be snuggled in my bed beside my husband again, having just made love. Yet there I was safely in his strong arms slowly falling asleep. I knew tomorrow would be horrible and sad yet I pushed those thoughts down, buried under as much denial as I could muster.

When I woke in the middle of the night, I didn't feel Orin against me. Then I flipped around and he was there, his hands folded behind his head as he stared at the ceiling. It was one of those times I couldn't figure out what was going through his head. I assumed Phillip was on his mind.

"Hey," I said noticing the sleepy quality of my own voice.

"Everything all right?" He glanced down at me then back to the ceiling.

"Have you slept at all?"

After a long pause, he said, "A little."

"Talk to me, Orin." I pushed myself up so that I could lay my head on his shoulder and ran my hand down his bare chest. For someone who got so hairy when he shifted, he was remarkably normal in his human form.

"I'm just thinking everything through. I'm very happy that you're home but my brother is dead. And I wouldn't change anything. Except maybe if I could take his place." He sighed. "Tomorrow, please don't take anything that happens personally. Diana is hurting."

"I deserve whatever she has to say anyway."

This time his gaze hit mine almost forcefully as if I could feel it.

"If you would never have met me or if I would have married Noah or Bradley, your family would still be intact," I told him. "None of this would have ever happened."

"My family is still intact, Lizzie. Do you still not understand? You're my family. We will get through this. Although I will take much more pleasure in ending the Balodis pack than I would have before."

"Was it too much earlier?" I asked quietly. He'd told me once that I could talk to him about anything so I had to know and wasn't embarrassed at all to ask that question. "Should I have not pushed you to be with me because I just needed to do something to help you feel better." My face flushed with those words. so maybe I was a little embarrassed to be saying it out loud.

He kissed me softly. "I needed you, Lizzie, but I also didn't want to hurt you if you were already hurt."

"You never hurt me, Orin. You heal me every day."

Our conversation came to an end with those words when Orin rolled over on top of me again. I felt his need without him telling me and was more than happy to oblige. I wasn't going to pretend to understand what was happening with him, how giving him access to my body the way he needed would make things better. I didn't care about any of it. I just wanted to be whatever would do him the most good. His fingers weren't as gentle, his lips more demanding but the more pressure he put on me the more I wanted until we both came apart and were left gasping for air. It was quick and demanding. It was what he needed.

He huffed out a breath and dropped his forehead to mine. I didn't think he realized how much rougher he'd been with me until he was done. I smiled up at him just to reassure that I was absolutely fine. I'd never known being with someone physically could be so good or in this case, help heal.

Since Orin was a shifter, his physical wounds had already healed.

This was for emotional healing.

In the morning, Orin was already gone when I woke, letting me sleep too late once again. He told me he'd never wake me when he was the reason I was up late. I'd asked him not to let me oversleep but apparently when it came to me, he couldn't be reasoned with. Right after I'd picked a black dress and the lowest shoes I owned, our bedroom door creaked open and Orin stepped quietly through like he was trying not to wake me. His eyebrows slammed down when he didn't find me on the bed but straightened when he found me by the closet.

"I meant to be back sooner," he said coming toward me. "I didn't want you to wake up alone."

"I'm not who needs to be taken care of today."

"You're the one I need to take care of always."

His eyes left mine to take in every curve of my body that he'd already memorized. "Everything is arranged for today. We need to leave in an hour."

Nodding, I said, "All right." But I also had a million questions that he began to answer without my asking as he pulled a fresh set of clothes out for himself.

"Dad made the arrangements and you can accomplish just about anything with enough money. Phillip will be buried right at the edge of the cemetery just outside of town. We will be alone and uninterrupted but have to move quickly and Phillip is already there."

That covered everything that had been rattling around in my brain.

Dressed and feeling incredibly solemn, Orin and I arrived at the cemetery. I noticed all the others huddled together near a freshly dug grave. Little Ruby was even quiet and my heart broke at all the things her father was going to miss. As we passed Ivan, I heard him growl low in his chest which got a pointed look from Orin. I knew by coming here, I'd be the focus of their anger, their grief, but there was no way I would stay home. I could take whatever any of them wanted to dish out.

Instead, I held Orin's hand tightly as they each

said something about Phillip. I don't know if it was on purpose or not, but they skipped me and I was so grateful for that. I didn't want to stand in front of his family to talk about a man I hadn't gotten to know nearly well enough while they looked at me the way they were.

When they were each done, the guys lowered the plain pine box that held Phillip's body, into the ground then covered it with dirt. Orin explained on the way over that this was how the pack did it. They did everything themselves to keep human involvement to a minimum. I can't be sure, but I would have sworn that I saw Orin's eyes fill with tears at one point. But being a man, he pushed them away. I wouldn't have thought less of him if he cried over the death of his brother, but men weren't raised to show emotion and he'd already shown me more than I ever expected.

Anton and Emmie left first, taking little Ruby with them and glancing around I found Diana sitting on a bench not far from us. She looked devastated which was expected. I didn't have children with Orin but if something happened to him, I'd want to crawl right in that grave with him.

Making my way over to her slowly, I watched

Karina, Roman's wife, mimicking my moves as if she didn't want me to be near Diana alone.

"Diana," I said softly, "I don't want to make things worse but I want to tell you how sorry I am."

"Sorry?" she snapped. "Why are you even talking to me? If it weren't for you my husband wouldn't be dead."

Couldn't argue with that.

"Diana, she didn't do this." Karina stepped in.

"Were you there when he died?" Tears fell silently down Diana's face.

I could only nod in return.

"He wasn't alone then? That's something at least." She thought for a moment. "Did he say anything? Orin has kept us away from you so I haven't been able to ask. I just want to know if my husband said anything before he died."

I slowly shook my head no. There wasn't a point in telling her that her name was the last on his lips when he hadn't had time to say anything else. I didn't think there was a point at least.

Flaming hot pain radiated from my cheek up to the bone and into my eye. I hadn't even seen her move so I couldn't prepare before she slapped me with everything she had. My eyes burned but I wouldn't cry.

"Diana," Karina gasped pulling the other girl away from me right as Orin pushed his body in front of me.

"Don't do this, Diana," he said gently but with a clear warning behind his words.

"I'm all right, Orin," I said because the last thing I wanted was for Diana's grief to be used against her. Yes, she hit me but her grief ran deep and while Orin had needed me in another way to help cope with the death of his brother, Diana needed someone to blame. I could be that for her.

"Come with me," he demanded through clenched teeth as he pulled me away from the cemetery.

He drove us slowly, taking the longest possible route back home, I thought to calm himself down. By the look of his gripped the steering wheel, his anger ran as deep as Diana's grief.

"You can't be angry with her," I said and his head snapped my direction.

"Like hell I can't be. She hit you. She's lucky she's a woman. If she weren't I would have ended her right then. No one touches you."

"She's upset. Nothing more." I didn't let on just how much my cheek hurt. She was a werewolf. She had strength.

When we got home, the rest of the family was already there. We entered the house two hours after we'd left and were met with a delicious aroma that said Emmie had been cooking. Traditionally, after a funeral, everyone went back to the family's house for a wake just like this. Another thing the werewolves had in common with the humans only for this funeral, it was just the family.

An uncomfortable silence awaited us as we entered the kitchen. The family was arranged around the table but Diana refused to look up at us. Emmie and Anton stood near the counter putting the finishing touches on the late lunch they were preparing and no one spoke for what seemed like forever.

"I don't suppose we can call a truce with the Balodis," Ivan broke the silence.

"They'll still be coming after Lizzie," Orin countered. "They won't stop."

"That isn't our problem." Ivan tightened his muscles before continuing. "We already lost Phillip. I vote we broker peace."

"And what?" Orin raged. "Trade her for that. Hell no, Ivan."

"You know this is about more than just Lizzie," Roman said to Ivan. I didn't understand what he meant because I didn't know the history between the two packs.

"And I don't care anymore," Ivan countered. "I'm taking my wife and we're going home." I'd noticed days ago that they never said where exactly they came from. that could have been their normal way of doing things or it hadn't been decided that I could be trusted.

"I want the men who killed my husband to pay," Diana said in a monotone voice that didn't sound at all like she had at the cemetery. Now it sounded as if the life had completely drained out of her with the anger she expelled before. "I deserve that."

The group fell quiet again. Truth be told, I wanted that for her.

"Then we need to know everything, Lizzie," Roman said gently.

"I don't know where to start." I pulled at the waist of my dress nervously. I didn't want to tell them anything but I'd do whatever they wanted. I'd been the cause of enough trouble.

"Start with who murdered my brother," Daniel finally spoke.

"His name was Gunther," I said. "I think he was the one who actually killed Phillip but there were three of them so I can't be absolutely positive. He's one of the ones that... " my voice trailed off and I looked at Orin hoping I wouldn't have to say it out loud again. The man tried to rape me. Though unsuccessful, that didn't mean Gunter didn't hurt me.

Orin's fists clenched against the sides of his body. He understood.

"The one that what?" Ivan demanded. When we didn't answer, he stood, "The one that what, Orin?"

I adjusted my weight from one foot to another and wet my bottom lip with my tongue. "Tried to rape me," I said softly so Orin didn't have to because I felt the anger rolling off him in waves.

The room fell silent and while I tried not to look at any of them directly, I could feel them all staring at me. A chair scraped across the floor as I imagined, someone tried to make the uncomfortable more comfortable. The silence became unbearable.

"We'll take care of this tomorrow," Daniel finally broke through everyone's thoughts as if they'd all already agreed to it.

The brothers all had wives. They could understand what Orin was feeling even if they didn't like me much. But the fact that those people killed their brother sealed their fate as soon as Phillip died.

There wasn't much talking at dinner that night. I

could barely eat a thing so because of the limited room, and the assumed need of the Vilkatas family to be close to each other, I set my plate on the counter and stood while taking in what little I could. Orin stayed beside me, his appetite pretty normal, cleaned his plate then part of mine as he tried to get me to take something in. I just couldn't.

My stomach was in knots in anticipation and fear of what was to come.

Chapter Twenty-Nine

I HEARD Orin in the room before my eyes ever opened and somehow I knew it was still early. Like my body hadn't gotten enough rest and my head was too heavy.

When I slowly opened my eyes, I found him rummaging through my clothes pulling out what I assumed I was going to wear that day. It wasn't surprising that he chose pants and a button-down shirt that he usually wore only for yard work. It spoke to what we were about to do.

"Am I going with you today?" I asked quietly.

His body stilled. The muscles along his arms and back tightened as he turned toward me but before he answered he came toward me and sat on the bed beside me.

He ran a hand down my hair then came up to cup my face.

"I don't like it but yes. You're the only one that can identify this Gunther person." Orin leaned down, brushing his lips across mine. "Though I wish you could stay back with my mother." Reading my face he added, "She will be here taking care of the children."

"I guess I should get moving then." But I didn't make an effort to do that. Nobody had said anything about what could happen, at least not where I'd been able to hear, but we all knew it. I also knew that I'd be the most vulnerable as the one non-werewolf, or half dormant werewolf, in the group. "I should have a weapon," I said once I finally got myself out of the bed. "You all can't be worried about me while you're doing what you need to do."

"Would you be able to use a weapon if you had it?"

"I don't want to die, Orin. Yes, I'd stop someone from killing me."

He nodded slowly then watched me dress for the day before we joined the rest of the family in the kitchen.

The entire group moved around the kitchen solemnly as they fueled their bodies for the coming battle. I had absolutely no appetite but Orin insisted that I needed to eat so I choked down as much as I possibly could. I'd be grateful that I did later, he said.

"We're ready to go," Anton announced as I put my plate in the sink.

All at once, they started to move like everything had been planned in my absence. A few went outside to wait for the rest of us but Orin had disappeared so I didn't know what to do. He'd want me as close to him as possible and I wouldn't want to be anywhere else. Just as I was about to go searching for him, he found me.

"I had to grab something for you," he said quietly wrapping a strap around my waist. When he was done I looked down to find a very large knife in a leather sheath hanging halfway down my thigh. "Just in case." Those dark eyes burned right into me. There were words I wanted to say right then but couldn't find my voice.

I wasn't stupid. I knew that their mission, our mission, was to murder the entire Balodis pack and they would be trying to end the existence of the Vilkatas. To help me understand the politics of pack life, Orin explained that the Balodis family was the governing body over their pack so that meant that there were more members than just that one family.

We could've found ourselves outnumbered and he couldn't promise that we'd beat the entire pack but he could ensure a power shift among them and when that happened, they'd be even more vulnerable.

After a quick squeeze, Orin pulled me by the hand so we could join the others. When I glanced back over my shoulder to the house next door, I saw Emmie gently rocking the baby and tried to put myself in her shoes. Losing a son just to have to watch your other kids walk off into a battle that could cost her, even more, couldn't have been easy. The thought almost brought me to tears.

Since I hadn't been part of the planning, I couldn't be sure exactly what we were doing but Anton seemed to be leading us back through the forest, across the edge of town then through another thick set of woods to the spot where Phillip died.

Nobody said a word for the longest time as we stood there remembering the events of just a couple of days before. My stomach tightened as the memories flooded through me. The blood, the sounds, the way that Phillip spoke to me. He was wrong if he thought that I was worth his death. But if I had to I'd spend the rest of my life, however short that may be, trying to prove him right.

"Is this where it happened?" Diana asked quietly. "I know this is where he was hurt. I can smell his blood. Is this where my husband died?"

"Yes," I whispered. I didn't want to tell her that I could still see the dark mark left by the blood that had poured from her husband's body.

"Lizzie, you have to lead us from here." Orin stepped into my side. "Do you remember where their place is?" Nodding quickly, I started out the way Phillip and I had come because I couldn't get away from that spot fast enough.

Every step I took, Orin was right there taking it with me. His presence gave me a confidence I'd never had before.

"Everybody knows what to do, right?" Daniel asked as we made our way closer to the house I'd been kept in.

"No," I answered honestly. From somewhere to my right someone snorted.

"That's because you just get to hide while we protect you," Nell spat at me.

"Um... no," I said back.

"Elizabeth," Orin said with a sigh. "You can't fight them. We're here to end something that was going on long before you came along. The only thing you can do is not make me worry about you."

"No." I stopped short causing everyone else to as well. "I'm not some inept human that you can just brush aside."

"Except you sort of are," Diana cut in. "I just want the wolf that killed my husband dead. I don't care about the rest of it. So let's get on already."

"Then why give me a weapon?" I glared at Orin.

"It's not like she'll use it," Nell said with a giggle.

"Like hell I won't." My words surprised them as did the force I put behind it. I was really getting sick of everyone making assumptions about me. Months ago, I would have hidden. That wasn't me anymore.

"Stop!" A low growl sounded from Orin's chest.

I started to protest but one look from him shut me up completely.

"You heard it, too?" Roman leaned in close to his brother and whispered. Orin gave a short nod so clearly something was happening.

"I don't have time to argue with you," Orin said to me through clenched teeth. "I'm your husband. You will listen to me. Stay back, Elizabeth."

My eyebrows shot up as he turned his back to me. There was a slew of words on the tip of my tongue that I wouldn't let loose. Couldn't let loose. Not to the detriment of the others.

But Roman, his mouth slid into a sly grin as he

spoke right into my ear. "Tsk, tsk, Orin's temper is coming through."

I narrowed my eyes at Roman and pushed him away, while keeping a small grin at bay, to join Orin at the front of our pack. That was the first time I claimed to be part of them. Something inside told me I'd used the right word. Like my dormant werewolf gene was nodding its approval.

What I saw had me wanting to run and hide the way Orin wanted me to. Shadowed figures made their way through the morning mist, maybe a dozen or so large men were stalking toward us. Some I recognized from the house, some I didn't. What I did know was that we were outnumbered.

"The tallest one in the middle with brown hair. That's Gunther." Trying to whisper, it was obvious everyone heard me, even those I didn't mean to hear when the Balodis pack each growled and someone yanked my arm hard enough to pull me to the back.

It was Karina. She didn't stop until we were further away from the about to battle packs.

"I'm supposed to take you back to the house." She kept us moving with a grip so tight I just knew there'd be bruises.

"I don't want to leave." I pulled against her but made no progress.

"Do you think I want to leave my husband right now, Lizzie? This is what was decided."

"Please. Karina, please. If something happens to Orin..."

She thought about that for all of five seconds then nodded and turned so that we could make our way off to the side where the others wouldn't notice us immediately. I couldn't hear anything going on but Karina could. She wasn't sharing the details though, even when I asked but I hated not knowing.

"Come on, Karina. I need... something."

She sighed. "Fine. Orin just promised to rip Gunther's throat out. They're basically goading each other, trying to see who has the biggest dick."

My eyes popped wide. Karina snorted and shook her head.

"Metaphorically speaking. They're competing to see who's more of a man."

Oh. The more I was around the Vilkatas family, the more sheltered I realized I had been my whole life.

Beside me, Karina sucked in a short breath and all hell broke loose around us.

Loud, terrifying growls filled the air. I expected to find them all shifting immediately but they didn't.

Why were they fighting in human form? I didn't know but it seemed like a better idea to shift.

"What happened?" I asked urgently.

"Gunther told Orin that his wife tasted delicious and not in a way that says Gunter had a bite of you. He meant it sexually."

Orin couldn't let Gunther get to him that way. When I turned back to Karina, she'd flipped around and was growling at something herself but I couldn't see what.

The world moved like it did when Olivia and I spun at parties.

My face slammed into a tree, scratching every inch of skin and I felt a small trickle of blood down my cheek. Even worse, Karina was about to take on two of the Balodis herself. One lunged, she jumped, the other caught her and I hear something crunch before she hit the ground.

Gaining my bearings, I pulled the knife out of the sheath on my hip and ran. I didn't stop until the blade sunk deep in the first man's back. A loud roar erupted from him. I felt like my ears would explode. I didn't care. I yanked the knife out and stabbed it again. He shook and rolled landing on top of me and crushing the air from my lungs.

Black spots filled my vision and my head become

so light I thought it'd float away. Once I could get some oxygen, I pushed everything else aside, sprung to my feet, grabbed the knife, and scurried over to Karina who looked about to be bested by a very large, dark man.

The knife was still safely in my grasp but he was on the other side of her about to strike. There was blood running down her leg and somehow I knew she was about to shift. Before she got the chance, I threw myself on top of her.

"Get off me, Lizzie," she grunted out.

"They can't hurt me," I said squeezing my eyes shut hoping that was still the case. "They need me. They can't kill me." Turning over, I found the man about to hurt Karina, stop his swinging arm.

"We can't kill you. We can certainly hurt you."

I swung the knife. He grabbed my wrist, yanking me to him, and started backing away. Karina shifted. From the beautiful dark-haired women into an equally dark-haired beast with a long snout and large, snarling teeth. It still made me take a step back, which pushed me further into Henry. Big mistake. His grip tightened causing me to drop the knife.

I thought he was going to run with me but he thought better of it, spun me away from him with such force that my foot caught and I hit the ground with an unimpressive thud. My head hit a tree stump sending my brain into a fuzzy world of confusion. Trying to shake that off, I willed myself to get back to that knife. The one that I left a hundred miles away. I couldn't see what Karina was doing.

Just before I got to her, I threw up. Not a good sign considering how hard I hit my head but I wasn't going to leave her there to fight on her own.

"Run," I told her shaking the fuzz from my head. "We need to run."

"I can't run, Lizzie. My leg is useless."

That's when I saw how badly she was injured. I wanted to check on her but first, I got the knife.

Henry charged again.

I swiped the blade hoping to make contact but since there were two of him, I couldn't be sure. So I just kept at it until I heard him groan and something wet and warm sprayed across my neck and chest.

He stumbled backward, his arms flailing, and got a hold of my hand. Taking me with him, the gurgling from his chest scared me. At least now I could see him, even if it was like he was in a tunnel. We were near a hill because it had given us a good view of the rest of the family but now it served another purpose. Henry kept pulling me.

At the very last second, I braced my shoulder

against a tree and Henry fell down the hill where I assumed he'd bleed to death.

I allowed myself two long breaths before shakily making my way back to Karina.

"Come on, Karina," I said helping her to her feet. Her arm went around my shoulder so she could lean on me as we made our way to a small alcove I'd seen on our way up.

We could hide there.

A tree had fallen and the foliage had tried to take the space back but for us, it became a little area where no one would see us. I set her down gently then wedged myself in beside her holding the knife in front of my face in case anyone else came along.

All the fighting after hitting my head created a buzz in my ears. The loud buzzing became my focus once we could take a breath. I couldn't hear anything and the harder I tried the less I could see.

The world before my eyes was fading fast.

Until I saw nothing.

Chapter Thirty

"Lizzie. Elizabeth." Orin's voice reached out to me like I was drowning and he was the hand that would pull me to shore. I wanted to be on shore with him. "Come on, Lizzie. Open your eyes. Please open your eyes."

I wanted to do as he said if for no other reason than to make the sound of panic leave his voice forever. But my body wouldn't obey my orders or his. It took every single ounce of resolve and energy I had left to open my eyes the smallest bit. The late morning sun hurt my eyes causing me to wince in pain. At first, I couldn't feel my body but then the tight muscles and aching from my fall kicked in and I knew I was alive.

"There she is," Orin smiled down at me. "Don't try to sit up just yet."

Listening to him, I focused on breathing and getting that dizzy feeling out of my head. It was the same feeling that Olivia and I used to make happen on purpose just to feel different. Now I didn't like it at all.

Once I felt ready, I began sitting up and of course, Orin was right there helping me along the way until I was upright. It was a full minute later before I could stand on a set of very shaky legs and was able to take inventory of the others.

A quick count let me know that we hadn't lost anyone but no one had come out unscathed for the most part. There were bruises already forming along with cuts and scratches. At least as far as I could see but everyone looked like they could use some sleep. Roman was basically carrying all of Karina's weight. He was shirtless and the missing item was hanging loosely on his wife. Which meant she shifted. I hadn't seen that.

At least they'd all heal pretty quickly due to being shifters. I however would heal at a human rate.

"Is everyone all right?" My throat felt dry and scratchy and sounded like it as well.

"More or less. What about you?"

"I'm fine," I said even though I wasn't. I didn't think I was going to die or anything but I certainly wasn't completely ok either. "I need to know what happened."

"At home. We need to go."

I didn't remember the trek back home but by the time we got there, I was feeling more like myself. We all fell into our house then moments later Emmie burst through the door. She moved from one of her children to the next checking them out and giving instructions to the less injured on what to do to help.

Until she got to Karina.

Getting my first really good look at Karina's legs made my stomach turn. There were three very long, very deep scratches up her calf.

"This is going to need to be closed up until she can heal." Emmie glanced up to Anton who moved as if he'd been given instructions. "Roman, go get your wife some clothes ready."

He shot up from the table sounding like he took the steps two at a time into one of our spare rooms. I could hear drawers opening and closing then he was back.

"Won't they just heal?" I asked Orin quietly.

"It will heal quickly but the worse the injury, the longer it takes.

"Everything's ready." Roman glanced from his wife to me then back. There were questions in his eyes just as their father came back with, what looked like, a doctor's bag.

"She saved me," Karina said then hissed as Emmie poured antiseptic on her wounds. "She stabbed one of them in the back when both were going for me. Then she threw herself on top of me like an idiot because she said they couldn't hurt her. Since they want her for breeding. She killed him, too."

Orin tensed beside me. "Why would you do that?"

"Hey," Roman stepped forward. "That was brave, Lizzie. Stupid but brave. And thank you. I'm kind of attached to my wife." Karina snorted behind Orin's shoulder.

"It was true. They couldn't kill me. The other guy even said so."

"He did," Karina agreed. "Can someone tell us what happened? We were kind of busy so we didn't see or hear much after Gunther said something about the taste of your wife."

"Disgusting beasts," Emmie shook her head and continued working on Karina's leg.

Finally, they told us. Orin lunged after

Gunther's comment about me and a full-on brawl erupted. By the way, the brothers talked, I knew they were keeping details out of it. They fought as men, shifted into werewolves. Blood was spilled on both sides. In the end, a couple ran off but the majority of the Balodis pack that were there that day were dead.

"Gunther included."

"Yes, I had the pleasure of taking care of him." Diana stood. "Now, I'm going next door to bathe their disgusting blood off me." And she was well covered. I hadn't noticed before. Daniel and his wife then Ivan and Nell followed her out leaving Roman, Orin, Emmie, Anton, Karina, and me.

"Where's the baby?" I asked.

"Napping," Emilija answered.

When Emmie finished wrapping Karina's leg, she came over to me, taking my face gently in her hands turning it gently to take in my own injuries.

"Come, *Dukra*, let me clean you up as well."

I let her lead me to a chair where she gently washed each scrape on the side of my face while my eyes stayed locked with Orin's. I'd be taking a bath anyway, but Emmie removed a few pieces of bark then dropped the antiseptic on the wounds making the air hiss between my teeth. It was the most care anyone had given me other than Orin. My eyes burned with tears, ones that I couldn't let fall. That would show my weakness amongst their strength.

Then Orin and I were alone. Roman had taken Karina upstairs so they could each wash the day away as soon as her leg had been taken care of.

"They're done now so we can head up." Orin took my hand gently.

"What does *dukra* mean?" I asked before I got up from the chair.

"Daughter."

That did it. There was no holding in the tears that had been brimming from Emmie's kindness. Big crocodile tears fell down my cheeks which brought Orin to his knees in front of me. His hands clasped my cheeks letting his thumbs wipe away the tears that were just replaced by more.

"Please don't cry, Lizzie."

"It's just... " I took in a deep breath so that maybe I wouldn't sound like a sobbing child. "My own father, my flesh and blood, barely called me his daughter unless he needed to remind me to obey but you're mother... she doesn't have to refer to me that way."

"Oh, baby, she wants to. You're one of us. You put yourself between a couple of werewolves. That means something to us."

My voice no longer worked. Instead, I just nodded as more tears fell.

I let him guide me, did what he said as the new information settled in my brain and I became more comfortable with the idea that I had a family. A family that would protect me and I would protect them. One where some members loved me, some respected me, and some would probably never even like me. That seemed pretty normal.

Clean and completely exhausted from the day, I crawled onto the bed. It welcomed me in a way it never had. Orin dropped beside me then pulled me in close.

"Let me know if any of this hurts but I can assure you that I never want to sleep without you as close as possible."

"This feels perfect."

"Everyone will rest for a while. Then soon the others will go home."

"Will we?" I asked quietly. I hadn't given moving a thought but it wouldn't matter. Where Orin went, I went. I had nothing here without him.

"We are home." He grew quiet. "Unless you want to leave. I can arrange that."

"No," I shook my head. "I'm comfortable here. It's what I know so for now, I think we should stay."

"So we'll stay. I have a feeling Roman and Karina will be moving in next door."

"I'd like that," I said with a yawn.

"I love you, Elizabeth. My entire life changed in the best ways possible the night I went to that ball. I watched you with Olivia spinning and dancing, turning down other men who asked but I had to meet you. It was more than the pull of the pack. You are beautiful and more open than anyone I've ever met. You and I are forever."

"I love you, too. Forever."

He pulled my lips to his, kissing softly as if I were fragile and might break if he was too rough. When we pulled apart, he tucked me into his side so he could rest his chin on my head and wrapped both arms around my body.

We fell asleep like that. It was the deepest most needed sleep of my life.

And I wouldn't have wanted to share it with anyone else.

My husband.

My protector.

My heart.

Chapter Thirty-One

THE SUMMER HEAT had finally started to retreat leaving us with lovely fall weather. The leaves were turning and everything seemed to have returned to normal. Orin's parents left a couple of days after the fight with the other pack, taking Diana and baby Ruby with them then Ivan and Nell followed half a day later. Nell and I had come to some sort of understanding that I didn't fully get but no one had tried to kill me since that so I was more than all right with it.

Daniel and Aras waited a full day before going home. I think they didn't want it to seem like they'd rather chew their arms off than be where I was, doing whatever they could to get away from me. I didn't care either way.

Just like Orin said, Roman and Karina decided to

stay in the second house Orin bought next door. I couldn't have been happier with their decision. In Karina I had more than a friend, I had a sister. But I also couldn't deny that I was over the moon that we had our house back to ourselves. Being alone with Orin was the one thing I craved above everything else.

Unfortunately, I hadn't seen Olivia much since everything happened. This wasn't too surprising. I wasn't part of her world anymore. She wasn't part of mine. My husband wasn't in her husband's circle so she had to move on to bigger and better things. I didn't blame her but, if I'm being honest, I still missed her and the years we'd spent together. Once upon a time, she'd been my only friend.

Stepping out into the cool afternoon air, I did something I would never have dared in my previous life. I bit into a bright red apple right there in the street. Father would have lashed me for something like that but I was hungry and no longer cared about being or appearing proper. I was the town girl that ran off with a man her father did not choose nor approve of. Who cared about the other stuff?

"Don't you look lovely today, Mrs. Vilkatas?" Orin's deep voice came up behind me right before he slid an arm around my shoulder. A gesture like that was something I'd seen often from people not of my father's class but never from his people. I preferred it this way.

"Thank you," I smiled up at him. I was wearing trousers a lot more often and found them so much more practical than skirts, but truth be told, my own style was still evolving. "Have a nice run?"

"The best. I love this time of year." He slowed his pace to match mine because we really had nowhere we had to be. This was our life. We didn't hurry anymore or rush from place to place. Our day wasn't a plethora of scheduled events, though there were some of those because I wasn't ready to let everything from my old life go.

"Is it a full moon tonight?" I asked.

"Yes. Are you keeping track?" Shrugging, I tried to keep any trace of a smile from my face. "Oh don't start blushing now. I know exactly why you like the full moon."

"I'll admit to that," I finally said. "But I like that whether the moon is full or gone completely." He pulled me even closer so he could kiss my forehead. "I went to my father's today."

"Lizzie, I said I'd go with you. I don't trust him."

"Actually it was pretty good." The skepticism was all over his face. "Really. I just gave him the journal back. He seemed surprised but I told him I always planned to return it."

"Is that all?"

"No," I sighed. "I asked him why he kept my mother's sister from me. Why he never told me about her."

One of the biggest revelations from my mother's journal was that the fourth non-shifting female was her sister. Now, she referred to them as a family, not a pack, and never mentioned being a werewolf but she did say that she and her sister were born without an important family trait. That they were hated and had to disappear though did mention the sister's last known address.

I'd taken a chance and written a letter that found her sister, Audrey.

"And?"

"He told me that my mother only ever said she didn't want me anywhere near her family so he assumed they weren't good people."

"Wow, he got something right."

"Orin!" I slapped his chest. "She married a human." His eyebrows shot up. "I received a letter from her today. She lives in Boston, has been married for fifteen years." I took a deep breath. "She has children, Orin."

His head snapped to me and his steps faltered to a stop. After glancing around quickly, he took my hand to lead me to the small park not far from where we'd stopped. We sat down on the closest bench. He leaned forward so that his elbows rested on his knees. This had been an awkward subject for us even though we'd only spoken about it twice.

Half of me came from the Balodis pack. A pack whose women were dying off in childbirth or produced one offspring that never shifted. My own mother died giving birth to me. I didn't know what that meant for the future of Orin and my children. If that was even possible. And neither did he. Though he did assure me that he could not care less whether our children exhibited the wolf gene. He just wanted them healthy and for me to make it out alive.

"How many?" he asked quietly. He didn't like to admit it because he didn't want me to feel responsible, but I knew he wanted children one day, not today, but sometime in the future. I was still too young he said. I'd been so oppressed in my father's house, Orin wanted me to have a chance to live before I even thought about starting a family.

"Three. Not one complication. Her letter said she could explain everything so that maybe... maybe one day we... "

"You know I love you regardless."

"Yes." I smiled. "I do know that. But I also know that I want a family. And I want it with you." I fell silent before telling him the next thing he wasn't totally going to like. "I want to go to Boston, Orin. I want to meet my aunt and hear stories about my mother from childhood. I want her to tell me why she didn't die in childbirth but my mother did."

He nodded softly. "It'll take a few days to arrange."

Orin was terrible at telling me no. Even more so since everything happened with the other pack.

"I think I can manage to keep myself entertained for a few days."

That statement alone brought a big, beautiful smile to his face. I loved seeing him happy and carefree without worrying about me or that someone was going to try to take me away from him.

"I think it's time to head home." His voice was so low and husky that it made every muscle in my body tighten and relax at the same time. that was a reaction reserved only for him. But since the fight, he had made me feel loved and desired every single day. He'd done that before but I saw something different in his eyes now.

After slipping my hand into his, we stood and

headed back toward the house. I wanted to run the entire way. Get there and out of my clothes as quickly as possible but I forced myself not to. To enjoy the quiet moments with my husband. To squeeze every second of build-up out of the experience knowing that there will be a wonderful payoff once we got there.

Things weren't perfect. We didn't know where the lost members of the Balodis pack disappeared to, though their numbers were so low that it would be suicide to try to take on our family, even with only three werewolves in town. Orin and I had resigned ourselves to the fact that having children of our own may be too dangerous for me. We still had hope. I went from no family to more than I knew what to do with and I was determined to add to it. I hoped my aunt would have some of the answers. There was a time when I wanted nothing out of life. I didn't dare to dream of something better. Now I wanted it all.

Things weren't perfect. But it was perfect for us.

Because he loved me.

We were together.

And now I was going to have the chance to get to know my mother.

I couldn't wait to get to Boston and see what secrets my aunt held.

He was my brother's best friend and off limits.

The world knows Silas Briggs as the baseball heartthrob on a hot streak. I know him as brother's former friend and my teenage crush.
Four years ago, he broke my young heart by making me think there could be something between us.

Then he left town and never looked back.

Now I'm back and working for the team, hoping that we can be friendly. Then I see him in person and friendship is the last thing on my mind.

START READING KISSING THE PLAYER TODAY

Do you love rock stars?

FOREVER GRAYSON

Forever 18 Book 1

One night three years ago is coming back to haunt me.

It was supposed to be one night then I'd never see him again. One night at a dive bar where I met someone who could scratch an itch.

He wasn't famous then.

Now he's a rock star.

A rock star whose manager just hired me to be the band's stylist. It's a dream job to me but it could be a nightmare.
Is it worse if he remembers me? Or worse if he doesn't?

START READING FOREVER GRAYSON NOW

START READING DAISY NOW

Cross *Courting Chaos Book* 1

When a sexy drummer mistakes me for a groupie and tries to kick me out of the venue, I'm willing to chalk it up to mistaken identity. Usually everyone knows me but I shouldn't assume. Now Cross wants to make it right ini the hope that my father won't kick his band off the tour.

In trying to make amends, Cross becomes my surprise protector when I accidentally snap some pictures of his bandmate in a bad situation and he wants them deleted.

Cross being my protector has me wanting something I've never wanted before... A sexy drummer.

Growing up with a famous father has taught me many things but the number one rule has always been NEVER FALL FOR A ROCK STAR.

I guess I want to break the rules.

START READING CROSS TODAY

After living under my father's rule, I'm about to break free.

My father has kept me on a short leash my entire life.

The Orin comes for me.

Finding out what he is... scares the hell out of me.

Finding out I'm his supposed mate... I don't know that I'll recover.

START READING MOONSTRUCK TODAY

Being the daughter of my people's leaders, I should understand protocol and appropriate behavior. Problem is, I understand both, I just don't follow them.

But I have a different plan.

There's a boy... now a man, who is supposed to be powerful. I want him on our side.

What I didn't know is that together, he and I might be unstoppable.

Now I just have to find him.

START READING THE GREMLIN PRINCE TODAY

START READING THE GREMLIN PRINCE TODAY

I'm a witch. Or so they tell me.

Finding out I'm a witch isn't even the weirdest part of my day. Having the guy who hated me in high school stand before me to tell me that I am, is.

Somehow, I'm supposed to learn spells and how to ground myself to the elements, fight the fact that I want him like I want air, and not freak out that my parents are part of a shadow coven trying to pull me over to the dark side.

Yeah. No problem.

START READING CURSED MAGIC TODAY

THE FALLOUT SERIES

A new adult romance series

Coming home is hard.
Finding out the boy you loved had a baby with your
former best friend... heartbreaking.

*START READING LAST GOOD THING
TODAY*

GAMBLING ON LOVE

A new adult romance series

Desperate times call for desperate measures so
Flannery Tate is selling her virginity.

START READING HIGHEST BIDDER TODAY

I you'd like to just keep up with my sales and new releases, you can follow me on BookBub!

Bookbub: https://www.bookbub.com/authors/ heather-young-nichols

Heather Young-Nichols is a USA Today Bestselling author of contemporary and paranormal romances. She writes swoony heroes and snarky heroines with a heap of romance.

When she's not writing, she's binging a show with her kids, watching baseball, or snuggling with her cuddly animals.

Find Heather on Social Media or by visiting her website.

heatheryoungnichols.com

facebook.com/heatheryoungnicholsauthor

instagram.com/heatheryoungnichols

amazon.com/Heather-Young-Nichols/e/B00KKTM54A

bookbub.com/authors/heather-young-nichols

tiktok.com/@heatheryoungnichols

www.ingramcontent.com/pod-product-compliance
Lightning Source LLC
Chambersburg PA
CBHW020332010826
48970CB00010B/79